VICTORY AT SEBASTOPOL

Historical Fiction by V. A. Stuart
Published by McBooks Press

THE ALEXANDER SHERIDAN ADVENTURES

Victors and Lords
The Sepoy Mutiny
Massacre at Cawnpore
The Cannons of Lucknow
The Heroic Garrison

THE PHILLIP HAZARD NOVELS

The Valiant Sailors
The Brave Captains
Hazard's Command
Hazard of Huntress
Hazard in Circassia
Victory at Sebastopol

For a complete list of nautical and military fiction
published by McBooks Press, please see pages 219–221.

THE PHILLIP HAZARD NOVELS, No. 6

VICTORY AT SEBASTOPOL

by

V. A. STUART

McBooks Press, Inc.
Ithaca, New York

Published by McBooks Press 2004
Copyright © 1973 by V. A. Stuart
First published in the United Kingdom by
Robert Hale and Co. Ltd., London

Cover: *British Naval Boat Taking Soundings Under the Batteries of
Cronstadt,* from a drawing by J. W. Carmichael, engraved by
E. Brandard. Courtesy of Mary Evans Picture Library

Library of Congress Cataloging-in-Publication Data

Stuart, V. A.
  Victory at Sebastopol / by V.A. Stuart.
      p. cm. — (The Phillip Hazard novels ; #6)
  ISBN 1-59013-061-8 (trade pbk. : alk. paper)
  1. Hazard, Phillip Horatio (Fictitious character)—Fiction. 2. Great
Britain—History, Naval—19th century—Fiction. 3. Great Britain.
Royal Navy—Officers—Fiction. 4. Crimean War, 1853-1856—Fiction.
5. British—Ukraine—Fiction. I. Title.
  PR6063.A38V545 2004
  823'.92—dc22

                                      2004009176

Distributed to the trade by National Book Network, Inc.,
15200 NBN Way, Blue Ridge Summit, PA 17214
800-462-6420

Additional copies of this book may be ordered from any
bookstore or directly from McBooks Press, Inc., ID Booth
Building, 520 North Meadow St., Ithaca, NY 14850. Please
include $4.00 postage and handling with mail orders. New York
State residents must add sales tax to total remittance (books &
shipping). All McBooks Press publications can also be ordered
by calling toll-free 1-888-BOOKS11 (1-888-266-5711).
Please call to request a free catalog.

Visit the McBooks Press website at www.mcbooks.com.

Printed in the United States of America

9 8 7 6 5 4 3 2 1

AUTHOR'S NOTE

With *the exception* of the Officers and Seamen of HMS *Huntress* and of Colonel Gorak and his daughter, all the characters in this novel really existed and their actions are a matter of historical fact. Where they have been credited with remarks or conversations—as, for example, with the fictitious characters—which are not actually their own words, care has been taken to make sure that these are, as far as possible, in keeping with their known sentiments.

Grateful thanks to Mr Ian Scott of Boston Spa, Yorkshire for technical advice on the Russian "infernal machine" and other explosives mentioned in the text.

My main sources of reference were *The Russian War,* 1855, edited by Captain A. C. Dewar; *History of the War Against Russia,* E.H. Nolan, 1857; *Illustrated London News,* 1854–55; *The Crimean War,* Philip Warner, 1972; *Surgeon in the Crimea,* George Lawson, edited by Victor Bonham Carter, 1968.

FOR MY DAUGHTER VALERIE STUART

with much love

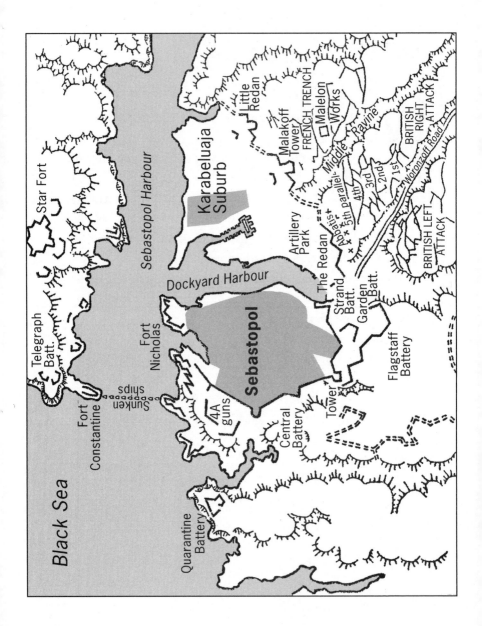

Black Sea

Star Fort

Telegraph Batt.

Fort Constantine

Sunken ships

Fort Nicholas

Sebastopol Harbour

Karabeluaja Suburb

Dockyard Harbour

Sebastopol

4A guns

Quarantine Battery

Central Battery

Tower

Flagstaff Battery

Garden Batt.

Strand Batt.

The Redan

Artillery Park

Abbtus

5th parallel

4th

3rd

2nd

1st

Malakoff Tower

FRENCH TRENCH

Malelon Works

Middle

Ravine

Little Redan

Woronzoff Road

BRITISH RIGHT ATTACK

BRITISH LEFT ATTACK

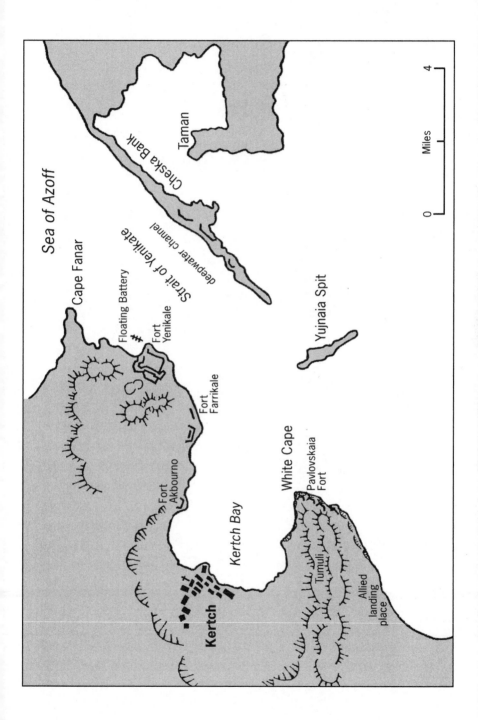

THE WAR IN THE CRIMEA

Notes on the main events from September, 1854–
May, 1855. The siege of the Russian naval base of
Sebastopol, on the Crimean Coast of the Black Sea, followed
the landing, on 14th September, 1854, of the Allied Expeditionary Forces of Great Britain, France, and Turkey at the Old
Fort, Kalamita Bay, some thirty miles to the north of their
objective.

Under the command of General Lord Raglan, a veteran of
Waterloo, the British force consisted of 26,800 men. Together
with sixty guns and about two thousand horses, they embarked
at Varna, on the Bulgarian coast, and crossed to the Crimea in
a fleet of fifty-five sailing transports towed by steamers, and
escorted by ships of the Royal Navy, whose second-in-command, Rear-Admiral Sir Edmund Lyons, was responsible for
the whole complex operation of transport and landing.

The French, commanded by Marshal St Arnaud, landed
twenty-eight thousand men and sixty-eight guns and the Turks,
who were heavily engaged in fighting the common enemy on
other European and Asian fronts, contributed a smaller force
of seven thousand. Although badly affected by an outbreak of
cholera, the Allied Armies defeated a strongly positioned
Russian army, with one hundred twenty guns, on the Heights
above the Alma River on 20th September, the British sustaining over two thousand casualties and the French nine hundred.

With only a small garrison of seamen and the 50-gun Star Fort to offer resistance, Sebastopol lay open to a determined assault from the north—an assault which Lord Raglan was fully prepared to undertake. Instead of this, however, General Canrobert—who had succeeded to the French Supreme Command on 23rd September—expressed the conviction that the city was impregnable from the north and, on his insistence, the Allies struck inland and marched in a semicircle to the south-east, where bases were established at Balaclava (British) and Kamiesch and Kazatch Bays (French).

The landing of the siege-trains, again at Canrobert's obstinate insistence, gave the Russians the time they needed to put Sebastopol into a state of defence. Admiral Korniloff, acting on the orders of the Russian Commander-in-Chief in the Crimea, Prince Menschikoff, scuttled seven of his line-of-battle ships across the mouth of the harbour, between the stone-built forts of Constantine (97 guns, in casemates, thirty feet above sea level) Alexander (56 guns, similarly mounted) and the 50-gun Quarantine Battery, thus effectively barring both harbour and docks to the Allied naval squadrons. Behind this barrier, eight sail-of-the-line were moored from east to west inside the booms, three of these heeled over so as to give their guns sufficient elevation to sweep over the land to the northward. The rest of the Russian fleet lay at anchor at the head of the harbour, with their guns covering its entrance.

The Russian Admiral—a courageous Officer, who was killed early in the siege—is said to have been heart-broken by the ignominious fate of the ships under his command. Yet there is little doubt that Sebastopol's long resistance was, in no small measure, due to Prince Menschikoff's farsighted decision to scuttle or immobilize his fleet within the confines of the harbour. Had he permitted Admiral Korniloff to sally forth, in time honoured fashion, to do battle with the Allied squadrons, Sebastopol would almost certainly have fallen to assault by sea and land within a few weeks—or even days—of the besieging armies' flank march to the south-east. As it was, lack of troops prevented a complete investment of the city and, throughout the year-long siege, the post road from Simpheropol in the north remained open. Menschikoff established his headquarters there and was able to send reinforcements and supplies into the town, whilst maintaining a large and mobile army outside, in the Valley of the River Tchernaya, which offered a constant threat to the thinly held British perimeter and the port of Balaclava.

It took the better part of three weeks, after the landing of the siege-trains at Balaclava and Kamiesch, for the Allies to haul their heavy guns into position on the Kheronese Upland overlooking Sebastopol and to establish the army camps and supply depots on the plateau. During these three unexpected weeks of grace, Colonel Franz Ivanovitch Todleben, a thirty-seven-year-old Prussian engineer, born in one of Russia's Baltic provinces, set to work to render the city impregnable to the threatened attack. He was a military engineer of genius and, under his direction the inhabitants of Sebastopol—men, women and even children—toiled day and night to repair crumbling fortifications and to construct a four-mile-long system of connecting earthworks and batteries in which he sited his guns.

To the north, the newly renovated Star Fort guarded the road from Simpheropol, along which Prince Menschikoff had, by 9th October, sent close on thirty thousand troops to reinforce the garrison. From east to west, in a semicircle, a series of heavily armed redoubts constituted the landward defences; the so-called Little Redan, with the Malakoff or White Tower, in front of which was a fortified hill known as the Mamelon. Further west, a huge bank of earthworks joined the formidable Redan to the Barrack Battery and, at the head of the Dockyard Creek, the Strand and Garden Batteries and the Flagstaff Bastion were connected to the Central Bastion and the semicircle was completed by more earthworks extending to Quarantine Bay and the battery sited there. In all, some 1,200 guns faced the Allied siege works on the Upland and the total of 126 guns which, in three weeks of herculean effort, had been dragged six to seven miles from Balaclava and Kamiesch to the top of the plateau.

The Royal Navy, in addition to manhandling guns which weighed from 42 cwt (the thirty-two-pounders) to 95 cwt (the sixty-eight-pounder Lancasters) also landed a Naval Brigade of upwards of three thousand seamen and Marines to assist in the siege, and 29 of the 73 British siege-guns were manned by seamen. Of the heavy guns, 56 were taken from ships of the fleet.

The first Allied bombardment, intended as a prelude to the long-awaited assault on Sebastopol by the land-based forces, opened at 6:30 a.m. on 17th October, and the combined fleets were ordered to attack the seaward defences in support. This they most gallantly did, pitting their wooden ships against the stone-walled forts at the mouth of the harbour, with little effect, in an engagement which lasted from noon until dusk. When they finally hauled off, with a great many ships damaged or on fire and over five hundred men killed or wounded, it was to learn that the land-based assault had not been launched, due to an eleventh-hour decision by General Canrobert not to commit his troops to the attack.

Thereafter the role of the Allied Fleets in the prosecution of the siege became a secondary one. A blockade of the Russian

Black Sea ports was established and ships-of-war—mainly the steam-frigates—kept the armies supplied with reinforcements and the materials of war. The port of Balaclava was small and quite inadequate as a base but it was the lifeline on which the British Army on the Upland depended and therefore, at all costs, it had to be held. The flower of the British cavalry—the famous Light Brigade—perished in a desperate battle to prevent a breakthrough by the Russians from the Tchernaya Valley, on 25th October, 1854. Out of a total of 675 men, 247 were killed or wounded and 475 horses were killed. On 5th November, the bloody battle on the Heights of Inkerman was fought and won in dense fog, a scant eight thousand British infantrymen—including the Brigade of Guards—having found themselves facing some sixty thousand of the enemy in a dawn attack. The battle was half over before French aid reached them, in the shape of General Bosquet's division but, when the Russians were finally driven back, they left an estimated fifteen thousand casualties behind them.

With the onset of the dread Crimean winter, the Allied Armies, in their exposed canvas tents, suffered appalling losses from disease—out of a total loss of 19,600 men, 15,700 British soldiers and sailors died from disease. The fleets also sustained heavy losses when a storm of hurricane force struck the Crimean coast on 14th November and, there being little or no shelter to which they could run, many ships foundered or were driven on shore and wrecked, the loss in transport and supply ships outside the congested port of Balaclava being particularly heavy. The steamship *Prince,* carrying protective winter clothing for the army on the Upland, went down with all hands and her entire cargo, and the French three-decker *Henri Quatre,* a steam-screw launched five years previously, was driven ashore at Eupatoria and smashed to pieces. It was decided to send the sailing ships-of-the-line back to England and to replace them, as far as possible, with steamers.

Sebastopol continued to hold out, despite losses from the Allied bombardment averaging one hundred fifty a day. Reinforcements poured in along the road from Simpheropol which lay outside the range of the Allied guns and, with her vast reserves of manpower, Russia's losses were more easily replaced than those of Britain and France, whose reinforcements could only come by sea. Supplies of grain and other essentials from depots on the eastern shores of the Sea of Azoff also reached the beleaguered city in substantial quantities, even in winter, via a second road which crossed the Putrid Sea by means of a bridge and linked up with the post road to the north.

No troops could be spared from the siege to cut this supply route and, in winter, ice precluded naval operations in the area but, with the coming of spring, Rear-Admiral Lyons, who had succeeded Vice-Admiral Deans Dundas as British naval Commander-in-Chief, pressed for the adoption of a plan of action which both he and his predecessor had long advocated. Convinced that only by depriving the garrison of its supplies could Sebastopol be forced to surrender, the Admiral urged that a small flotilla of light draught steam-frigates and gun-vessels be sent into the Sea of Azoff for this purpose. In order to gain entry, the fortified towns of Kertch and Yenikale, whose batteries guarded the narrow Straits of Kertch, would have to be taken and occupied and the Admiral asked for a comparatively small detachment of troops to be made available for ten to fourteen days.

Lord Raglan wholeheartedly supported the proposed expedition as a means of shortening the siege; so, too, did Lyons' French colleague, Admiral Bruat. The British Army, however, which had been severely depleted during the winter and which had still to defend its long and vulnerable perimeter, could spare only twenty-five hundred men. As had so often been the case throughout the Crimean campaign, the final decision rested with the French Commander-in-Chief, whose army had recently been augmented by the arrival of twenty-five thousand fresh troops.

Canrobert agreed, with reluctance, to supply seven thousand infantrymen but, as a result of telegraphic instructions from the Emperor, he ordered the recall of the French ships and troops within a few hours of their arrival off the Kertch Straits. The British, unable to proceed alone against an estimated ten thousand Russians, were compelled to abandon the initial attempt to capture Kertch and enter the Sea of Azoff, and they returned to Sebastopol on 6th May. Canrobert, aware that he had been placed in an intolerable position by having had, once again, to go back on his word, resigned the French Supreme Command, and, on 19th May, 1855, he was succeeded by General Pélissier. Within three days of Pélissier's appointment, the second expedition to Kertch was under way, this time with the enthusiastic cooperation of the new French Commander.

All the foregoing events have been covered by earlier novels in the Hazard series.

CHAPTER ONE

Phillip Horatio Hazard, commanding Her Majesty's steam-screw sloop-of-war *Huntress*, of 14 guns, swung himself up into the mainmast shrouds and, twenty feet or so above the deck, put his glass to his eye, peering anxiously into the murk about him.

He could see little or nothing of the land he knew to be within less than half a mile of his ship's port quarter even from this vantage point, and the midshipman he had sent aloft to supplement the masthead look-out had not, as yet, reported sighting the White Cape, on the southern extremity of the Bay of Kertch or the formidable Pavlovskaia Fort by which it was guarded.

Directly ahead, the entrance to the Yenikale Strait lay shrouded in a pall of low-lying fog, which the pale afternoon sunlight had seldom been able to penetrate . . . and visibility, he knew, would become worse when the sun sank. Nevertheless on this occasion, Phillip Hazard welcomed the fog, since it promised to make his present task—if not easier—at least not quite so fraught with peril as it might have been.

He lowered his Dollond and glanced down at the lines of marker-buoys which, under the supervision of Mr Burnaby, the master, men of the duty watch were setting out in readiness on the after part of the upper deck, his dark brows meeting in a thoughtful frown as he counted them. The Russians, he was aware, had buoyed the deep water channel off the Cheska Bank to the east but they had also constructed extensive earthworks on the seven-mile-long spit of marshland, behind which they had set up batteries of 36-pounder guns to command the passage. These guns, crossing fire with the floating battery and the fort at Yenikale, barred the deep water channel to all but their own shipping. For this reason, he had been ordered to sound and buoy an alternative channel on the western side of the narrow strip of water, by means of which an Allied naval squadron might enter the Sea of Azoff during the next 48 hours.

Captain Moore, of HMS *Highflyer,* his immediate superior, had made a preliminary survey some weeks ago in the small 6-gun *Viper,* and had warned him that, in places, the water shoaled to give a depth of less than three fathoms and that there were numerous silting sandbanks but . . . Phillip gave vent to an audible sigh as he descended to the deck. Moore had gone in for the purpose of reconnoitring the proposed landing beach at Kamiesch-Bourno, where the troops would be put ashore for the attack on Kertch. Using the return of a captured carriage—the property of the Russian Commander, Baron Wrangel—as an excuse, the *Viper* had made her approach in daylight, after signalling her intentions. His own orders, on the other hand, were to enter the Strait under cover of darkness and to get as close as he could to Yenikale without making his presence known to the enemy, if he could avoid it . . . which meant that he would be unable to use his engines.

He had decided to keep steam up and the screw lowered, however, in case of emergency. Whilst by steering east towards the Yujnaia Spit, he could give the Pavlovskaia Fort a wide berth and might slip by Akbourno unseen, he knew that if the

40-gun battery at Ferrikale opened up on him from the north side of the bay he would have to make off at full speed, since the passage he was seeking lay within range of most of those forty guns. The *Huntress* would have no defence against them apart, that was to say, from her speed and manoeuvrability under engines and her own two pivot-mounted Lancaster guns, on the upper deck. Her draught was light; like a number of other ships in the British Black Sea Fleet, the *Huntress* had been specially designed and built for operations in the shallow inland Sea of Azoff. With even a scant two fathoms of water under her keel, she would be in no danger of grounding.

Even so, there were other dangers which had to be taken into account. Captain Moore's survey had, of necessity, been restricted by his obligations under the truce. There might well be sandbanks which his soundings had failed to reveal and, should the *Huntress* run on to one of these at full speed, she would be at the mercy of the shore guns, as helpless as a stranded whale, left high and dry by the receding tide. A silent approach was therefore essential, so that the gunners in the fort did not detect her presence and open fire . . . or at any rate, Phillip thought wryly, not until after he had dropped his buoys and was ready to make a cautious run for it into the obscurity of the misty darkness. Once out of range, he . . . something caught his eye and, with a smothered exclamation, he raised his glass again. The glass was of little use and he lowered it.

"Masthead there!" he called sharply, cupping his hands about his mouth. "Do you see anything? Breakers off the weather bow?"

"No, sir," came the prompt reply, in a boy's shrill treble. Then, after a pause, "Nothing, sir."

He must have imagined the breakers, Phillip told himself.

Midshipman Patrick O'Hara was a keen-eyed, alert youngster and his gig's midshipman. For all his youth, he was a tried and trusted veteran of this war, accustomed to accept responsibility and to command men of more than twice his age with the assurance that came with professional competence. He was not the kind to relax his vigilance, even for a moment—had there been breakers visible from the masthead, O'Hara would have seen and reported their presence. Phillip snapped the Dollond shut and began to pace the quarterdeck with slow, measured strides, in an effort to calm his taut nerves.

The ship was under as much sail as she could carry but, in spite of this, the light, fitful southerly breeze was barely keeping steerage way on her and he again found himself wishing that he could use his engines. In a situation like this, the engines were invaluable; if the wind dropped any more, he might have to lower boats in order to tow her into the channel, he thought glumly—there would be nothing else for it, if he were to complete his buoying and return to the Fleet rendezvous off Kamiesch by first light. The preliminary soundings would probably have to be taken by boat, in any case and . . . the mist cleared unexpectedly and, in a momentary break in the dank, greyish-yellow clouds of vapour, he glimpsed a rocky headland rising steeply out of the sea ahead and to port.

Midshipman O'Hara saw it too and made his report with commendable speed and accuracy. "It looks like the White Cape, sir," he finished eagerly.

It undoubtedly was the White Cape, Phillip saw, recognizing the square outline of the fort and the white sandstone cliff from which the headland took its name, and then the mist closed in once more, hiding both land and buildings from his sight. The ship was on the course he had plotted with Captain Moore and there was no sign of life from the shore; he felt some of the tension drain out of him and his voice was calm and level when he gave the order to permit the Lancaster guns' crews to stand down for a brief respite. The immediate danger was past, the first hurdle cleared and, once the White Cape was safely astern, he could bring her about, tack across the open expanse of Kertch Bay and put a man on the lead when he closed the coast again. He resumed his measured pacing of the deck, the charts he had studied and memorized in his mind's eye as he paused to peer into the binnacle before ordering a slight correction of course.

There was no reason to anticipate trouble while crossing the bay—the *Huntress* would be more than a match for any enemy ship she might encounter there and he intended to give the fort of Akbourno, on the southern arc of the bay, as wide a berth as he had given Pavlovskaia. The Ferrikale battery was less easily avoided and the fog was a mixed blessing, making it infernally difficult to pick up landmarks or judge distances with any accuracy. The wind, too—such as it was—was backing again . . . anxious not to lose way, Phillip sang out a warning to the Officer of the Watch to trim after- and head-yards and strode, frowning, to the weather hammock netting.

He would come about in another fifteen minutes, he decided and would endeavour to approach Ferrikale from the Kertch side of the bay. It was going to take very nice judgement indeed to slip the *Huntress* past the battery unseen . . . nice judgement and more luck than he could reasonably count on, even with the fog to hide her. He would have a chance if he could deceive the gunners into mistaking her for one of their own small war steamers on her way up channel from Kertch although, without knowing their recognition signals, he would require more than luck to succeed in his attempt at deception. Nevertheless, it was worth trying.

The minutes ticked slowly by. The line of faintly disturbed water he had been watching disappeared to leeward and he expelled his breath in a pent-up sigh.

"Bring her about, if you please, Mr Cochrane," he said crisply and gave his instructions for the necessary change of course.

Anthony Cochrane, the young red-haired Officer of the Watch, who had been one of his *Trojan* Officers, gave him an alert, "Aye, aye, sir," and repeated the order into his speaking trumpet. "Ready about, Bo'sun's Mate!" The pipe sounded, there was a thud of bare feet on the deck planking as the duty watch took up their stations for tacking, and the quartermaster eased the helm down in obedience to Cochrane's shouted command.

"Helm's a-lee!" The spanker-boom was hauled amidships, forcing the stern to leeward and, as head and fore-sheets were let go, the sail started to shake, spilling their wind. "Raise tacks and sheets . . . haul well taut the mainbrace! Handsomely, lads!" With the mainyards braced round, the jibs were hauled over and sheeted home. "Head braces!" Cochrane ordered, as the main course started slowly to fill. "Of all haul!" His orders, relayed by the boatswain's mate of the watch, were obeyed with swift efficiency as, his gaze on the mist-shrouded canvas above him, he trimmed sail to the light breeze.

Phillip watched, conscious of a sense of pride in his ship and in the seamen who manned her. Most of them had been civilians a little over a year ago—the same men whom his late First Lieutenant, Ambrose Quinn, had contemptuously described as "ploughboys and counter-hoppers." They had done well, he thought . . . it was no longer possible to pick out those who had been fishermen or coastguards from Quinn's ploughboys.

"Right the helm, Quartermaster," Lieutenant Cochrane ordered. "Brace up the mainyard, look lively, lads!"

"Marker-buoys ready, sir. Shall I relieve Mr Cochrane of the deck?" The elderly master was beside him and Phillip turned to give him an answering smile and a nod of assent. It was good to have old Burnaby in charge of navigation again; they had served together in the *Trojan* and it had taken all his powers of persuasion—and Burnaby's—to arrange his transfer to the *Huntress*. Captain Crawford had, understandably, been reluctant to part with him, since men of his skill and experience were hard to come by, but eventually Burnaby's own patiently repeated requests had achieved the seemingly impossible and, although Phillip had had to dispense with his Third Lieutenant in order to have the master appointed, he was well satisfied with the exchange. Burnaby was worth his weight in gold to his young and comparatively inexperienced ship's company.

"Have Mr O'Hara relieved at the masthead, if you please, Mr Burnaby. Once we're across the bay, it might be as well to relieve all look-outs every half hour—this fog is damnably trying on the eyes."

"A wise precaution, sir," the master agreed. He scowled at the swirling clouds of moisture which hemmed them in and shook his grizzled head. "It's getting thicker. I fancy it won't disperse till well into the night."

"Well, that should suit us." Phillip shrugged. "So long as it doesn't delay the Fleet rendezvous tomorrow." They discussed the course to be followed and, when the watch changed and Burnaby went to take over the deck, Phillip turned to find his brother Graham, now acting as his First Lieutenant, standing at his elbow.

He made his report with correct formality. Since the

restoration of his commission, Graham Hazard had become a changed personality and their relationship—although, as Commander of the *Huntress,* Phillip still out-ranked him—had been established on a new and happier footing. Not quite as it had been in their boyhood, of course; Graham was the elder by seven years and those lost years, when he had drifted round the world, sometimes as an Officer but more often as a seaman in the merchant service, had left their mark on him. But he was a conscientious and able First Lieutenant, under whose taut yet always just administration the ship's company had shaken-down in a manner Phillip had almost despaired of, when Lieutenant Quinn had been his second-in-command.

"You're going in now, are you, Phillip?" Graham asked, as they crossed to the weather side of the quarterdeck. "You aren't waiting till dark?"

"No point in waiting." Phillip gestured to the opaque curtain of fog which closed them in. "Burnaby doesn't think this will clear much before morning—and he's usually right. In any case, there's no wind to disperse it, is there?"

"Or to take us into the Strait," his brother observed. "If you still intend to go in under sail."

"It'll be devilish slow work," Phillip admitted. "But I daren't risk using the screw unless I have to—and only then if the batteries fire on us and we have to haul off fast."

"Then let us hope the gunners aren't keeping too vigilant a watch . . . and that the fog impedes them more than it impedes us!"

"Amen to that!" Phillip echoed. He grasped his brother's arm. "Let's walk, shall we? As always, I should appreciate your advice, Graham."

Pacing the deck together, they discussed what would have to be done, attempting to allow for any unexpected complications and, deeply concerned for the safety of his ship as some of the more unpleasant possibilities were considered, Phillip said feelingly, "I must confess that I'll be damned glad when this is over. The fort at Yenikale mounts something in the region of forty guns, according to Moore—about half of them of heavy calibre. My nightmare is that I'll run us aground on some sandback we know nothing about, right under their muzzles! Our charts are by no means reliable, as you know . . . but they're all we've got, so I suppose we'll have to do the best we can with them."

Understanding his feelings, Graham eyed him sympathetically. "You said you wanted a good man on the lead, Phillip. I've detailed Jackson."

"A good choice," Phillip approved. He lifted his glass to his eye and lowered it again almost immediately, with a rueful smile. "For God's sake—I must be seeing things! All the same, Graham, I could swear . . ." he thrust the Dollond into his brother's hand. "Do *you* see riding lights? There, look, abeam of us . . . oh, damn this miserable fog!"

Graham looked obediently, then lowered the glass and wiped the moisture from its lens before training it once more in the direction Phillip had indicated. "No, I can't see anything. Wait a minute, though . . . I believe you're right. There *is* something and it's not on shore. By heaven, Phillip, I think it's a ship! And she's at anchor. Curse this fog, I can't see her now! I'll go up to the crosstrees, shall I, and see if I can make her out?"

"No, wait—young O'Hara's just back on deck. Mr O'Hara!" The midshipman scampered over eagerly and came to attention in front of his Commander, his oilskin jacket streaming with moisture. It had been cold and damp during his vigil aloft and his teeth were chattering. "S-sir?" Phillip pointed to the flickering light, now clearly visible off the starboard bow and the boy reddened in dismay. "I—I'm awfully s-sorry, sir. I didn't see anything from the masthead, not even when you hailed, sir. S-shall I go back and—"

Phillip shook his head. "No, youngster, you cut along below and change into dry clothes. It's not your fault—the way the fog's swirling about, you could not be expected to see that light from the masthead. Off you go—I only wanted to confirm that you hadn't seen it. Who is the look-out who relieved you?"

"Williams, sir."

A reliable man, Phillip reflected . . . and there had been no hail from Williams either. He glanced at Graham as Midshipman O'Hara, in obedience to his nod of dismissal, touched his cap and ran off in search of a change of clothing. "One of the enemy gunboats, do you suppose?" he suggested. "They have four or five lying off Yenikale according to Captain Moore. Steamers, brig-rigged and armed with long thirty-twos. And . . ." the germ of an idea was beginning to form in his mind and he added thoughtfully, "The chances are she hasn't seen us . . . we're showing no lights. If she *had* seen us, she would have anchored under the protection of the battery, would she not?"

"Yes, I imagine she would. But"—Graham gave him a searching glance, sensing his sudden preoccupation with the anchored ship—"what have you in mind, Phillip? You're not thinking of trying to take her, are you?" It was evident, from his tone, that he did not expect his question to be taken seriously.

"Well . . ." Phillip hesitated, peering with narrowed eyes into the fog. The light showed again and this time he caught a brief glimpse of the Russian vessel. It was enough and he said forcefully, "Yes, damn it, why not? It would not be difficult."

"She'll run for the battery the moment she sights us," his brother objected. "And that will effectively put paid to our entering the channel. Besides if she—"

Phillip cut him short. "She won't sight us now. If we stay on this tack and then wear and bring-up between her and Akbourno, we could lower a couple of boats and cut her out without any trouble. But we must go about it quietly—I'll warn Burnaby." He crossed the deck with long, impatient strides and, reaching the master's side, requested him to issue no shouted orders. Burnaby dutifully passed on these instructions but he looked puzzled and Phillip gave him a brief explanation, wasting no words. When he indicated the approximate position of the enemy steamer, the master's faded blue eyes lit with a gleam of apprehension but he offered no comment.

Graham, however, appeared to share his concern. "I'm not questioning your decision, Phillip," he said, lowering his voice. "But may I know *why* you want to cut out the brig? Are you afraid that she might alarm the batteries?"

"No, no," Phillip assured him. "If she hasn't seen us now—and I'm pretty certain she hasn't—we're in no danger on that account."

"Then why waste time on her?"

"Because we could use her to make our survey of the channel, don't you see, instead of risking this ship?"

"Put a prize-crew aboard her, you mean?" Graham sounded suddenly less doubtful and Philip permitted himself a brief smile.

"Yes, that's what I mean," he returned. "Jackson to take soundings, and a party to lay out the marker-buoys—a dozen men would suffice. The gunners on shore are unlikely to fire on the brig if they sight her—they'll recognize her as one of their own ships. They must have seen her in the Strait hundreds of times, so they'll presume that she's going about her legitimate business. As to wasting time . . . we'd be able to use her engines and that, you must admit, would save us a great deal of time and effort."

His half-formed germ of an idea was beginning to take shape and to reveal a number of advantageous possibilities and Phillip enlarged on these, point by point. There was an element of risk involved, of course, but only to himself and the boarding party, not to the *Huntress*. She would be safely out of range of the batteries and, in fact, need not enter the channel at all, provided all went well. "Even if I should run the brig on to a sandbank," he added, "there'll be no serious harm done. You can stand by with the *Huntress,* can you not, Graham, ready to pick us up if necessary?"

His brother eyed him in frowning silence but Burnaby came unexpectedly to his support. "The Captain's right, Mr Hazard," he asserted with conviction. "If you'll forgive me for putting my oar in, sir. There would be far less likelihood of those batteries firing on the brig than on this ship and that's a fact . . . and being able to use engines, for a task like this, would halve the time required, as you don't need me to tell you."

"I don't deny that," Graham answered. "It's a most ingenious idea and I believe it would work but . . ." he broke off, avoiding Phillip's gaze. "There's just one thing wrong with it."

"Well?" Phillip prompted, as the master tactfully moved out of earshot. "What do *you* think is wrong with it?" There was a slight edge to his voice. Although technically his subordinate, Graham was still his elder brother; controlling his impatience, he invited quietly, "Tell me—I'm listening."

Graham's expression relaxed. "You always listen to me, don't you, Phillip? I'm grateful, believe me—but you are in command of this ship and I'm your First Lieutenant. You—"

"What has that to do with it, for God's sake?"

"Everything, my dear fellow. It is a First Lieutenant's duty to spare his Captain by taking command of such minor operations as boat and landing parties. Yet it would seem, from what you have just been saying, that *you* intend to lead the cutting-out party and, when the brig is taken, to command her yourself." Graham smiled but his tone was reproachful. "I am right, am I not—that *is* what you intend?"

"Yes," Phillip admitted. "It is." He peered into the fog, conscious of an unreasonable feeling of resentment. It was time Burnaby wore ship, his mind registered and then saw that the duty watch were going silently to their stations. "Do I require to explain my reasons to you?" he demanded, turning to face his brother again.

Graham's smile vanished. "You do not have to, of course, but for all that I should like to hear them. I'm not Quinn, you know—you can rely on me to carry out your orders to the letter."

"Oh, for pity's sake, I know that, Graham! But the responsibility for sounding and buoying the channel is mine. I cannot resign it to you, whether it is undertaken in this ship or aboard a captured enemy vessel. As to the brig . . ." Phillip sighed, his brief anger tempered by the realization that his brother was right, so far as the capture of the brig was concerned. Naval custom decreed that all such operations should be commanded by a senior Lieutenant, as Graham had reminded him. But if his plan proved a failure or if the crew of the Russian ship put up a strong resistance then that, too, would be his responsibility—his and his alone—and it went against the grain to send two boatloads of his men to face a danger which he himself did not share. Besides, he . . .

"I understand," Graham put in, before he could offer this

as a reason. "But permit me, if you please, to lead the cutting-out party. I don't imagine that there is likely to be much risk attached to it or that the crew of the brig will attempt to oppose our fellows, particularly if we succeed in taking them by surprise. All the same, Phillip, it is I who should incur what risk there is—not you. Would you have me fail in my duty?"

"No, of course not. But devil take it, Graham, the brig may be armed to the teeth, you know! She may turn her guns on you and blow your boats out of the water before you've even had a chance to board her and—"

"In that case, my dear Phillip, the *Huntress* will stand to lose her First Lieutenant," Graham countered cheerfully. "But she will still have her Commander who, I don't doubt, will blow the brig out of the water before proceeding to carry out his orders to sound and buoy the channel. Isn't that so?" His smile returned and he put an arm about Phillip's shoulders, eyeing him with affectionate mockery. "As the late unlamented Ambrose Quinn was wont, all too frequently, to remind you—you are new to command, sir. And command has certain disadvantages, does it not?"

Phillip, recognizing defeat, ruefully echoed his brother's smile. "Yes, it would appear to have," he conceded and, when Graham hesitated, he said crisply, "Well, carry on—volunteer your boarding party and stand by to lower boats. We've delayed long enough."

"You mean that, Phillip?"

"Of course I mean it. Young Grey had better command the second boat, I think, if you're agreeable, and I'll put O'Leary on the forward gun to cover you. We don't want any firing obviously, if it can be avoided, but issue rifles to about a dozen reliable men and cutlasses to them all. If you need help, send up a red flare—I'll have Cochrane standing by with the cutter."

"Aye, aye, sir," Graham acknowledged and left the quarterdeck to volunteer his boats' crews. Phillip sent for the acting gunner, O'Leary, and put him in charge of the forward Lancaster gun and, when the *Huntress* wore round, he again ascended the mainmast shrouds in the hope of obtaining an early sight of the brig. It was, however, Able-Seaman Williams who sighted her from the masthead, and his relief who—obedient to the order to preserve silence—came shinning breathlessly back to the deck to report her position to the master. Burnaby, with his usual skilful precision, brought the *Huntress* to, as Phillip had instructed, between her and the northern extremity of the bay and the boats were rapidly lowered, each with its complement of armed and eager seamen, to row across the short expanse of fog-enshrouded water now separating the two ships.

Phillip watched, hiding his apprehension, until the fog swallowed them up and the muffled creak of oars faded into silence. Then, having given Anthony Cochrane his orders and seen the cutter lowered, he left the deck in old Burnaby's capable hands and made his way forward to await the outcome from the vantage point of the forecastle, with O'Leary and the crew of the Lancaster.

The huge gun, weighing close on five tons, had been run out on its pivoting slide-carriage and trained in the direction of the still unseen Russian brig, and Gunner O'Leary himself, lips parted in his familiar gap-toothed grin, stood close behind it, the trigger line looped about his right hand. He was gazing into the curtain of mist and swearing luridly and with hardly a pause as if, by the sheer force of his invective, to compel his target to reveal herself. Neither he nor the six men who composed the Lancaster's crew heard their Commander's approach; so intent were they all on their search for the brig that none turned or moved from his station, until a warning cough from one of the auxiliary powder-men brought O'Leary's head round. His harsh injunction to the offending seaman to "cease his bloody plochering," was bitten off short when he recognized the new arrival and he said apologetically, "Beg pardon, sorr—I'd no idea 'twas yourself."

"All right, Mr O'Leary, carry on," Phillip bade him as he, too, stared vainly into the fog. The boats ought, by this time, to be more than half way across, he thought and, with difficulty, refrained from cursing the poor visibility as fluently as O'Leary had just done. "Are you able to make her out?" he asked, aware that it was unlikely.

The gunner shook his head. "Divil a sign of her, sorr, for the past ten minutes. But I'll have me sights on her the instant there's the smallest clearance in the fog, don't you worry. She'll not get away from dis beauty." He slapped the great iron gun barrel with a bony hand.

"You are to hold your fire until I give the word," Phillip reminded him. It had been partly in order to issue this reminder that he had come forward; he knew Gunner O'Leary's enthusiasm for action and knew, too, the big, raw-boned Irishman's pride in his guns and in the crews he had so patiently worked up to their present high standard of efficiency to man them. The reminder probably wasn't necessary but it was a precaution and, to make his wishes absolutely clear, he added sternly, "Even if you sight the brig and even if she should open fire on us, you understand? The threat of this gun should be quite enough so, if I order you to fire, put a shot across her . . . well overhead. I don't want her damaged—I have other plans for her."

"Aye, aye, sorr," O'Leary acknowledged dutifully but his expression was a trifle injured. Glimpsing his face as he turned, Phillip relented and offered a brief explanation of the purpose of the cutting-out party and was glad he had done so when he saw a delighted grin spread over the Irishman's craggy countenance. "Now dat's what I call a grand idea!"

"You think so?"

"B'Jaysus I do, sorr!" the gunner exclaimed, chuckling. "'Twill make them Roosians look the quare eejits, so it will, when we go steaming down the channel right under their noses, in one o' their own ships!"

Phillip found his enthusiasm oddly reassuring and some of his misgivings faded as O'Leary, with a wealth of picturesque detail, enlarged on the impending discomfiture of the guardians of the Yenikale channel. He had a weakness for O'Leary's special brand of rugged Irish humour and resilient cheerfulness and, indeed, for the man himself. They had gone through a great deal together since the days when the one-time "Queen's Hard Bargain" had acted as his orderly during the battle for Balaclava. In fact, he reminded himself, he owed his life to Joseph O'Leary and . . .

"Sir—" The gun captain murmured a low-voiced warning and Phillip spun round, eyes and ears straining into the vaporous darkness. The brig must have had steam up, he realised, for suddenly he heard the throb of engines and then the threshing of water as her paddle-wheels started to rotate. She must have seen the boats or heard the splash of oars as they approached her, and was about to take refuge in flight. Probably she had slipped her cable; there had been no sound which might have betrayed her intention but obviously her Captain considered the loss of an anchor a small price to pay to avoid the capture of his ship.

"Will I put a shot across her now, sorr?" O'Leary asked. Phillip shook his head. "No, wait for my order. Quiet, all of you!"

He listened intently, in an effort to judge the brig's position and the direction in which she was heading from the sound of her engines, but the fog distorted all sounds and, apart from the fact that she was further away than he had imagined, he learnt nothing. Pray heaven she did not fall foul of his own ship as she made her blind bid for escape, he thought, and started aft at a run, only to slow his pace to a dignified walk a moment later.

Burnaby had the deck and he was the *Huntress's* most capable and experienced watchkeeper; he would have heard the threshing paddle-wheels and would take what evasive action was necessary—or possible—without waiting for orders. And he had wit enough to know that the need for silence was past, so far as the brig was concerned, and that he could use the screw if he deemed it prudent to do so. Regaining the quarterdeck without giving the appearance of undue haste, Phillip found that, as he had confidently expected, the master was well in command of the situation. With men standing by the head braces and the helm amidships, he was taking what advantage the light breeze offered to make a stern board, steering by means of the topsails and head yards. Phillip joined him, making no comment beyond a nod of approval and then, as suddenly as they had started up, the brig's paddle-wheels ceased churning.

In the ensuing silence, both men crossed to the starboard side and Phillip, moving more briskly, was the first to discern the ghostly outline of their quarry, about two cables' length distant and, still with way on her, heading north towards Akbourno and the protection of the shore batteries, as he had guessed she would.

"Well, there she is, Mr Burnaby," he observed, at pains to sound calm and unruffled. "But I'm damned if I can see either of our boats, can you? Unless—" He put the Dollond to his eye.

"Beg pardon, sir—I can see one of them!" a boy's excited voice announced from the rigging above his head. "Fast to her midships chains, sir, port side. And our fellows must have boarded her . . . I can only see one man in the boat, sir."

Recognizing Midshipman O'Hara's piping treble, Phillip permitted himself a brief smile. The boy was right, he saw, as a small gust of wind opened a rift in the low-lying fog—one of the boats had secured alongside the brig's port quarter. He could see no sign of the other but men were moving on the Russian's upper deck and there were shouts and a muffled cheer, which . . . there was a vivid flash and his acknowledgement to O'Hara was drowned by the crash of a single gun.

It was the only shot the brig got off and it whined harmlessly high above the *Huntress*'s masthead, to fall into the water well astern. Then the fog closed in about both ships once more—thicker and more impenetrable than ever, it seemed—and Phillip waited in an agony of impatience, listening to the subdued shouts and cries, his imagination conjuring up a picture of the hand-to-hand battle now being waged in the darkness aboard the enemy vessel. If only one boatload had managed to board her, they would be heavily outnumbered, he told himself, and cursed the fog which prevented him from seeing the second boat. It was, of course, possible that Graham had divided his small force and sent the young acting mate, Grey, to run in under the brig's counter so as to enable both parties to board her simultaneously, but her sudden dash under engines might well have taken Grey by surprise, with the result that his boat had failed to reach its objective.

If, instead of being secured to the brig's starboard side, Grey's boat had been left astern, then . . . Phillip glanced round at Burnaby, intending to order the screw lowered. There was nothing to be gained by silence now. The sound of the brig's engines and certainly the discharge of her gun would have carried to the batteries and alerted the garrison at Ferrikale and he needed the speed and mobility his own engines could give him if he were to close her. However skilfully old Burnaby might back and fill, he could not be sure—in this apology for a breeze—that he was maintaining his station relative to the Russian ship. She had no sail set and might drift anywhere after slipping her cable. "Mr Burnaby," he began and broke off, sick with relief, as a burst of cheering shattered the silence.

The cheers were spasmodic and swiftly suppressed but they were unmistakably British cheers and the knot of young Officers gathered on the *Huntress*'s deck and in her lower rigging echoed them heartily, an example which was followed by the seamen. Phillip, too pleased by the outcome himself to play the martinet, turned a deaf ear to them and old Burnaby's faded blue eyes were suspiciously bright as he murmured a heartfelt, "Thank God for that!"

Two or three minutes later, Grey's voice sounded across the intervening distance, distorted by the speaking trumpet he was using. "*Huntress* ahoy! Captain, sir—the First Lieutenant's respects and I'm to tell you that the brig *Constantine* has struck to us."

His announcement was greeted by renewed cheers but this time Phillip, taking the speaking trumpet Burnaby held out to him, ordered them sharply to desist, and the young mate added, "We have six men wounded, sir."

"Seriously wounded, Mr Grey?"

"Only one, sir—Ordinary-Seaman Wright. We also have fourteen or fifteen Russian wounded and about 35 prisoners. Mr Hazard asks if he may transfer them to the *Huntress* and I am to request you to come aboard as soon as convenient, sir."

Phillip frowned. Wright, he recalled, was one of Ambrose Quinn's despised "counter-hoppers"—a twenty-year-old draper's assistant from Clerkenwell, mustered as a waister. He gave permission for the transfer to be made, the wounded to be sent across first, added a quick, "Well done, all of you!" and then turned to the master. "Send the cutter to take off prisoners, Mr Burnaby, if you please, and call away my gig. And perhaps you'd pass the word to the assistant-surgeon to prepare for casualties." He hoped fervently that Brown, the inexperienced ex-medical student—to whose care all these wounded men, British and Russian, must soon be entrusted—would prove equal to the task, and then thrust the fear that he might not firmly to the back of his mind. There was always O'Leary, who had spent so long in the *Trojans*'s sick bay with a crushed leg that, when it came to dealing with serious injuries, he had more experience than Brown. O'Leary, he knew, would volunteer his aid if Brown were unable to cope and at least poor young Brown had no false pride. He was well aware of his limitations and would ask for help, if he needed it.

"You may have the forward pivot gun secured, Mr Burnaby," Phillip said, when the master came to report that his gig had been lowered and Cochrane, in the twelve-oared cutter, was on his way to take off the crew of the brig. "Keep all the guns' crews standing by their guns for the time being. I'm sure the engineers will be able to provide boiling water for cocoa by the time the wounded come aboard and . . ." he added a few detailed instructions as they descended to the entry port together. The master's gnarled fingers went to the peak of his cap. "God go with you, sir," he offered, his voice low. "And good luck!"

"Thanks, Mr Burnaby," Phillip answered. He could only hope that he had made the right decisions, he reflected wryly, as he stepped down into the waiting boat. The fog seemed thicker, in the gig, than it had from the *Huntress*'s quarterdeck and even the sharp-eyed Midshipman O'Hara, who was at the tiller, failed to see the pinnace approaching with its cargo of wounded, until the muffled splash of oars indicated its position. The boat was coming slowly towards them and Grey's voice answered Phillip's hail, sounding a trifle strained as he reported that the unfortunate Wright was in a bad way.

"He's not conscious, sir," the mate added. "We've done what we could for him but I'm afraid his back's broken."

Phillip listened in dismay. This was neither the time nor the place to enquire how the ex-draper's assistant had received such an injury—Graham would report on it, in due course. Probably the lad had fallen, somewhere in the darkness of the brig's deck, during the fight for its possession. Or he might never have gained the deck—a slip, as he was attempting to board, could have sent him tumbling back into the boat again and if he had struck a thwart with sufficient force, then a fractured spine might be the least of his injuries. Pray heaven that O'Leary would know what to do for him, even if Brown did not . . . Grey called out something and, as he had before, Phillip thrust his doubts and fears to the back of his mind, aware that the time for self-reproach would also come later.

It was still impossible to make out more than the hazy outline of the other boat but, squinting anxiously into the murk about him, he saw something else—a flat, wooden object floating on the surface of the water about twenty yards ahead and to starboard of his own boat. A piece of flotsam, he decided, and then looked again, puzzled by something about it that wasn't usual. For one thing it was too smooth and regular in shape to be driftwood and for another what looked like a strand of wire trailed from it, as if . . . Grey's boat emerged from the gloom and, before Phillip could shout a warning, its bows struck the strange floating object a glancing blow. The next instant there was a blinding flash, which lit the foggy darkness to blood-red clarity and was followed by the fearsome roar of an explosion.

The pinnace disintegrated—oars, thwarts, and the stout timbers of which it was constructed went spinning skywards in a confused jumble of barely recognizable fragments, some of which returned to the surface of the water as brightly burning debris. There they flickered until the shock-waves from the explosion extinguished them, briefly illuminating the bobbing heads and white faces of four or five swimmers . . . *four or five swimmers,* from a boatload of twenty or more? Half-blinded, his ears still ringing from the blast, Phillip stared unbelievingly about him and then, as fingers grasped weakly at the gunwale of the gig, he leaned forward to drag the swimmer into the sternsheets beside him. He was a Russian, his head roughly bound in a bloodstained cloth, and he lay gasping on the bottom boards of the gig, unable to speak.

More heads appeared from the now pitch-black darkness: Phillip yelled to the cutter to aid in rescuing them and Cochrane, who had appeared from nowhere like the bobbing heads, needed no urging. Leaving him to pick up the nearest survivors, Phillip took the gig to where an oar floated, miraculously intact and, to his stunned amazement, recognized the white, unconscious face of Ordinary-Seaman Wright, the seriously injured man, of whose chances of survival young Robin Grey had earlier despaired. He was wrapped in a tarpaulin, with two oars secured to either side of his broken body—evidently to protect him from further injury when he was being lowered into the boat—and these had kept him from sinking.

Grey himself trod water beside him and, although he looked shocked and was bleeding from a cut on the head, he responded cheerfully to O'Hara's shrill cry of recognition, as the gig drew alongside him and willing hands reached out to assist him from the water. "I'm all r-right, sir," he insisted, making a valiant effort to still his chattering teeth. "The water's rather cold, that's all. Have a care, Cox'n, as you bring that poor young devil Wright aboard," he added. "I d-don't think he can take much more."

"He's dead, sir," the coxswain told him, his tone apologetic. He glanced enquiringly at Phillip who, tight-lipped, confirmed his assertion. "We'll transfer his body to the cutter. You, too, Mr Grey—the sooner you get back to the *Huntress* and into some dry clothes the better. You did all you possibly could for poor young Wright," he added, sensing Grey's anguished disappointment.

Robin Grey gulped. He was just seventeen, Phillip reflected pityingly and, although he had met with violent death all too often in his short naval career and had himself been severely wounded the previous year, when serving with the Naval Brigade on shore, this was probably the first time that he had ever felt personally responsible for the death of a man under his command. Removing his boatcloak, Phillip draped it round the boy's dripping shoulders and said gently, "It wasn't your fault, Mr Grey. Don't blame yourself."

"No, sir," the mate responded flatly. "But he . . . poor little devil, sir, he took a blow from a marline-spike that was meant for me, when we were boarding the brig, and it knocked him back into the boat. It would have done for me, sir, if it had landed—I'd have had my head split in two if Wright hadn't flung himself in front of me." He drew a long, shuddering breath and then asked, frowning in perplexity, "What caused the explosion, sir, do you know? I suppose we must have hit something . . . but what do you think it was, sir?"

"I don't know," Phillip admitted truthfully. "But I intend to find out, if I can." There had been rumours, he was aware, that the Russians had perfected an explosive device, designed to be left floating in channels and harbours open to Allied naval attack and containing a charge of powder which—rendered by some means impervious to sea water—blew up on impact. But these were only rumours; he had paid little attention to them until now. Now, he thought grimly, it would behove him to give the matter his urgent attention since, if the channel he had been ordered to survey should prove to be blocked by any of the infernal things, the Allied fleets would be unable to use it until they were found and removed. And that might take days and jeopardize the success of the troop landings . . .

An almost naked body drifted slowly into sight and Phillip recognized the white, lifeless face of Grey's coxswain. He leaned over into the icy water, impelled by an instinct stronger than reason to try to recover Leading-Seaman Ryan's mortal remains, so that the Christian funeral, to which the man was entitled, might be performed on board the ship in which he had served. But, even as his numb fingers closed about the seaman's shoulder, he drew back, appalled by the glimpse he had caught of the hideously mutilated body. It was better not to inflict this horror on the crew of the gig, he told himself, and murmured a few words of the Burial Service before relinquishing his hold and allowing the corpse to drift away. O'Hara and his own coxswain crossed themselves and then hastily looked ahead, to where the cutter was approaching them.

Lieutenant Cochrane hailed him with the news that, aided by the second boat, which had been sent from the brig to join him, he had picked up twelve survivors and Phillip's anxiety eased a little. "Four Russian wounded are missing, sir," Cochrane reported. "I spotted a couple of them, swimming as hard as they could for the shore, but I doubt if they'll make it. We tried to pick them up but they vanished in the fog. Five of our men are badly hurt—shall I take them to the ship, sir?"

"I have Mr Grey and a Russian to transfer to you," Phillip called back. "And the body of Ordinary-Seaman Wright. Come alongside, if you please." The transfer was effected without mishap and, when both rescue boats were pulling across to the *Huntress,* Phillip told Midshipman O'Hara to take him to the brig. He found his brother anxiously awaiting him, with the unwounded Russian prisoners lined up under guard on the forecastle.

"Thank God you're all right, Phillip," Graham said. "I was really worried for a while, until I heard Cochrane say he'd picked up most of our fellows, so I take it that it might have been worse."

"We lost two men and five are badly hurt," Phillip told him, with conscious bitterness. "Grey's boat was blown to pieces." He supplied what details he could but, when he started to describe the mysterious object which had apparently caused the explosion, he saw his brother's mouth tighten ominously.

"Come and take a look at this, Phillip." Graham picked up a lantern and led the way to the starboard side of the brig's upper deck. Holding the lantern high, he pointed to a cone-shaped wooden container, with a flat top some three feet in circumference, which was suspended from what appeared to be a specially constructed rack, slung well clear of the ship's side, just forward of her paddle-box. "Well?" he demanded. "Does this contraption bear any resemblance to the object you saw strike Grey's boat?"

Phillip gingerly inspected the four-foot-high cone, careful to avoid contact with any of the wires protruding from beneath the flat iron-bound and bolted top. So the rumours had not been exaggerated, he thought grimly—this was the so-called

Russian "infernal machine" concerning which there had been considerable speculation among the ships of the Baltic Fleet, which had encountered them off Cronstadt and in the Gulf of Finland. The *Merlin* had been struck by one and suffered some damage, he recalled, although she had not been put out of action. Nothing of the kind had, as yet, been reported in the Black Sea theatre to the best of his knowledge but he was conscious of a bleak feeling of dismay as he turned to answer his brother's question with an affirmative nod.

"Yes," he said slowly, "I fancy this must have been very like the object I saw. Most of it was submerged but the shape and the flat top are similar—I noticed the flat top particularly. I imagine that there's an inner watertight casing to house the charge and that it's detonated by means of those wires . . . they'll be attached to some sort of firing mechanism inside the casing, no doubt. A pretty diabolical contraption, is it not?" He glanced about him with narrowed, searching eyes. "Do you know if this is the only one on board?"

"It's the only one *left* on board," Graham told him. "The one that blew up Grey's boat was dropped over the side—I rather think in the hope that the *Huntress* might run on to it— when the Captain realized that he'd been boarded. The others, according to him, have all been dropped and left floating in the approaches to Yenikale and—"

"In both channels?" Phillip put in, his mouth suddenly dry. "Did he tell you how many have been dropped, for God's sake?"

Graham shook his head regretfully. "The Captain is not very communicative, I'm afraid. All I was able to get from him was the boast that there are now enough obstructions of various kinds to bar the Sea of Azoff to our ships. But I take leave to doubt that there can be all that many floating bombs, Phillip.

The *Highflyer* and the *Vesuvius* have had the Strait under constant observation and they've reported nothing unusual. Besides, these are new weapons and damned dangerous to handle—they'd have to be carried in launching-racks, rigged for the purpose, like that one there. There's another on the port side and each can hold three bombs, so . . ." he shrugged. "Even if she's made two trips, this brig can only have dropped eleven of the things and one's accounted for."

"I hope you're right." Phillip frowned. This was a most unwelcome complication but . . . "Where is the Captain now?"

"I sent him below, to his cabin, with Gunner's Mate Thompson on guard. I thought you'd want a word with him."

"I do indeed." Phillip's voice had an edge to it. "And I'm going to keep him on board, Graham, until we've cleared every last one of his infernal machines from the Kertch side of the Strait. If he can't or won't tell me where he dropped them, then by heaven I'll run his ship through the channel regardless, until he cracks!"

"He's a tough customer," Graham warned. "He won't crack easily. But"—he led the way below—"see for yourself."

CHAPTER TWO

Graham's assessment of the *Constantine*'s Commander was amply borne out when Phillip attempted to question him. He was a tall, thickset man of about forty, with close-cropped black hair and heavy beard, whose expression of sullen indifference gave nothing away and whose answers, in thickly accented French, were defiantly uninformative. Even when Graham addressed him in his own language, he responded with shrugs and headshakes and, beyond admitting that his name was Kirkoff, he refused to be drawn.

"Tell him," Phillip said at last, losing patience, "what I intend to do, if he won't give me the information I require. And make him believe I mean it, if you can."

Graham translated and, for the first time, the brig Commander's deep-set dark eyes betrayed a hint of uneasiness, as he replied at some length. "He says," Graham repeated, "that he is a prisoner-of-war and he demands to be transferred to the *Huntress* with his men and accommodated in accordance with his rank, until an exchange of prisoners can be arranged. He also wishes you to . . ." Exasperated, Phillip cut him short. Time was passing and many lives might be lost, he thought angrily, if the infernal machines this man had dropped in the channel were not removed—or rendered harmless—before the Allied flotilla under Jack Lyons's command passed through it on the way to Yenikale and the Sea of Azoff. If Kirkoff would not talk willingly, then he would have to be coerced into doing so, whatever his rights as a prisoner-of-war. He . . . there was a tap on the door and Midshipman O'Hara entered, cap in hand.

"Yes, Mr O'Hara?"

"Mr Cochrane's compliments, sir, and all wounded and the prisoners have been transferred to the *Huntress*," the boy announced. His gaze strayed with unconcealed curiosity to the glum-faced Russian Captain and Phillip said quietly, "One moment, Mr O'Hara. Thompson, escort Captain Kirkoff on deck, will you, and mount a guard on him. I'm keeping him with us and I'd like to keep you in charge of the guns, if you're willing to stay. There's no compulsion—the prize-crew will all be volunteers."

"I'll stay, sir," the gunner's mate answered promptly. He grasped his prisoner's arm none too gently and started to propel him towards the open cabin door.

"Look over the brig's guns when you've detailed a guard," Phillip called after him. "They're long thirty-twos, I fancy, and we may need them. Check the magazine, too, while you're about it." Hearing Thompson's acknowledgement, he turned back to the waiting midshipman. "Now, Mr O'Hara—you say Mr Cochrane has returned aboard?"

"Yes, sir. I'm to tell you that he's brought an ensign and the marker-buoys, on instructions from the master, and he's loading them aboard this ship. He has also brought Jackson, sir, with a lead-line, and the second engineer and two of his fellows, as you ordered. Bo'sun's Mate Driver is with them and your steward, sir. Mr Burnaby said you were to be informed that they all volunteered to join your prize-crew."

Burnaby, a good man that he was, had forgotten nothing,

Phillip's mind registered, although he had left no instructions concerning his steward, Higgins.

"Thank you, Mr O'Hara," he said formally. "Ask Mr Cochrane to have the marker-buoys stowed on the after part of the upper deck, if you please, and say that I'll want a tow-line rigged astern for the cutter—he can take off the cutter's crew in the quarter-boat. And, if he hasn't already gone below, perhaps you'd better tell Mr Curtis that I shall require engines within the next fifteen or twenty minutes, so he would be as well to inspect them before we part company with the *Huntress*. Then you can stand by to take off the First Lieutenant *and* my steward—I shan't be needing a steward. Have you got all that?"

"Yes, sir. But I . . ." O'Hara shuffled his feet nervously, making no attempt to depart on his errand and Phillip prompted, with a hint of impatience, "Carry on, Mr O'Hara. The First Lieutenant will not be long."

"Sir, I . . ." the boy's cheeks were pink but he held his ground. "If you please, sir, may I volunteer for the prize-crew? You'll need an Officer, surely, sir, and I *am* your gig's mid-shipman, after all . . ." and a rattling good young Officer into the bargain, Phillip reminded himself, in spite of his lack of inches. He had intended to keep Grey with him, as the senior, but in the circumstances . . . he hesitated and then inclined his head. "Very well, Mr O'Hara. In that case, tell your cox'n to stand by to take off the First Lieutenant."

"Aye, aye, sir. Thank you very much indeed, sir." O'Hara sped off, as pleased and excited as if he had been given pro-motion, instead of the chance to risk his neck, Phillip thought ruefully. But in time of war, fourteen-year-old midshipmen could not be treated as boys; they were naval Officers, with the duties and liabilities, as well as the privileges of their rank and, he supposed, he had reason to be thankful that Cadet Lightfoot, who had recently celebrated his twelfth birthday, hadn't also offered himself as a volunteer. He swore under his breath and Graham observed, as if he had voiced his thoughts on the subject of O'Hara audibly, "You'd have broken the poor little devil's heart if you hadn't let him stay."

"I know that. But—"

"But it hurts, does it not?"

"Like the devil," Phillip admitted. "He's a mite too keen to chance his arm for my liking but—" he shrugged. "He'll go a long way in the Service, if he's given the opportunity."

"If he survives to be given it, you mean," his brother countered shrewdly. "And so will you, my dear Phillip! This is a risky enterprise. I wish you'd permit me to—"

"No!" Phillip retorted, an edge to his voice. "This risky enterprise, as you are pleased to call it, is my responsibility. You've done your share."

Graham sighed. "Very good. But you know perfectly well that I shall never make flag-rank, whereas you may one of these days if, like young Paddy O'Hara, you live long enough! But there it is, I suppose." He reached for his cap and asked, with a swift change of tone, "How many men do you intend to keep with you, Phillip? Shall I call for volunteers before I return to the *Huntress?*"

"I'd be grateful if you would." Phillip considered the question. "Curtis has his complement for the engine-room, but Thompson will need six gunners and, with Jackson on the lead, I'll need a reliable quartermaster and a couple of hefty lads to heave those marker-buoys over the stern. They can double as look-outs, at a pinch, and I'd better have a man to keep an eye on Captain Kirkoff, I suppose."

"Another ten men, then. You're whittling your crew down rather drastically, aren't you?"

"I want no more than I can take off in the cutter."

"Very well." Graham's expression was carefully blank but a small muscle twitched at the angle of his jaw as he said, "And my orders? You'll permit me to stand by, will you not, in case you need assistance?"

"At the entrance to the channel and out of range of the batteries," Phillip told him uncompromisingly. "Don't take any risks with the *Huntress,* Graham, whatever happens to the brig. You understand, I—"

"Am I to let you drown?" Graham protested. "Or be blown sky-high by one of Kirkoff's infernal machines, without lifting a finger to help you?"

"You can send a boat if necessary. I'll soon let you know if I need assistance, don't worry," Phillip assured him. "If the fog's too thick for a rocket to be seen, I'll give you a succession of long blasts on the steam whistle." He laid a placatory hand on his brother's arm. "For heaven's sake we'll have the cutter, and those infernal machines don't carry a big charge. Even if we have the misfortune to strike one head on, we should have ample time to abandon ship before it sinks us."

"I trust you will, Phillip."

"Of course we will. But if I do ask for help, send in the quarter-boat, under Cochrane's command. Don't bring the ship in or engage the batteries without specific instructions. That channel has to be buoyed and, if we fail, it will be up to you to see that it's done, you understand?"

"I understand." Graham's voice was flat but, to Phillip's relief, he did not argue, although it was evident that he did not find these instructions particularly palatable. He moved towards the door of the cabin and added, his voice still without expression, "Kirkoff was attempting to destroy his confidential papers when I interrupted him. He got rid of a number but there are some charts next door, which you might care to examine before you come on deck. I only glanced at them but there's a chance you might find them better than ours."

"Thanks—I'll have a look at them." There was a small chartroom opening off the main cabin and, entering this, Phillip turned up the lantern which was hanging there. By its light, he saw that the table was littered with an untidy mass of books and papers and seating himself, he started to make a careful search for anything which might prove useful or informative. All were in Russian and therefore incomprehensible to him; some bore official seals and appeared to be orders, a few probably current but most, judging by their faded appearance, long outdated. A battered signal manual caught his eye and he opened it, to find a thick sheet of folded draught paper thrust between its pages, as if in a clumsy attempt to use the manual as a hiding place. His interest aroused, he spread the sheet out in front of him, to purse his lips in a silent whistle of pleased astonishment, for there could be no mistaking the neatly executed series of diagrams at which he was now looking.

Despite their Russian text, they were easily comprehensible in their step by step illustration of the design and construction of the floating bomb that had blown Grey's boat to pieces, the counterpart of which he had seen hanging from a rack attached to the brig's upper deck. There was the coneshaped container, there the flat wooden top, with the three iron bolts by which it was secured to its base. Each part had been given a distinguishing letter or figure, so that he was able to see that the charge was housed in an inner casing—as he had supposed—held in place by a thick ring of gutta-percha which, in turn, was fitted to an iron ring above it.

The firing mechanism appeared simple but ingenious. A primer of some kind—probably fulminate of mercury, Phillip decided, unable to decipher the Russian text—was placed in a small flush container above the charge, with a rigidly held percussion nipple at one end. The percussion hammer, for setting off the explosion, was operated by two wires, which acted as trigger-lines. These, he saw, passed inside the central ring and, to enable the bomb to be transported safely, their ends were brought through to the outer side of the casing where, in order to render it active, they had to be joined under tension. On impact—that was to say when the flat top of the bomb was struck by a passing vessel—the wires parted, releasing the trigger-lines and, the charge being ignited, the infernal thing exploded. The diagram illustrated the tools required for the purpose of connecting the wires but offered no guidance as to what method to employ when reversing the process. Once activated, it seemed, the bomb remained dangerous for as long as . . . he frowned. For as long as the outer casing remained water-tight and he could only guess at how long that would be. For some hours, certainly, but more probably for several days.

His excitement at his unexpected discovery somewhat dampened, Phillip hunted among the scattered objects on the chartroom floor and finally found the tool-kit for which he had been looking, in a leather case, half-hidden behind a pile of books. The case contained some strips of gutta-percha—presumably to provide insulation or protection for the wires—an auger, two pairs of pliers and a small, oddly shaped wrench; the latter, he supposed, for removing the bolts which held the flat top of the bomb in place.

He slid the case into his pocket and, returning to the table, swiftly thumbed through the signal manual in the hope of learning the enemy's current recognition signals but without success, for the manual was long outdated. There were, however, several charts of the Straits and of the Sea of Azoff itself, including the one by which Captain Kirkoff had evidently been navigating. In addition to the usual symbols, this was marked with a number of inked-in circles and annotations, some in black and others in red ink and Phillip stared at them for several minutes, in an effort to decide whether they were intended to indicate recently constructed artificial obstructions or the presence of floating bombs. They could be either or both; he had no means of knowing for certain, unless the Russian Captain could be prevailed upon to tell him or unless Graham could decipher the notes. He reached for dividers and a ruler and started to make a few rapid calculations, when there was a tap on the door of the main cabin and O'Hara's voice broke into his thoughts. "Sir!"

"Well, Mr O'Hara?"

As always, O'Hara had run with his message and was out of breath.

"First Lieutenant's compliments, sir, and I'm to tell you that he has selected the prize-crew and embarked the rest of the boarding party in the quarter-boat. He asks, sir, if he may have a word with you before he returns to the *Huntress*."

Phillip nodded. "Ask the First Lieutenant to step down here, please." He looked at his watch. "Have you a report from the engine-room?"

"Yes, sir—Mr Curtis is ready with engines and the coal-bunkers are two-thirds full, sir. And the gunner's mate has reported both guns serviceable. He's brought up ammunition from the magazine—it's all shell, he says, sir—and the guns are run out and loaded, on the First Lieutenant's instructions. We're ready to get under way, sir."

"Thank you, Mr O'Hara. We'll get under way as soon as I've had a word with the First Lieutenant." Phillip gave his orders with deliberate lack of haste, detailing the members of his depleted crew to the stations at which, for the time being, they could be most usefully employed. "See that the boarding party leave their rifles with us," he added. "We may need them."

"Aye, aye, sir." The midshipman was off, his new status as second-in-command of the brig *Constantine* belied by the undignified speed of his departure.

"No reason to run, Mr O'Hara," Phillip called after him in mild reproof. "I shall be at least ten minutes with the First Lieutenant."

Graham joined him in the chartroom a few moments later. "I've been trying to pump our prisoner again," he announced, before Phillip could speak. "But the damned fellow has shut up like a clam. I've been thinking, though, in the light of his refusal to co-operate, could you not wait for an hour or so, Phillip, and let me go and find the *Vesuvius?* If I report the situation to Captain Osborn, he may be able to procure you some technical help. The Army will have explosives experts, even if we haven't and—"

"They won't be necessary," Phillip put in impatiently.

"Not necessary? What about those infernal bombs?"

"I think I can deal with them. You see, I—"

"For God's sake, how?" Graham demanded harshly. "O'Hara's just told me you want our rifles but you'll certainly risk the batteries opening up on you if you attempt to blow them up with rifle or gunfire—flying the Russian flag won't protect you. And it will be a devilish tricky business if you try to tow the accursed things clear of the channel. Even securing a line to one is liable to explode it—you saw what happened to Grey's boat."

He sounded so deeply and genuinely concerned that Phillip made an effort to hide his impatience. "You may certainly go and find the *Vesuvius,* my dear fellow, whenever you've a mind to—there are some charts here that Jack Lyons will find extremely useful, especially if Sherard Osborn can deliver them to him before he leaves the Fleet rendezvous. You were right about their being an improvement on ours . . . but look at these diagrams, will you, before you say any more?" Relinquishing his seat at the table, he offered the purloined Russian diagrams for his brother's inspection. "They show exactly how the charge is stowed in those bombs and how it's detonated, do you see? I found them stuffed into an old signal manual, by a stroke of luck—Kirkoff must have tried to hide them there. Obviously he didn't want them to fall into our hands."

"No, obviously he didn't." Graham examined the drawings, his expression relaxing visibly as he did so. "I'm relieved, for your sake, that you found these, Phillip. At least you will not be working completely in the dark, although it still isn't going to be easy to disconnect the trigger-lines in the water, you know, with most of the bomb submerged. In fact, I doubt if it can be done . . ." he started to go into technical details but Phillip cut him short.

"There must be a way of doing it. If Kirkoff cannot or will not help—well, we have one of his bombs on board. I can test my theories on that, before we enter the Strait." He spoke with more confidence than he felt and, uneasily conscious that time was passing, drew his brother's attention to the marked chart. "What do you make of these inked-in circles, Graham? Do you suppose they're meant to indicate where the bombs have been dropped? I'm aware, of course, that they may have drifted but if we know where Kirkoff set them in position initially, it might offer a rough guide to where they are now."

"Very rough, I fear, unless the Russians have some means of anchoring them. There's nothing shown on the drawings, is there?"

"No. But presumably they've only been in the water for a few hours—Kirkoff must have been dropping them when we came up with him."

"Yes, I should imagine he was . . . and others, too, perhaps. With no tides, they won't have drifted far, of course." Graham bent over the chart, studying it with furrowed brows. "If these circular markings *do* indicate where the bombs were dropped, it looks as if most of them are in the deep water channel off Taman, to the eastward, doesn't it? But they could be sunken ships or artificial barriers—particularly this line here, look, where Captain Moore reported a great deal of coming and going by steamers, towing laden boats. Didn't he say that they were heaving stones and piles of timber into the Taman side of the channel, nearly a month ago?"

"Yes," Phillip confirmed. "He said they were hard at it— damn, I'd forgotten about that, Graham!"

"But you need not concern yourself with the deep water channel," Graham pointed out. "If these *are* floating bombs, then—provided the squadron is warned of their presence—the damned things can be blown up easily enough in daylight, after our troops have landed and occupied the batteries. If these black circles are meant to represent obstructions of some other kind, it will still be useful to know exactly where they are located. And talking of warning the squadron, shall I make a fair copy, on one of the other charts, so that it can be delivered to the *Miranda?* It won't take me long."

"Make the copy for me," Phillip suggested. "And omit the notes, because I can't make head or tail of them. I take it they're in Russian—can you make any sense of them?"

Graham shook his head regretfully. "I should need a dictionary and more time than we have now, I'm afraid. I can make myself understood in Russian but I can't read or write it." He picked up a pen. "Pass me that bottle of red ink, Phillip, would you? Thanks . . ." he worked with deft speed. "These charts are more accurate than any we've got, you know, and they give a depth of at least two fathoms, right up to Yenikale . . . even four, in places. You should have little trouble getting through the channel on this side, Phillip, because look . . . whatever these mysterious circles are supposed to signify, there are only five—no, six of them. It seems evident that the enemy aren't expecting our attack flotilla to attempt the western channel, although there's no doubt that it is navigable for light draught vessels. If they were expecting anything of the kind, they would have dropped more of their infernal machines on this side of the Cheska Bank, don't you think?"

"They probably consider the batteries a sufficient deterrent," Phillip answered. "Or perhaps Kirkoff was supposed to replenish his supply." He glanced anxiously at his watch. "Have you nearly done?"

"Very nearly." Graham's pen moved rapidly, the nib squeaking under the pressure he put on it. "There, that's it, I think, when the ink dries. Phillip, if I may, I'd suggest you steer nor' by east until you sight Ferrikale and then stand out into mid-channel. It will be safer, for one thing and for another, if these markings do indicate floating bombs and they're not secured, the current will carry them inshore."

Peering over his brother's shoulder as he traced the course to be followed, Phillip's earlier optimism returned. The channel was narrow, it was true, but it existed. He would go straight through, he decided, as Graham advised, setting the marker-buoys out as he went, and postponing his search for the bombs until he had carried out his orders and was on his way back. The brig would be less likely to arouse the suspicion of the gunners on shore if she made a bold, direct run up to Yenikale and, thanks to Kirkoff's excellent charts, he could dispense with a survey boat, sounding ahead of him. On the return run, he would have to make a careful search for any bombs or other obstructions which constituted a danger to the passage of Jack Lyons's flotilla through the channel and deal with these as best he might. It would probably be impossible to avoid arousing suspicion when he was thus engaged . . . unless Captain Kirkoff could be persuaded to tell him how the bombs could be defused, he would have to blow them up and the resulting explosion would undoubtedly bring the batteries' fire down on him. But . . . he sighed. Time enough to cross that hurdle when he came to it. There was always the possibility that Kirkoff might be prepared to reveal the brig's recognition signal; even the taciturn Russian might become more amenable, he thought grimly, were failure to reply to the batteries' challenge to result in his ship coming under fire.

Graham rose, rolled up the marked chart he had been copying and tucked it under his arm. He asked, as they left the chartroom, "I imagine you'll wish me to report with this to the *Vesuvius* right away, Phillip? Or am I still to be permitted to stand by in case you require assistance?"

Phillip's hesitation was momentary. "Right away, if you please. If anything should go wrong, it will be when we're on our way out of the channel, I fancy—but you'll hear if we're fired on."

"Very good." Graham did not attempt to question his decision. Reaching the deck, he looked about him, observed that the fog was as thick as ever and then held out his hand.

"*Au revoir* and the best of luck, Phillip, my dear fellow. I'll be standing by to pick you up in a couple of hours—sooner, if the fog lifts. And be careful how you handle Kirkoff—he's an ugly customer, if ever I saw one, and he knows his rights as a prisoner-of-war."

"I'll be careful," Phillip said lightly. He waited until the gig cast-off and then turned to his youthful second-in-command, who was standing expectantly at his elbow. "Very well, Mr O'Hara, let us get under way. Inform Mr Curtis that I am ready for engines, if you please." He crossed to the binnacle and, when the steady throb of the brig's engines heralded O'Hara's return, gave his orders with crisp brevity.

"Aye, aye, sir." The boy hesitated, eyeing him uncertainly. "Shall we dowse lights, sir?"

Phillips smiled down at him. "A Russian ship, approaching Russian guns, would do so openly, showing her deck and navigation lights, would she not? To all intents and purposes, we are a Russian ship, Mr O'Hara, so we shall do precisely that, you understand?"

"Yes, sir," O'Hara acknowledged. "I understand, sir."

It was to be hoped he did, Phillip thought, his smile fading as he peered once more into the illuminated compass bowl in front of him. The *Constantine's* paddle-wheels gained momentum, churning the water to foam and the dark silhouette of his own ship vanished into the fog.

"Steer nor' by east, Quartermaster," he ordered.

"Nor' by east—aye, aye, sir," came the answer. A tall, black-browed Cornishman named Trevelyan was at the wheel, he noted approvingly, a man with nearly eighteen years' service and—until Ambrose Quinn had had him flogged on some trumped-up charge the previous year—an exemplary record. It was typical of Trevelyan to volunteer for both boarding party and prize-crew; the flogging had not embittered him, as such harsh punishment frequently did. He was a good choice, an excellent helmsman, especially under sail . . . the brig responded a trifle sluggishly to her helm and, his lined brown face twisting into a grin, the quartermaster compared her, with good humoured blasphemy, to a mulatto woman with whom, it seemed, he had once co-habited.

Eyes on the compass bowl, Phillip affected not to hear the witticism but the corners of his mouth twitched as he ordered a correction of course. Turning again to the alert O'Hara, he said, "I have a matter to attend to which will take me ten or fifteen minutes, Mr O'Hara, but it need not concern you. You will be in charge of the deck. Maintain this course and speed— I shall have finished what I have to do before we're likely to close the north side of the bay but inform me at once if you sight any other ship. And keep a sharp look-out . . . here, take my glass, I shan't be requiring it."

The midshipman gave him a pleased "Aye, aye, sir," and, the Dollond in the crook of his arm, started to pace the narrow confines of the brig's quarterdeck with the slow, measured tread of a seasoned watchkeeper. Satisfied that his keen young eyes would miss nothing, Phillip picked up a lantern and, crossing to the rack from which the cone-shaped bomb was suspended, he swung himself up into the mainmast shrouds in order to make a second and more careful examination of the flat wooden top and the wires running from beneath it.

From this vantage point and in the light of his newly acquired knowledge of the firing mechanism, he saw, to his dismay, that the trigger-lines had been connected. The bomb, therefore, was no longer in a state when it could be moved without risk. Conscious of an unreasonable feeling of disappointment, he descended to the deck and, stepping to the forward side of the bomb rack, levered himself on to the top of the paddle-box. By lowering the bomb a foot or two in the net which held it, he could, from where he was now positioned, alter or adjust the wires. By the same token, he could probably unbolt the top casing and lift it right off, so as to expose the inner chamber but . . . he swore under his breath, realizing that it was out of the question to attempt anything of the kind once the trigger-lines had been set. The smallest error and the charge would explode, with disastrous consequences, not only to the brig but to any man within range of the blast, including himself. He had a mental vision of poor Ryan's mangled body and felt the sweat break out over his own.

Damn Kirkoff for having activated those trigger-lines, damn his treacherous Russian soul to perdition! Scowling at the tautly stretched wires, Phillip forced himself to make a cautious fingertip exploration of the thick wooden sides of the bomb's barrel-like outer casing. In a spirit of optimism induced by his possession of the diagrams, he had counted on his ability to work out some simple way in which the bomb could be rendered harmless. He had been prepared, if necessary, to strip this one down in order to find a method that would serve equally well when he had to deal with one of its counterparts, floating in the waters of the channel but . . . he sighed in frustration. If he could not test his theories on the only example of the foul contraption that he was likely to find high and dry, then his chances of success were slight, if they existed at all. As it now was, this bomb was useless for his purpose; indeed it was dangerous and his best course would probably be to jettison and blow it up, even at the risk of alerting the batteries.

Of course, if he did so, he would be committed to dealing in the same manner with any others he might encounter in the channel, with the added risk of their proximity to the shore, but he had little choice, he thought glumly. The bombs could not be destroyed silently, the infernal things had to be exploded, unless . . . he drew in his breath sharply. Unless he could devise a means of puncturing the outer casing, so as to flood the charge with water. Undoubtedly this would deprive the bomb of its menace as silently and effectively as he could possibly wish . . . but was the idea feasible?

His questing fingers moved over the casing, seeking a flaw and finding none. The wood was smooth, tightly held by two iron hoops and at least three inches thick—*too* thick, the devil take it! Even with the top held securely in its specially designed rack, it would take time to bore through a three-inch thickness of hardwood. When the bomb was afloat and largely submerged—as it would be in the channel—the task would take much longer and a single hole might not suffice.

Nevertheless it might work, Phillip told himself, and was tempted to try. The bomb would have to be lowered very carefully into the water, with the net still enveloping it, so that he could keep it under control—in fact, he would probably have to go down with it to make sure that its descent was not impeded. Once in the water, he would need a boat to take the heavy cone in tow and remove it to a safe distance from the brig . . . he glanced round. The *Constantine* carried two boats on her starboard side, one a small, four-oared gig, which would serve his purpose admirably, and he would have to take two men with him, one to hold the boat steady, the other to assist him to dispose of the bomb. Thompson was the obvious choice as his assistant; he was accustomed to dealing with explosives and he would not lose his head. Besides, the big gunner's mate was an intelligent man—shown the diagrams, he might come up with some more practical solution to the problem than his own.

And there was Kirkoff . . . Phillip's mouth twisted into a grim little smile. Captain Kirkoff had earned the right to join the bomb disposal party, if anyone had, he thought cynically . . . and the experience might loosen his tongue. Lowering the lantern, he vaulted down from the paddle-box and, taking out his watch, saw to his relief that it was not yet eight o'clock. He had told O'Hara that he would need ten minutes for his inspection of the bomb and he hadn't taken much more than that but, in another fifteen minutes or so, Ferrikale Point and the first of the Kertch batteries would loom up through the foggy darkness, and all his attention would have to be concentrated on getting the brig safely past.

He needed more time and he would have to take it, he decided; more haste, in this case, was liable to result in less speed. He could not enter the Strait with that infernal bomb hanging from its davits above the deck, it would be asking for trouble. The bomb had to be destroyed and a delay of an hour or so would not make much difference—he could be into and out of the channel before dawn, given a modicum of luck. Given a little more, he could be in and out without the enemy being aware of his presence . . .

"Mr O'Hara!" His mind made up, Phillip called O'Hara over and instructed him to stop engines and bring-to. "And pass the word for Gunner's Mate Thompson," he added.

"Aye, aye, sir." O'Hara's round, cherubic face was the picture of astonishment but he was too well trained to ask questions. Even when, the order to the engine-room passed on smartly, Phillip told him to stand by to lower the four-oared gig, he expressed no more surprise than could be conveyed in a dutiful acknowledgement. When Thompson came running aft in response to the summons and the steady throb of the engines ceased, Phillip motioned them both to follow him and crossed to the bomb rack. He said, gesturing to it, "That bomb is set to explode. I'm going to jettison and destroy it before we proceed any further but the question is how. Take a good look at these, Gunner's Mate." He unfolded the sheet of diagrams and set the lantern beside it on the deck. Thompson obediently dropped to one knee in order to examine them, his expression as puzzled as O'Hara's had been a few minutes before.

"Take your time," Phillip bade him. "And you can inspect the bomb itself, from the paddle-box, if you want to—but have a care how you handle it. Then tell me what *you* think is the best way to render it harmless, having regard for the fact that this probably won't be the only one we shall have to get rid of . . . and that some may be too close to the shore batteries for comfort."

"You mean you don't just want to blow it up, sir?" Thompson suggested.

"Yes, that's what I mean."

"It's a tall order, sir," the big gunner's mate demurred.

"I'm aware of that," Phillip admitted. "As a last resort, we'll have to blow them up—the channel has got to be cleared for our attack flotilla tomorrow morning and there may be half a dozen of the things floating about there now." He explained briefly and O'Hara, who had been leaning over Thompson's shoulder, straightened up to meet his gaze in shocked understanding.

"Was it one of these bombs that did for Mr Grey's boat, sir?"

"Yes, almost certainly it was, Mr O'Hara," Phillip answered. The boy, too, must have glimpsed the body of Grey's unfortunate coxswain, he thought, and it did not take very much imagination to conjure up a horrifying vision of the damage which half a dozen of Kirkoff's floating bombs could cause, among the boats of a flotilla putting ashore. Midshipman O'Hara, he was aware, possessed a lively imagination and he said, with intentional sharpness, "See to the gig for me, if you please. I want a fender rigged over the stern and one pair of oars will suffice—you can remove the others. Oh, and I shall require a lantern. Stand by to lower when I give the word."

The horror faded from the youngster's eyes. "Aye, aye, sir. But . . ." he hesitated. "Sir—"

"Well?" His mind busy with details which had yet to be attended to, Phillip's tone was still sharp. "What is it, O'Hara? And where's Captain Kirkoff, where's the prisoner, do you know?"

"On the fo'c'sle, sir, with the forward gun's crew, I think. Shall I send for him?"

"No, I'll get him myself. What did you want to ask me?" Phillip waited, concealing his impatience.

O'Hara avoided his gaze. "Well, I . . . are *you* going in the boat, sir? I mean, are you going to blow up the bomb yourself?"

He could hardly delegate a responsibility of this kind to his second-in-command, Phillip reflected, reminded of Graham's obstinate insistence on leading the boarding party. "Yes," he asserted, "I am, Mr O'Hara. I shall take Thompson and one other man with me. You will remain in command of this ship and, if anything should go wrong or if for any reason I should fail to get back, you are to rejoin the *Huntress* and hand over your command to the First Lieutenant—is that clear? He's gone to report to the *Vesuvius* but he should be back here within a couple of hours."

"Yes, sir, that's clear. But, sir . . . I—" He was still looking anxious, Phillip realized, and he said reassuringly, "Don't worry, youngster, I intend to handle that bomb with kid gloves. And I shall probably take Captain Kirkoff with me, to ensure that nothing goes wrong. He hasn't been exactly co-operative so far concerning his bombs and I have it in mind to try and loosen his tongue, if I can. So . . ." he smiled and, after a moment's uncertainty, O'Hara grinned back at him.

"Now I see, sir. Thank you for telling me. I'll go and attend to the gig, sir."

Phillip made his way forward. The wind, he noted, had freshened a little and was still backing—another point or two and the fog might start to disperse. He looked at his watch, hoping that it would not lift too soon, and returned the time-piece to his pocket with a wry grimace. He had seldom, if ever, *wanted* a fog to persist but tonight he wanted it badly, for just a few more hours . . .

CHAPTER THREE

P *hillip* ascended the companion-ladder to the forecastle and, at the sound of his approach, the men squatting round the long, Russian thirty-two pounder broke off their desultory conversation and scrambled to their feet.

"All right, carry on," he bade the gun captain and they squatted down again, eyeing him with a curiosity which discipline precluded them from putting into words. "We're going to get rid of an encumbrance we shall be better without," he offered in explanation, sensing that their curiosity was mingled with a certain anxiety. "It ought not to take very long. If the gunner's mate and I can't put it out of action between us, you may have an opportunity for some target practice with that gun—so keep on your toes, my lads."

The gun's crew exchanged knowing glances. "It's a bomb, sir, ain't it?" one of them asked. "A new kind of floating wooden bomb them Ruskies have invented?"

"That's about the size of it," Phillip admitted. "And when we get it into the water, you'd better make yourselves familiar with the look of it afloat, because there may be more of the same sort where we're going. They're not too easy to spot when nine-tenths of the casing is submerged." He left them to digest this warning and crossed to where the squat figure of the brig's Commander stood, shoulders hunched against the dank chill of the night, watching his approach with ill-concealed resentment, which found explosive expression as soon as he was within earshot. He listened in silence to the spate of words, flung at him in fluent but gutteral French, from which he learnt that his prisoner found the company of common sailors distasteful and that of the insolent oaf detailed to stand guard over him particularly so.

"I am an Officer of the Imperial Russian Navy, *monsieur*," the Captain reminded him furiously. "You have taken possession of my ship and made me your prisoner, for what purpose I do not know. But the usages of war demand that you treat me with the respect and consideration due to my rank. These men are animals! If you have no Officer to whom you can entrust my care, then permit me to retire to the privacy of my cabin where I may, at least, be spared the foul-mouthed insults of your men."

When the tirade at last petered out, a Cockney voice observed dryly, from the shadows at his back. "'E don't arf rant on, do he, sir? Bin at me this past arf hour to take 'im below, out o' the cold. But I told 'im 'e'd 'ave ter wait until you give me the word."

Recognizing the voice of his steward, Phillip asked curtly, "Higgins, what are *you* doing here? I told the First Lieutenant I did not need you. In fact I sent an order by Mr O'Hara for you to return to the *Huntress*."

"Yessir," Higgins agreed. He limped forward, slapping the butt of his Minié rifle in smart salute. "I volunteered to stand sentry on 'is Nibs—beg pardon, sir, the Captain, seeing as you didn't need me. But I wasn't given no order to go back to the *'Untress,* sir, and when the First Loo'tenant called for volunteers, I stepped forward, thinking I could make meself useful, like."

"I see." There was no reason to doubt his word. Like

O'Leary and Treveyan, Able-Seaman Higgins was a long service man, who knew exactly what liberties he could take
within the strict disciplinary limits of the lower deck and was
careful never to exceed them. His limp was a relic of his service ashore with the Naval Brigade, when a shell-burst in the
Diamond Battery had wounded him severely, but he was otherwise perfectly fit and, in the six months since he had joined
the *Huntress,* he had become a first-rate steward, conscientious
in the performance of his duties, cheerful and even tempered—the last man to behave insolently to any Officer. All
the same, Kirkoff's charges were serious ones and they could
not lightly be dismissed. The Russian was cold and out of
temper; almost certainly, he had exaggerated the affront to his
dignity but, equally certainly, all chance of gaining his cooperation would be lost if he were offered no redress. Pressed
for time though he was, Phillip knew that he would have to
investigate the prisoner's complaints and, if necessary, pun-
ish the offenders.

"Shall I carry on, sir?" Higgins ventured.

"No, not yet. Captain Kirkoff tells me that you've insulted
him, Higgins." Phillip eyed him sternly. "What have you to say
to that, pray?"

"*Me,* sir—insulted 'im? Oh, no, sir!" The steward's expression was one of honest bewilderment. "I ain't said nor done
nuffink to 'im—nuffink like that, I give you me word. I just
carried out me orders and kept 'im 'ere, nice an' quiet, like
the First Loo'tenant said."

"And the others?" Phillip demanded. "The gun's crew? The
Captain is not impressed by their discipline or their language."
Which, he thought, was a rather toned-down translation of
Kirkoff's actual words but the slur on his men still rankled. "I
want the truth, Higgins, because I cannot permit a prisoner-
of-war to be abused by men under my command. Come on,

now, I've no time to waste—have any of you been disrespect-
ful or used foul language to this Officer?"

Higgins headshake was emphatic. "No, sir," he answered
gravely. "As Gawd's me witness—we was yarning a bit, me and
the gun's crew, just passing the time. But not to 'im, sir. No
one's shown 'im no disrespect. In any case, sir, the prisoner
don't understand English, so 'ow can 'e accuse me of insulting
'im? 'Ow can 'e say as any of us was using foul language? It
took me all me time to make 'im understand why I couldn't
take 'im below and . . ." he broke off with a smothered gasp,
as the Russian Captain spun round to strike him a stinging
blow across the face with the flat of his hand.

If the blow was unexpected, so too was the stream of vitu-
peration which followed it, in a confused mixture of French,
English, and Russian. To Phillip's relief and his own infinite
credit, Higgins offered no retaliation. A thin trickle of blood
ran down his chin from his bruised and battered mouth but
he said nothing and, in a telling demonstration of the British
naval discipline his accuser had questioned, he remained
rigidly at attention, staring through the angry Russian as if
unaware of his existence.

Two of the gun's crew, who had been watching, started
towards them but Phillip waved them back to their gun. What
little sympathy and respect he had felt for the *Constantine*'s
Commander swiftly evaporated and he said coldly, "I regret
that it will not be possible to send you below, Captain. I require
your assistance in disposing of the unpleasant object which
formed part of your cargo, so perhaps you will be good enough
to accompany me." To Higgins, he said, lowering his voice,
"Good lad, you behaved admirably . . . now escort the prisoner aft, if you please. And if he should strike you again, you
have my permission to ground your rifle on his foot."

"Aye, aye, sir," Higgins acknowledged, a gleam in his dark

eyes. "Thank you, sir." He gripped his rifle purposefully and Captain Kirkoff, recognizing defeat, moved sullenly towards the companion-ladder. "It's my belief, sir," the steward added in a hoarse whisper, "that the Captain understands a mite more English than 'e's bin letting on—and they do say as listeners never 'ear good of themselves, don't they, sir? Maybe 'e took exception to summat me and the gun's crew was saying about the Ruskies, when we was yarning, sir."

"Yes," Phillip agreed. "He probably did. So oblige me by keeping a guard on your tongue in future."

"I will indeed, sir," Higgins assured him contritely. This was the nearest to an admission he was likely to get from his steward and, he thought, the nearest he wanted to get, in the circumstances. Higgins had taken his punishment and had deserved to, since it now seemed improbable that the Russian Captain would co-operate willingly with his captors . . . but clearly the alleged insults had been unintentional and the incident was best forgotten. Remembering Graham's parting words, Phillip sighed. "All right, my lad—we've wasted enough time. Escort your prisoner aft and look lively," he ordered and strode briskly over to where Thompson was standing beside the bomb rack. "Well, Thompson, what about it?"

The gunner's mate shook his head despondently. "It'll have to be blown up, sir—there's no other way that I can see . . ." he went into technicalities, to which Phillip listened, frowning.

"I don't want to risk using the guns," he objected. "The bomb will be a small target in this fog, as you don't need me to tell you. Several shots might be needed to sink it and that would reveal our position to the batteries. Even rifle shots would be heard, you know."

"Yes, sir, I thought of that, so I prepared a small charge

and a slow match." Thompson displayed an oilskin-wrapped package for his inspection. "If we tow the bomb to a safe distance, I can set this charge on the lid, sir, clear of the water and she'll go up about ten minutes after the fuse is lit—longer, if you want, I can adjust the length of the fuse. The percussion wires will snap when the lid blows but we'll be out of the way by then."

"And how do you propose to tow the bomb to a safe distance?" Phillip asked.

"I can rig a couple of towlines to the net, sir," Thompson answered promptly. He pointed to the bomb rack. "The release-gear is designed to drop the bomb clear of the net but I think I can fix that. Then, if the boat's lowered first, we can haul the lines taut so as to keep the bomb well away from our hull. It shouldn't be too difficult to shift, sir, if we take it slowly."

"Well done, Thompson," Phillip approved. It was a compromise but, he supposed, it would have to do—he was running out of time. "You're quite sure there's no way to put the damned thing out of action without exploding it? No way of sinking it or of letting water into the inner chamber, by boring holes in the casing or through the lid? There'll be others, remember, that we shall almost certainly have to deal with when we're buoying the channel."

Thompson shook his head. "I wouldn't care to try boring holes in it, sir," he said positively, backing up his statement with further technicalities. "I had thought of attaching a weight, heavy enough to send the whole contraption to the bottom but them trigger-lines only need a touch to release them—the weight of water would do it. Come to that, sir, I wouldn't altogether fancy dropping bombs like this off, even with the ship under way, like the Russians have been doing, seemingly. In anything like a sea or when she's at anchor, it'd be downright dangerous because—" from behind him, Captain Kirkoff growled something unintelligible. Eluding Higgins' attempt to restrain him, he thrust the threatening rifle barrel contemptuously aside and pushed past Thompson to confront Phillip, his bearded face dark with rage.

"You intend to buoy the western channel, Captain?" he accused, in fluent English. "In *my* ship, so that your fleet may attack Kertch and Yenikale?"

Phillip motioned the indignant Higgins to come to a halt at his prisoner's back. Facing the Russian, he answered quietly, "Yes, sir, that is my intention."

"You will not pass our shore batteries unchallenged," Kirkoff warned. "Or the obstacles we have placed in the channel."

"With your assistance, Captain, I am confident that we shall," Phillip countered, smiling. "Should the batteries challenge us, you know the correct recognition signal and it will save time—and the possibility of damage to your ship, as well as loss of life—if you will reveal it."

"I shall reveal nothing," the Russian told him sullenly. "Your suggestion is an insult, sir. I am a prisoner-of-war, I cannot be coerced into assisting you."

"As you wish." Watching him closely in the dim light of the deck lantern, Phillip shrugged with well simulated indifference. "Your ship is, I am sure, familiar to all your gunners and, in this fog, our failure to reply to their challenge may well pass unnoticed. That is a chance we shall have to take." Again he saw a flicker of uneasiness in the prisoner's angry dark eyes and hastened to follow up his momentary advantage. "I've examined your charts, Captain, and even without your aid, I anticipate no difficulty in negotiating the obstacles, which are clearly marked. Some of them are floating bombs, are they not, similar to the one we are about to dispose of?"

He gestured to the bomb rack and added, in explanation, "To safeguard my crew, I propose to scuttle that one, as you probably heard, before we enter the channel."

"Scuttle?" Kirkoff's heavy black brows met in a faintly puzzled scowl but beneath them, his eyes were bright with malice. "Do you mean that you will jettison the bomb?" he enquired. "And sink it by gunfire?"

Phillip shook his head. "Oh, no, Captain—that would alert the batteries, would it not? And they would be certain to challenge us. We are going to tow your bomb to a safe distance and set a small charge on top of it, timed to go off when we are clear of the area."

Captain Kirkoff stared at him in shocked dismay. "By the Holy Virgin!" he exclaimed. "*That* is not the way to destroy so dangerous a weapon! You will blow yourselves up if you attempt to take it in tow—these bombs can only be destroyed by gunfire."

His words and the vehemence with which they were uttered almost carried conviction—almost but not quite—and Phillip hesitated, uncertain whether or not to believe him. It would suit his book, undoubtedly, if the shore batteries *were* alerted and a prolonged burst of gunfire—even from what appeared to be one of their own ships—could not fail to send every gunner in the forts to his post, to peer, portfire in hand, into the murky darkness. On the other hand, the Russian might be telling the truth. He knew more about his infernal bombs than anyone else, although Thompson was no fool when it came to handling explosives and he had given careful thought to the problem of their disposal. It was possible, of course, that he might have erred in his reckoning, even with the diagrams to help him and, if he had, the consequences would be appalling . . . but *had* he?

Still undecided, Phillip turned, intending to consult the

gunner's mate again, but instead he found Midshipman O'Hara at his elbow and was reminded of his earlier decision to take the prisoner in the gig with him, in the hope of loosening his tongue. The mere threat of this might do so now, he thought, in view of Kirkoff's real or pretended alarm at the suggestion that his bomb might be taken in tow and it would do no harm, surely, to force the truth from him?

Glancing aft, he saw that the gig had been hoisted out, with men attending the falls, and his hesitation ended. "Ah, Mr O'Hara," he said. "Are you ready to lower?"

The midshipman touched his cap. "Yes, sir," he answered eagerly. "Fenders rigged, as you instructed. Ready to lower, sir." An impish grin spread over his small, pink-cheeked face as he looked at the prisoner. "Shall I carry on, sir?"

"Lower away, Mr O'Hara, and secure amidships until I'm ready to relieve you." The boy scurried off to take his place in the stern of the gig, his shrill commands to his crew of two to perform their task handsomely rising about the creak of the lowering tackle.

Phillip smiled to himself. There were few more efficient junior Officers in the Service than this youngster, he reflected and, as he had told Graham, O'Hara would go a long way, once he had overcome the habit of doing everything at breakneck speed. Then, meeting Kirkoff's baleful gaze as the gig splashed into the water, his smile faded and he said, with icy courtesy, "I'd be obliged if you would accompany me to the boat, sir, to assist in the disposal of that bomb before we proceed. I'll accept your parole if you are willing to give it and—"

"My *parole?*"

"Your word that you will not try to escape, sir. Escort the Captain, Higgins, if you please. Thompson, I want you to rig towlines and take charge of—"

The Russian Captain's reaction was swift and violent.

"You are mad!" he shouted. "All the English are mad! *I* shall give you no assistance!" He spat his contempt at Phillip's feet. Both Higgins and Thompson, incensed by the insult to their Commander, attempted to close on him and drag him forcibly away but the stocky Russian resisted their efforts. White with rage, powerful arms flailing, he hurled abuse at them in any language that came to his tongue. "Do not lay hands on me, you misbegotten curs! Verminous animals! I am an Officer, lately in command of this ship, and a prisoner-of-war—you have no right to violate my person! Call off these men, Captain," he appealed wrathfully to Phillip. "Under the usages of war I demand protection from them!"

Mindful that there was some justice in his claim, even if there had been none for his earlier outburst, Phillip snapped an order and the two seamen, breathing hard, obediently stood back. "I offered to accept your parole, sir," he pointed out, at pains to speak without heat. "If you will give it, then—"

"I will give you nothing." Kirkoff spun round, his expression suddenly ugly. Without warning, he struck the unsuspecting Thompson across the back of the neck, felling him instantly and, when Higgins hesitated before trying to grapple with him, he robbed the man of his rifle as if it were a plaything in the hands of a child and drove the butt of it hard into his stomach. The steward crumpled gasping to his knees, impeding Phillip's ill-timed lunge and, moving with astonishing agility for one of his bulk, Kirkoff broke free and made for the paddle-box.

He vaulted on to it and, expecting him to dive overboard in a bid to escape, Phillip yelled a warning to the boat below and grabbed him by the ankle, only to receive a savage kick in the face which sent him reeling. When he recovered his balance, he saw through a bloodstained haze that the Russian had an axe in his left hand. With this—kept, no doubt, for emergency in case the release-gear jammed—he started to hack at the ropes from which the bomb-net was suspended, dropping the rifle in order to use both hands to more effect. His purpose was now all too clear . . . fool that he was not to have realized it before, Phillip reproached himself and, in a despairing attempt to prevent him from achieving it, he made a leap for Kirkoff's straining back.

He was seconds too late. The first rope was already severed when he gained a precarious foothold on the paddle-box top and, in the brief struggle that ensued, he found himself out-matched and out-manoeuvred by a heavier and more powerful opponent, who paid no heed to the Queensberry Rules and seemed possessed of a maniac's strength. Twice the Russian broke from him to slash at the remaining release-rope; once he managed to wrest the axe from him but lost it again when Higgins endeavoured bravely, if clumsily, to come to his aid. The second time, the rope parted under a frenzied assault and, watching helplessly from the prone position into which he had been flung, Phillip saw the bomb drop into the water.

It sank, rose to the surface almost immediately and was carried by the momentum of its fall to within a foot or two of the starboard paddle-wheel. There, with its tautly stretched trigger-lines awash, the deadly thing floated on the slight, oily swell, needing only a puff of wind or the chance pull of the current to drive it against the paddles . . . that or a well aimed rifle shot to explode it.

Dear God, the rifle! Higgins's Minié lay between them, within his reach, and Phillip stretched out a hand but Kirkoff was before him, kicking his hand away and swearing as he stooped to pick up the weapon. He followed the kick with another, which connected painfully with Phillip's face but now there were half a dozen men milling about the paddle-box, with Thompson and the quartermaster, Trevelyan, making determined efforts to mount it, and the Russian had to fend them off with the butt of his weapon before he could take aim. In spite of this, he contrived to keep them at bay and had the rifle to his shoulder when Phillip forced his bruised and battered body to a final effort and, in a parody of a Rugby tackle, sent him flying into the waiting arms of the men on the deck below.

As he fell, the Minié went off, almost unheard in the confused clamour of voices, to discharge its single ball harmlessly into the air. Kirkoff continued to battle furiously with his captors but even his incredible strength was to no avail against so many with scores to settle and Phillip, staggering dazedly to the edge of the paddle-box, was compelled to intervene, in order to save him from serious injury.

"All right, my lads, that's enough," he bade them thickly, fumbling for a handkerchief with which to wipe the blood and sweat from his face. One eye was rapidly closing and it was an effort to hold himself upright but somehow he managed to do so and his vision started to clear a little when he returned the stained scrap of linen to his pocket.

"What shall we do with the bastard, sir?" Higgins asked truculently, as he and Jackson dragged the prisoner, none too gently, to his feet. "If I 'ad my way, I'd tear 'is ruddy guts out and—"

"Belay that, Higgins!" Phillip's tone was curt. "Take him below to his cabin and don't let him out of your sight until we're able to deliver him to the Admiral—but keep your hands off him, understand? Thompson, up here and see how much of the net you can salvage—we shall need it to tow that bomb away. The rest of you . . . back to your stations and keep your eyes skinned. Look lively, now, we're not out of trouble yet. I'll be in the boat, Thompson."

"You're in no state, sir," Thompson ventured. He vaulted on to the paddle-box, eyeing his Commander with concern. "Why, you can't hardly stand and your face . . . that Russian bastard made a proper mess of your face, sir."

"I'm fully aware of that," Phillip assured him irritably. "But that infernal bomb is of more concern to me at the moment, so for pity's sake, get to work on the net, will you, so that we can get the blasted thing out of the way of the paddles before it does any damage. It's lying too close for us to risk warping the ship astern, I'm afraid, so we'll *have* to tow it clear. However, we can count ourselves lucky that it didn't blow up when it hit the water."

"That we can, sir," Thompson agreed feelingly. Taking his knife from his belt, he swung himself on to the empty bomb rack, whistling tunelessly under his breath. Phillip was about to descend to the deck when the whistling abruptly ceased and he heard the seaman call his name in sudden alarm.

"What the devil's the matter, Gunner's Mate? You sound as if—"

"It's Mr O'Hara, sir . . . he's pulling across to the bomb, in the gig, sir, alone as far as I can make out . . ." Thompson broke off, muttering blasphemies. "It looks as if he's got a boathook and he's backing up, stern-first. My God, sir, I do believe he's aiming to tow the bomb away by himself!"

Phillip's first reaction was one of impotent anger. Confound O'Hara, he thought, confound him for a scattered-brained young idiot! Surely he must have overheard enough of the earlier discussions with Thompson to realize with what care that bomb had to be handled? Yet here he was, with complete disregard for the orders he had been given, apparently about to take a boathook to it!

The sweat cold on his temples, Phillip peered downwards, praying that he would be in time to stop the boy before he attempted any such act of madness. His vision was still blurred but he could just make out the gig, with O'Hara bareheaded and in his shirtsleeves, crouching in the stern, the boathook gripped firmly in both hands. He had shipped his oars and his elbows were resting on the matting fender for support but the bomb was barely inches away and Phillip knew that it would be inviting disaster to do or say anything which might break his concentration or startle him into making a sudden movement.

"Boat there!" he hailed softly, no trace of anger in his voice. "Don't look up, Mr O'Hara, but listen to me, if you please."

O'Hara's fair head lifted a fraction but did not turn.

"I'm listening, sir. Don't worry, though—everything's all right and I know what I'm doing." He sounded resolute, if a trifle apprehensive but this, Phillip reflected wryly, was more likely to be because his unauthorized action had been discovered than because he feared the consequences of it. O'Hara had never lacked courage, had never shrunk from doing his duty, as he saw it, and no doubt imagined, in his innocence, that by risking his life in this quixotic, single-handed venture, he was sparing others from having to risk theirs. "I'm taking every care, sir," the boy added, in a burst of confidence.

"Good." Phillip knelt, unbuttoning his watch-coat. "But I'd rather you didn't do any more on your own. Can you haul off, without touching the bomb?"

There was a brief hesitation. "No, sir, I don't think so. I have the boathook attached, you see. If I let go, I may send it into the paddles . . . it's yawing a bit, sir. Must be the current."

"Then hold fast, Mr O'Hara," Phillip ordered, conscious of a sick sensation in the pit of his stomach at the thought of what might happen should the youngster fail to do so. He heard Thompson jump down beside him and asked, lowering his voice, "Did you get the net?"

"I have it here, sir."

"Good man! Off with you now and tell the bo'sun's mate to lower a second boat as fast as he knows how—from the port side. Tell him he's to pull round, under our counter, and stand off until I call him in . . . right? Then come back here. I'm going down to Mr O'Hara with the net and I'll need your help, because it will take two of us." Phillip shrugged off his coat, shaking his head impatiently to Thompson's offer to exchange their roles. "Jump to it, man! But don't shout any orders or let the boat's crew kick up a shindy—if that boy loses his head, it'll be all up with him."

"Sir!" O'Hara's voice floated up from the darkness, sounding less confident, as if the realization of what he was up against had become suddenly and alarmingly apparent to him. "The bomb's yawing an awful lot, sir . . . I—I don't think I can hold it. I'll *have* to fend it off or—or try to take it in tow, because the gig's drifting too, sir. You see, I—"

"Wait, lad!" Phillip besought him, working at frantic speed to complete the preparations for his own descent. He secured a stout line to the frame of the bomb rack, attached the end of the net to its extremity and let both snake down into the water a few yards ahead of the gig. There was no time for finesse now, he told himself, kicking off his boots—whatever he did carried an element of risk but O'Hara's situation would brook no delay. His original plan had been to encompass the sunken portion of the bomb-casing in the salvaged net, using a boat to haul the net into position from a safe distance by means of long towlines, paid out as the net was let down from the brig's paddle-box. But now he knew the distance would have to be shortened and a swimmer would have to do what the boat should have done . . . "Hang on for another couple of minutes," he told O'Hara. "I'm coming down to you."

"I'll try, sir," the boy promised breathlessly and lapsed into silence, fighting his lonely battle against panic. Phillip glanced down, unable to suppress a shiver when he saw how far round both bomb and gig had drifted. Then Thompson rejoined him, with the news that the second boat was being lowered and he steadied himself, making an effort to speak calmly and without haste as he explained what he intended to do.

"Right, Mr O'Hara," he warned. "I'm coming now. If you can—"

"There's no need, sir," the midshipman called back, his shrill young voice unexpectedly cheerful and unafraid. "I've got the hang of it, honestly I have. The Russian Captain was talking through his hat when he said you couldn't tow these bombs, because you can, sir. This one's coming quite easily. All you have to do is hold it steady. You—" his voice was lost in the dull boom of an explosion.

As its predecessor had done, the bursting bomb shed a bright, glowing radiance over the dark water on which it had been floating, a glow that was reflected in all its hideous clarity by the shifting banks of vapour overhead. The brig shuddered, as shock-waves struck her hull and rebounded, to lose themselves in the foaming maelstrom from whence they had arisen. Phillip was knocked off balance, when Thompson cannoned into him; regaining his feet, he stumbled to the edge of the paddle-box, the blood pounding in his ears, to stare about him in shocked disbelief. Where, on the previous occasion, there had been the bobbing heads of one or two swimmers to offer hope, now—apart from a few smouldering scraps of shapeless wreckage—there was nothing to be seen, no sign to indicate that either the gig or the boy who had been crouching in its stern had ever existed.

"Sweet Mother in Heaven!" Thompson whispered. "Oh, sweet Mother in Heaven . . . he must have grabbed hold of the trigger-lines or caught them with his boathook, poor little sod! I suppose . . ." he glanced, in white-faced uncertainty, at Phillip. "There'll be no hope of finding him, sir?"

Sick at heart, Phillip shook his head. "I doubt it but we shall have to try. Call the boat in, will you? Tell Driver to pick me up." He went over the side, aware that it was a forlorn hope but driven by his own grief and pity to make the attempt. The intense cold of the water as he entered it afforded some relief to his pent-up feelings. He made a conscientious search, deliberately shutting his mind to everything but the task he had undertaken, refusing to let himself remember O'Hara's voice as he had heard it a few moments before the thunder of the exploding bomb had silenced all other sounds.

Memories would return to haunt him, he knew. He would hear the voice of his conscience, echoing that of the boy he had failed to save, until his own dying day; and there would be questions—unanswered and unanswerable questions—to torment him when his spirits were low and when the decisions inseparable from command had again to be made. He could not absolve himself of responsibility for O'Hara's death or for young Wright's or even for Ryan's—they had been his men and he had sent them to their deaths—but now, whilst he still had orders to carry out, he dared not allow himself to think of them.

When the boat picked him up, with the expected report of failure, he abandoned the search and ordered Boatswain's

Mate Driver to pull over to enable him to inspect the starboard paddle-wheel. Damage to it was slight and, relieved on this account at least, Phillip motioned towards the entry port.

"All right, Bo'sun's Mate, get your boat hoisted inboard and look lively—I want to get under way as soon as I can. You'll take Mr O'Hara's place and act as my second-in-command on deck."

"Aye, aye, sir," Driver acknowledged. He was an ambitious young regular seaman but his voice expressed no pleasure at his temporary elevation in rank. All the boat's crew were subdued, their faces glum—O'Hara had been popular with the lower deck and his loss had come as a shock to them, the more so, perhaps, because of the circumstances surrounding it.

Back on board, Phillip lost no time in putting them to work and, with the return to accustomed routine, the habit of discipline reasserted itself and they set to with a will, their grief—like his own—thrust temporarily into abeyance. Only when the brig was on course for Ferrikale did he yield to Thompson's urging and change into dry clothing borrowed, the gunner's mate told him with a grin, from Captain Kirkoff.

"No sign of life from the batteries, sir," he added, his tone faintly puzzled. "But they must have heard the explosion."

They could hardly have failed to, Phillip thought grimly. He sent Thompson to stand by his gun and subjected the fog-shrouded coastline to a lengthy scrutiny from the mainmast crosstrees before coming to the same puzzling conclusion. There were lights, gleaming faintly through the fog, but no undue activity that he could make out and, having instructed Driver to prepare a signal lantern and to summon him immediately should there be a challenge from the shore, he went below to make a final study of the marked Russian chart.

Higgins, on guard over the sullen Kirkoff, reported that

the prisoner was lying on his bunk, apparently sleeping.

"'E ain't said much to me, sir," the steward enlarged. "Except to call me one or two sorts o' verminous animal and order me not to lay me filthy 'ands on 'im. So I left 'im be— if 'e can sleep through that there infernal device of 'is going off, then good luck to the booger . . . begging your pardon, sir." He hesitated and then ventured diffidently, "Is it true that Mr O'Hara's a goner, sir? You didn't find 'im?"

"It's regrettably true," Phillip confirmed, tight-lipped. "And we were unable to find him." He bent over the chart, the contours and figures blurred and indistinct as he endeavoured to concentrate on them, and Higgins wisely returned to the subject of his prisoner.

"You won't get nuffink out of 'im, sir, not in 'is present mood, you won't . . . that is, sir, if you was thinking of trying. 'E says as you've violated his rights as a prisoner-of-war."

"I probably have," Phillip agreed, without contrition. He rolled up the chart and got wearily to his feet. "We are about to close the Ferrikale batteries, Higgins, and if they challenge us, we've no answer—make sure Captain Kirkoff knows that, will you please? And if we're fired on, you can bring him on deck at the double, laying your filthy hands on any part of his person you find expedient in order to get him there."

Higgins grinned appreciatively. "Aye, aye, sir. I'll see 'e knows that too, sir. But if you'll permit me to offer you a word of advice—with respect, sir, I mean it—you'd be better off if you was to drop 'im overboard and let 'im swim for it, instead of 'anding 'im over to the Admiral."

"Oh, for heaven's sake, man!" Phillip exclaimed in exasperation. "This isn't the time to indulge your sense of humour—I'm in no mood for jokes."

"I'm not joking, sir," Higgins assured him. "That Russian

bastard's out to get you. 'E as good as told me that 'e's going to make an official complaint against you, the first chance 'e gets, and—"

"Well, he can try." Phillip dismissed the suggestion with a shrug, too tired to take it seriously just then. "Carry on, Higgins," he added sternly. "The prisoner is *your* responsibility and I don't want any more trouble from him. I'll have you on a charge if he even attempts to escape, do you understand?"

"Yessir, very good, sir. I thought I ought to warn you, that's all." Higgins snapped smartly to attention, acknowledging the reproof without resentment.

Phillip returned to the deck and promptly forgot the prisoner and his steward's misgivings concerning him. There were other, more pressing matters to be dealt with than Captain Kirkoff's future complaints; the brig was within range of the enemy shore batteries now and the success or failure of his mission in the balance.

"We'll stand in boldly," he told Driver. "And try to fool them. Be ready with that signal lamp. If we're challenged we shall have to make some sort of reply or they'll fire on us. Hold the lamp low, so that it's partly obscured, and make your signal slowly and awkwardly, as if you're a poor hand at it."

"No trouble about that, sir," the petty officer answered, with glum satisfaction. "I *am* a poor hand, sir, always was." He looked pale, Phillip noticed, and his fingers, as they tested the signal-shutter, were not quite steady but he managed a grin at his own wry admission of his inadequacies as a signaller and padded purposefully forward to take up his position by the starboard rail.

To Phillip's consternation, the fog thinned as the distance between ship and shore gradually lessened. Glass to his eye, he was able to make out the distant silhouette of the fort of

Ferrikale from the deck a second or two before the masthead look-out sang out a warning. Following Graham's advice, he ordered the necessary change of course and stood out into mid-channel without reducing speed, so as to weather Ferrikale Point and the earthwork gun batteries positioned on its slopes. He expected at any moment to be challenged but, to his heartfelt relief, no challenge came.

There were lights gleaming from the fort and he could dimly see men moving about the earthworks but either the gunners recognized the *Constantine* and supposed her to be going about her legitimate business or else the fog had lulled them into a sense of false security. For whatever reason, the disturbance in the bay and the sound of the exploding bomb did not appear to have alarmed them and they allowed the brig to pass unmolested. Finally satisfied that his ruse had succeeded, Phillip mopped the beads of sweat from his brow and sent Leading-Seaman Jackson to get the lead going in the forechains.

"Right, Driver," he ordered, when his new second-in-command joined him in response to his summons. "Take the two spare hands from the after-gun and start laying out those marker-buoys. I'm going to reduce speed in a few minutes and steer by the chart . . . we've got nearly four miles of channel to mark, so you'll have to be sparing with the buoys." He gave detailed instructions and Driver, gaining in confidence now, nodded his understanding.

"Aye, aye, sir. What about the signal lamp, sir?"

"You can leave it with me," Phillip told him. "We're not likely to be challenged until we come abeam of the Yenikale fort—and with luck, perhaps not even then. But I shall have to take two more men off the guns because I shall need messengers. Pass the word for Gunner's Mate Thompson, if you please."

Thompson appeared promptly, with the two men he had asked for and, having despatched one to the engine-room with the order to reduce speed, Phillip entrusted the task of relaying the leadsman's calls to the other.

"Your responsibility will be to look out for any more of those infernal floating bombs, Thompson," he added. "I propose to destroy any which are likely to obstruct the channel on our return passage, if possible—I don't want to delay now, in order to deal with them, if it can be avoided. For one thing, it would certainly draw the attention of the gunners in the fort to us and for another I want to lay out our buoys before the fog lifts. I'll be steering by this chart of Captain Kirkoff's, which has artificial obstructions marked, as you can see." He spread out the chart on a hatchway cover and indicated the markings which Graham had copied so carefully. Thompson bent over it, listening attentively to his explanation, as Jackson's voice sounded faintly from the fore-chains.

"And a half six, sir!" the messenger repeated.

Phillip rolled up the chart. He could discern a star almost directly overhead, he realized, and another to the northeast . . . the fog still swirled over the deck and lower yards but overhead it was clearing, rolling seaward from the dark bulk of the land and borne by a freshening off-shore breeze.

"Fog's lifting a bit, sir," Thompson observed.

"Well, that should make your job a little easier—and mine, too, come to that. All right, carry on, Gunner's Mate." Phillip laid a hand briefly on the seaman's broad shoulder. "Do the best you can—I'm not expecting miracles. I know how hard these blasted bombs are to spot in the water."

"Suppose I don't spot any, sir?"

"Then that will be all to the good, because it will probably mean they've drifted on shore, out of the channel. But that's too much to hope for, I'm afraid—Captain Kirkoff knew what he was doing when he dropped them off. All *I* hope is that we don't run on to one ourselves." Phillip sighed. "Put all your gun's crew, except the captain, on look-out and make sure they keep their eyes skinned. One man had better lie out on the jib-boom, at least until the fog lifts."

"By the mark five, sir!" the messenger called, as Thompson returned to his station at a run. Then, a moment or so later, "And a half four, sir!"

The channel was shoaling rapidly, Phillip's mind registered. He barked an order to the quartermaster, feeling the tension start to build up inside himself again, and sent his second messenger to the engine-room to request a further reduction in speed.

"Second buoy away, sir!" Driver reported, his words accompanied by an audible splash, as the threshing paddle-wheels slowed and the throb of the engines faded to a low pitched hum.

"By the deep four, sir!" came the shout from the leadsman.

"Steady as you go, Quartermaster," Phillip said. He swung himself up into the mainmast shrouds, feeling the wind fresh on his cheeks as he climbed.

CHAPTER FOUR

The wind continued to freshen and back round, finally dispersing all except a few isolated patches of fog, which lingered at a little over deck height above the water. The night sky, though overcast, revealed occasional glimpses of an almost full moon, by whose fitful light Phillip was able to keep an observant eye on the high ground of the western shore.

Seeing nothing to cause him alarm, he waited until the bristling gun emplacements of Ferrikale were left well astern and then ordered a cautious increase in speed. The little *Constantine,* miraculously unchallenged and apparently unnoticed, steamed slowly up the channel, sounding and laying out her buoys as she went. Conditions were ideal for his purpose, Phillip told himself—indeed, they were better by far than he had anticipated—yet he continued to feel tense and uneasy. He steered by Captain Kirkoff's chart and set course for Yenikale, now barely three miles distant, constantly sweeping both sea and shore with his night glass. The inked-in markings on the chart still puzzled him; if they were intended to note the position of obstructions in the channel, the darkness hid these from him, but he gave each a wide berth, aware that he would have to make a more careful investigation before leaving the Strait.

The first he sighted and was able to confirm was in the

form of a sunken ship, lying on her side in the shallows, her splintered mainmast jutting skywards at an acute angle. She had almost certainly been driven on to the rocks in some long-forgotten storm and left to rot there, he decided, until the need to utilize any available object to block the narrow channel had led to her being dragged off, to find her last resting place on top of a sandbank, on the shore side of the channel. The only danger she appeared to present was to the unwary, in fog or darkness, but her position had been marked in red ink on Kirkoff's chart and, for this reason, Phillip cut his engine speed to dead slow and steered well clear of her.

He was thankful he had taken these precautions when, coming abeam of her, he noticed the two lengths of heavy chain cable which connected her battered bows to some unidentifiable sunken object—possibly another wreck—lying almost in mid-channel. An excited hail from Thompson, a moment later, drew his gaze to a bomb, wallowing in the disturbance caused by the *Constantine*'s paddles, and the gun captain spotted a second lying just beyond the barrier formed by the chains.

Two bombs, Phillip thought, and felt the muscles in his throat tighten as he trained his glass on the flat, innocent-seeming wooden top of the nearer of the two evil contraptions—two out of a possible six, if Graham had been right in his interpretation of the Russian chart. If he had and if the red circles indicated the presence of bombs, then the rest had been dropped between here and Yenikale.

He strode impatiently to a deck lantern and studied the chart again. There were two red circles *below* his present position—he and Thompson had missed them, so they would have to be located and put out of action on the return passage, as these two would, unless . . . he hesitated, the glass to his eye again. He was anxious to complete his mission but they had made good progress—more than half the four-mile length of channel had been buoyed—and this was a diabolical obstruction, one into which an over-eager Commander in Jack Lyons's squadron might well blunder, even in daylight and in spite of the buoys, if he failed to remove it. And in these circumstances, he could not be sure that he would make the return passage unscathed or with time to spare . . .

"Messenger!" he called. "Tell Mr Curtis to stop engines. Bo'sun's Mate, avast heaving those buoys and stand by to let go the bower anchor. Pass the word for the gunner's mate."

Thompson came running aft, a gleam in his dark eyes when Phillip told him of his change of plan. "I can do it, sir," he answered promptly. "And I have charges prepared—I set Ellis to work on them as we came up-channel, thinking you'd want them, sir. The only thing I need to know is how long a delayed fuse you want."

"I'll need fifteen minutes, to get us clear. Can you place the charges without any danger to yourself or the boat?"

The gunner's mate grinned. "That I can, sir—with a boathook. Poor young Mr O'Hara had the right idea but he . . . well, he didn't quite go about it in the right way. Can I take Ellis with me, sir?"

Phillip nodded. It went against the grain to leave this risky operation to his two seamen gunners but now he had no alternative, for there was no Officer to whom he could hand over command. "Carry on," he said briefly. "But for pity's sake, have a care, lad!"

"I will, sir," Thompson assured him. The boat put off, five minutes later, with Driver's two spare hands at the oars and Thompson and his gun captain crouching in the bows. Phillip waited, his mouth dry, following their every move with anxious eyes until the darkness swallowed them up. Within less time than he had believed possible, they were back and Thompson reported cheerfully that both charges had been placed in position.

"It went without a hitch, sir. I had Ellis steady my arm, just to make sure, and they went on, sweet as you please, with the boat well away from both of them."

"Well done, Gunner's Mate," Phillip said, with sincerity. "Well done indeed! I'll see that your conduct is brought to the Admiral's notice as soon as we get back to the Fleet."

"Thank you, sir." Thompson reddened and added practically, "With any luck, when those bombs go off they'll take the wreck with them—they'll take the cables for sure. And that's a good job done, sir—I wouldn't like to think what trouble that unholy contrivance might have caused to some of our ships, if it'd been left where it was. D'you reckon there'll be any more like that one, sir?"

Phillip shrugged. "Yes, I'm afraid there may be. But at least we know how to deal with them now—or I trust we do. All right, back to your station and don't take your eyes off the water for a split second. Bo'sun's Mate . . ." he gave his orders briskly, feeling some of his earlier optimism returning but, on course for Yenikale once more, he had to fight against the temptation to consult his pocket watch as the minutes ticked by and he listened tensely for the expected explosion. Fifteen minutes passed and the towering ramparts and tall watch towers of the fort of Yenikale were in sight, silhouetted against a lightening sky . . . yet still there was no sound save the throb of the *Constantine*'s engines and the rhythmic churning of her paddle-wheels, broken by an occasional shout from Driver, as he and his crew threw another marker-buoy over the stern.

Dear God, Phillip wondered, his heart sinking at the prospect, could Thompson's charges have failed, after all, to do their work? Had water seeped into the oilskin covers in which they had been wrapped or the fuses spluttered into extinction for the same reason? Perhaps Kirkoff was right, perhaps the only way to destroy his infernal machines was by gunfire. Perhaps . . . oh, to the devil with Kirkoff! Had not O'Hara's death proved, beyond all doubt, that these bombs required only a touch to set them off? And Thompson was a reliable man, he would have seen to it that his charges were watertight. It was a pity he'd had no Bickford fuses but . . .

"And a quarter three, sir!" The messenger whispered the words as if he, too, were listening with bated breath for the sound that did not come and feared that his own raised voice might preclude his hearing it.

He ought to relieve Jackson on the leadline, Phillip thought and opened his mouth to bid the messenger exchange places with him when, muted by distance, he heard the dull crump of an explosion. It was followed, seconds later, by another and, from what seemed a long way astern, he witnessed the now sickeningly familiar spectacle of blazing particles of wood hurtling into the air, to descend as smouldering flotsam on the dark, heaving surface of the water. This time, however, he welcomed both sight and sound and it required a conscious effort to stop himself joining in the triumphant cheers of his men. The cheers were subdued and he let them relieve their pent-up feelings before issuing a mild reproof.

"All right, that'll do, lads—remember where you are. We'll be for it if you don't watch out."

The cheering ceased but even the phlegmatic Trevelyan's lined brown face wore a boyish grin, which widened when a cannon spoke from Ferrikale, echoed by a second and a third, and several shells burst in the region of the sandbank on which the wreck had lain.

"Thikee 'aven't 'arf wakened en up, sir," he said derisively.

"Oi reckon as them bastards think they've caught one o' our ships in that auld booby trap o' thern. Well, let en waste ammunition—they be shuttin' the stable door after the 'orse 'as gone an' no mistake!"

They would also alert their comrades in the Yenikale batteries, Phillip thought ruefully, as the firing continued unabated and, now that they were roused, might be expected to stand to their guns for what remained of the night. He sighed and thrust the thought of the probable consequences to the back of his mind. At least the abortive cannonade would help to raise the morale of his own men, at a time when they needed it most—the crucial test was about to come, he was only too well aware, when the last buoy went over the stern and the *Constantine* prepared to make her escape from under the muzzles of the Yenikale guns.

They would need luck—even more luck than they had had already, he told himself and repeated his sigh, as the moon broke through a bank of cloud to spread a silvery carpet on the deck at his feet. Whilst in semi-darkness and low lying fog, the true nature of the brig's activities might not have been apparent to any watchers on shore, in this damnably revealing moonlight, he could not hope to conceal her presence or her purpose for very much longer. Lights were springing to life from end to end of the squat, stone-built fort; men crowded on to the ramparts, others ran across to the floating battery on the foreshore and Phillip watched through his glass as a cavalry patrol galloped off towards Ferrikale, presumably to ascertain the cause of the commotion.

"And a half two, sir!" the messenger sang out, his voice restored to its normal pitch and sounding incongruously cheerful. His next call gave a depth of only two fathoms—the channel was shoaling again.

"Slow ahead engines," Phillip ordered. He consulted the chart; the last of Kirkoff's two red-ink circles lay ahead and to starboard, if his memory was not at fault . . . yes, there they were, clearly marked and within range of the fort. Too close for him to attempt to deal with yet, he decided regretfully, because all hell would break loose if he did. He would have to drop a buoy, when he sighted the accursed things, and sink them with the brig's stern gun when he came about, depending on the resultant confusion to aid his escape. As yet there had been no challenge; the garrison of the fort appeared to be too occupied with what was going on down channel to notice or concern themselves with the *Constantine*'s unobtrusive arrival.

"By the mark two, sir . . . and shoaling!" He heard Jackson's call, before the messenger could relay it. The chart indicated the shoal and he snapped a correction of course to Trevelyan.

"Ease your wheel a point to starb'd, Quartermaster—ease it, mind! Bo'sun's Mate, let go a buoy there!" He glanced back, over his shoulder, at Driver and his sweating crew. There were only four of the marker-buoys left now. Thank God, this—the essential—part of his mission was all but completed, and a sixteen-foot-wide channel buoyed as far as Yenikale. But where the devil were those bombs? Thompson had made no report— with the moonlight to help him, surely he . . .

"Ship fine on the port bow, sir!" The masthead look-out's hail took Phillip by surprise and he spun round, fumbling for his glass as he made for the port-side shrouds. "She's a steamer, sir," the look-out amplified. "About half a mile away and approaching fast. Looks like a gun-vessel, sir!"

He was right, Phillip saw, when he focused the Dollond on her. She was a steam-sloop, of a type which had been observed frequently in the Strait, flush-decked and mounting six guns, and she was coming at full speed, evidently from her anchorage off Cape Fanar, at the entrance to the Sea of Azoff. As he watched her approach, he saw a light flash from her upper deck, vanish and flash again and the look-out called excitedly, "She's making a signal, sir . . . and the fort is acknowledging!"

Was she making her number, Phillip wondered, or the general recognition signal? There had been no challenge from the fort but . . . glass to his eye, he noted the number and duration of the flashing light signals. Two short, a long and a short from the gunboat . . . one long and three short flashes from the fort. The signals could mean anything; the Russian naval code, as far as he knew, bore no resemblance to the British. He considered sending for Captain Kirkoff and then decided against it, as the gunboat doused her lamp—Kirkoff, judging by his past performance, would not interpret the signals for him and might even deliberately misinterpret them. But he had gained something, perhaps, from what he had seen—if the fort should make a belated challenge, he would reply as the approaching gunboat had done, in the hope that she had made the recognition signal. If his hopes were unfounded, he would be no worse off than he had been before.

"Masthead, there!" he hailed. "Report any change of course by the enemy steamer!"

"Aye, aye, sir," the look-out acknowledged. "She seems to be reducing speed, sir, but she's still on the same course."

The Ferrikale guns had ceased fire now—no doubt it was on this account that she had reduced speed, Phillip reasoned, as he descended again to the deck. She was probably a watchdog, there to guard the channel against intruders but this time her services were not being called upon and it was to be hoped that she would return to her anchorage.

"And a half three, sir!" the messenger shouted.

"Last buoy but one away, sir!" Driver's voice sounded relieved.

"Avast heaving, Bo'sun's Mate . . . hold that last buoy," Phillip ordered. They were clear of the shoal now and too close to the fort for comfort; every instinct he possessed warned him to turn and run while there was still time. He had carried out his orders but . . . there were still those two floating bombs unaccounted for, those two ominous red circles on the captured Russian chart and he could not, in all conscience, make his escape until they were located. "Gunner's Mate . . ." He cupped his hands about his mouth but Thompson, forestalling the question, gave him a prompt and puzzled assurance that he had seen nothing. He checked the chart again . . . could the infernal machines have drifted? Or had Kirkoff failed to drop them, had he, perhaps, intended to do so when the fog lifted and he was on his way back to the gunboat anchorage? This was a distinct possibility but . . . Phillip swore softly and wearily to himself. He *had* to be sure, he would have to circle the area to make sure—damn it, in this moonlight, if the bombs were there, they must be visible. Feeling the palms of his hands clammy, he crossed to the wheel and gave Trevelyan his instructions in a flat voice that successfully hid his own misgivings. Then, after a brief word of praise to Driver and his crew, he despatched the two seamen aloft to act as additional look-outs, with orders to report anything suspicious they might sight floating on the surface of the water.

"Stand by with the signal lamp, Bo'sun's Mate," he added. "Our change of course may well bring a challenge from the fort, if they're keeping a vigilant watch. If it should—make two short and a long and a short, when I give the word. But remember, you're a poor hand at signalling. And keep the lamp well down."

"Aye, aye, sir." Driver mopped his damp face. He had

scarcely picked up the lamp when, as Phillip had feared, a light flashed from the fort. He waited until the signal had been repeated and then said, "Right, Driver—do your worst!"

The boatswain's mate obeyed. He made a commendably awkward job of it and the light from the fort flashed a third time.

"Deck there!" The masthead look-out's hail was urgent. "Enemy steamer's flashing now, sir. A succession of short flashes. I think she's making to us, sir."

Was she, Phillip asked himself, training his glass on her, or was she signalling the fort? She hadn't altered course yet but . . . he saw her head come round, an instant before the masthead look-out confirmed his observation. Perdition take her, the gunboat was coming to investigate!

"Driver!" he called sharply. "Make one long and two short flashes to her—but wait till she's completed her turn. And pass the word to Jackson to get back on deck right away."

He would have to alter course himself in a minute or two, he thought. Alter course and run for it . . . the little *Constantine* would be no match for a six-gun sloop-of-war and, with his depleted crew, he could not hope to use her two guns to much effect, particularly if the fort joined in the hunt. He raised his glass to his eye again, as the fort—still seemingly dissatisfied with Driver's signals—sent at some length. They were evidently suspicious but they could not be sure that there was anything wrong as yet, so probably they would leave things to the gunboat. Probably but not certainly; he knew he could not bank on their doing so once he started running, although they would be reluctant to fire on a ship they must recognize as their own, however eccentric her movements. Lowering the glass, he glanced up at the Russian ensign fluttering limply in the breeze and wondered for how much longer it would protect him.

"Enemy steamer's increasing speed, sir," the masthead look-out warned.

She was definitely setting course to intercept him, Phillip saw, although she had not run out her guns, which suggested that she did not expect to meet an enemy. He thrust the Dollond into his breast pocket and, hands clenched at his sides, deliberately turned his back on her as he considered the alternatives open to him.

Every second he delayed would add to the danger of discovery, he was aware. His best, if not his only chance was to get away at full speed now, at once, before the gunboat closed him and before either fort or gunboat realized that there was an enemy, sailing under false colours, in their midst. With a start of almost a quarter of a mile and the element of surprise to help him, the odds would be in his favour—as far as Ferrikale, at all events—and he owed that much, surely, to his men? Kirkoff's thrice-damned bombs would have to be abandoned, it was too late to hunt for them now. If they were there at all, they must have drifted but the newly-buoyed channel was clear for Jack Lyons's flotilla in the morning and for his own ship now—and he could count on a fast run down it, perhaps even on out-distancing his pursuer.

Only . . . he expelled his breath in a pent up sigh, sick with the realization that he could not use the channel. If he did so and the gunboat came after him, her Commander would undoubtedly see the buoys, would see and understand their purpose, and his night's work would all have been for nothing.

What the devil *could* he do, then? Run, clear of the buoys and take the risk of going aground on a shoal . . . no, for God's sake, that was out of the question, the risk was too great. If he ran, it was the channel or nothing and, if the gunboat gave chase, he would have to engage and stop her, because she could not be allowed to return to Yenikale with intelligence of the buoyed channel.

The only other course of action left to him was to endeavour to bluff his way out—to head towards the enemy ship, as if he had nothing to fear from her and depend on her sheering off, her curiosity satisfied. But would she sheer off, would that satisfy her Commander's curiosity? Phillip shook his head in frustration. It wouldn't, damn it—if he were in the other Commander's place, it wouldn't satisfy him. He could, he supposed, send for Kirkoff if he had to, he could hold a pistol to the fellow's obstinate head and try to force him to co-operate, either by disclosing the correct recognition signal or by speaking to the gunboat but . . . Kirkoff wasn't to be trusted. He . . .

"Deck there!" The masthead look-out yelled. "The enemy steamer's running out her for'ard gun, sir! And she's making again with her signal lamp—continuous long flashes, sir!"

She was calling on him to stop, Phillip knew. It was no use attempting to bluff, he must either obey the command or run . . . the decision had been made for him and the knowledge that it had came almost as a relief.

"Messenger!" The young seaman was at his side, white faced, a flicker of fear in his eyes. "Tell Mr Curtis I want all the speed he can give me," Phillip bade him. He smiled reassuringly into the boy's frightened eyes. "Then you can stand to your gun. That's what you came for, is it not—a chance of some gun practice at the enemy's expense? Well, you may get it, lad, if you look lively with that message to the engine-room, so off with you!"

"Aye, aye, sir." The seaman echoed his smile a trifle uncertainly before scurrying off on his errand. Phillip turned to Treveyan. "Hard a-starb'd, Quartermaster. Steer by the buoys when you sight them." Driver, he saw, was signalling to the

gunboat which, significantly, made no reply. "Belay that,
Bo'sun's Mate, and take charge of the after-gun. I want all gun's
crews to close up and . . ." he was interrupted by a stentorian
bellow from Thompson.

"Bomb, sir—dead ahead!"

Phillip's reaction was instinctive rather than reasoned, as
his hands joined Trevelyan's on the wheel. The brig responded
to her helm but, with so little way on her still, her response
was slow and the bomb perilously close. Both he and the quartermaster stood as if turned to stone, waiting for the inevitable
explosion and the jarring crash against the *Constantine*'s hull
which would follow but—incredibly—nothing happened. She
must have avoided disaster by a matter of inches, Phillip
thought, scarcely able to take in the fact that they were safe.
Then he heard the throbbing rhythm of the engines change
as Curtis, all unaware of what was going on outside the dark,
oily confines of his engine-room, gave him the increase in
speed for which—a very long time ago, it seemed—he had
asked. Forcing his numb limbs to obey him, he crossed to the
rail but the bomb had vanished in the churned-up water astern.

"Channel up ahead, sir," Trevelyan observed, when he
returned to the wheel. Lifting a brown hand, the quartermaster pointed to where the last buoy they had dropped bobbed
gently in the moonlight, forty or fifty yards ahead and to port.
"Steer along o' them buoys, you said, sir."

"Yes," Phillip affirmed. "Steer by the buoys. We'll give that
gunboat a run for her money, if she comes after us."

The Cornishman gave vent to a low, amused chuckle. "If'n
she does, sir, mabbe she won't clear thikee auld bomb as tidy
as we done. We was mortal lucky to 'ave missed 'er."

His words and the hope they held out raised Phillip's flagging spirits. Perhaps it was a faint hope but the bomb had

undoubtedly drifted—the gunboat's Commander would have no more idea of its position than he had had, a few minutes ago. If his ship hit it, the foul thing might not stop him but it would certainly slow him down, and there was one way to make sure that he gave chase. Phillip's gaze went again to the ensign staff—he could haul down the Russian colours and hoist his own.

Eyes narrowed, he measured the distance between himself and the fort and reluctantly dismissed the idea. Had the gunners on shore been in their earlier state of lethargy, the gamble might have been worth taking; as things were, however, it would be madness, an act of bravado which he could not possibly justify. If he were to have even a fighting chance of bringing the *Constantine* and her crew past Ferrikale unscathed, he dared not risk anything in the nature of an invitation to the Yenikale gunners to fire on her. As it was, they would have telescopes trained on her, watching her every movement and her sudden, precipitate departure—when the gunboat had signalled her to stop—would no doubt be causing considerable speculation. The fact that they hadn't yet opened fire on her could only mean that, as he had calculated, the flag she was flying was her protection.

"Deck there!" The masthead look-out hailed. "Enemy steamer is making a succession of long flashes, as before, sir!"

Phillip picked up the signal lamp. Aware that it was probably useless, he made one long and three short flashes—a repetition of the fort's first signal. The reply was not slow in coming and it, too, was a repetition, whose meaning left him in no doubt.

He said grimly to Jackson, who was standing a few yards away, coiling down his lead-line, "Pass the word for the gunner's mate, will you, and then go below and tell my steward to bring the prisoner on deck. You'd better lend a hand with him—he may not be too keen to come and I don't want him running amuck again."

"Leave him to me, sir," Jackson answered with relish. "I'll see he's not given the chance."

Thompson reported promptly. "Sir," he began, "I'm sorry I . . ." whatever apology he had intended to make was drowned by the roar of a gun, heralded by a bright orange flash from the enemy steamer's deck. It was a warning shot, aimed well over the *Constantine*'s bows and—like the signal—its meaning was plain. The Russian Captain was calling on the brig to heave-to and explain herself but, presumably because he still supposed her to be under the command of a compatriot, he waited even longer than he might have done for her to comply with his demand.

Phillip watched the roundshot ricochet across the flat, moonlit surface of the water. She was using a long range gun, his mind registered, loaded with shot, not shell . . . Lord, if only he had the *Huntress* now, with her sixty-eight-pounder Lancaster, he would make short work of her! For a moment, anxiety possessed him and he found himself regretting the absence of Gunner O'Leary, whose uncanny skill and accuracy with any gun might have turned the scales in his favour. But he had left O'Leary aboard the *Huntress* to tend the wounded and bolster the confidence of poor, incompetent young Brown and it was no use, at this late stage, wishing that he had not done so. He had Thompson, who was a good man by any standards, even if he lacked O'Leary's artistry, and he would have to do the best he could with the Russian thirty-two-pounder.

"It'll be a stern chase, won't it, sir?" Thompson suggested. "Do you wish me to lay the after-gun?"

Phillip nodded. "Yes—relieve Driver, if you please, and hold your fire until I give the order."

"*Hold* our fire, sir? Even if she fires on us?"

"That's right," Phillip confirmed. "So long as we don't return her fire, her Commander may go on thinking we're one of theirs—or have a few doubts on that score, anyway. I want to keep him guessing, in the hope that he'll decide not to follow us into the channel. But if he does come after us, we'll have to stop him . . . he mustn't be allowed to get back to the fort or our buoys will be gone by morning. Tell your gun's crew that . . . it may make it easier for them to wait, if they know why they're waiting. There's always the chance that her Commander may run her on to that bomb we missed just now, before he sights our buoys, but it's a pretty slim chance, I'm afraid."

"With respect, sir, I reckon it's a better than even chance," Thompson asserted. "That's what I was starting to tell you. Those bombs are just about invisible in this light, not like the buoys. I never saw the one we missed until we were almost on top of it—I'd have sung out a lot sooner if I had, believe me, sir. And Ellis thought he spotted a second, about thirty feet astern of mine, though he couldn't be quite certain. All the same"—he gestured to the gunboat, which was following the *Constantine*'s course at top speed, like a bloodhound in pursuit of a breast-high scent—"she'll be for it if she holds her present course. I'd take a bet on it, sir."

"I hope you're right," Phillip said, with more conviction than he felt. "Tell your gun's crew that, too—it'll give them something to think about while they're waiting to bring their gun into action."

"Aye, aye, sir. I'll make a book on whether she scores a hit or a miss." Thompson was smiling to himself as he made his way aft.

A second shot from their pursuer whined overhead, to splash into the water a bare twenty feet from the *Constantine's* starboard quarter and Captain Kirkoff, emerging from the quarterdeck hatchway between his two escorts, winced visibly as his eyes followed its flight.

"What is this madness?" he demanded of Phillip.

"No madness, sir. One of your gun-vessels has opened fire on us. Our replies to her signals failed to satisfy her. That is why I sent for you. I—"

"Then she will blow *my* ship to pieces!" Kirkoff said bitterly. He, too, glanced at the ensign and scowling, held out his hand. "Your glass, Captain." Phillip yielded his Dollond and walked with him to the rail. "That is the *Tarkhan,*" the Russian informed him. "She mounts six guns, of the *canon-obusier* type which, you may recall, a squadron of the Imperial Navy under Admiral Nachimoff used to some effect at Sinope. He destroyed a Turkish fleet and the harbour defences."

"I recall the occasion, sir," Phillip admitted coldly. The gunboat fired again, two shots in swift succession, which straddled the straining brig. Her gunners were well practised, he was forced to concede; her shooting could not have been more accurate. She signalled once more, as if in a final attempt to restore her errant sister to sanity and Captain Kirkoff snapped the Dollond shut.

"She is ordering you to heave-to," he said, with a return to his former arrogance. "You have no choice but to obey, Captain . . . unless you are anxious to die."

Phillip picked up the discarded signal lamp and offered it to him. "*You* have a choice, sir," he suggested. "Make a signal she will understand—make your number."

"You offer me such a choice?" The Russian took a menacing pace towards him as if to knock the lamp from his hand and Higgins, alarmed, leapt forward, rifle levelled at his prisoner's chest. Disdainfully Kirkoff raised both arms in a gesture of surrender. "And if I refuse, Captain," he enquired mockingly. "You will, no doubt—since you have so little regard for the usages of civilized warfare—order this cretin to shoot me?"

He had spoken in French and his tone was deliberately provocative but Phillip kept his temper.

"No, sir," he returned quietly. "I shall leave your fate in the hands of your countrymen and their *canons-obusiers*. I have no intention of heaving-to and you will remain with me on the quarterdeck, if you please. Higgins!"

"Sir!" Higgins obediently stood back, rifle grounded, his expression carefully blank. Jackson grasped the Russian's shoulder and, with an impeccable, "If you please, sir," led him away. The trio had scarcely reached the port side of the quarterdeck when a shell from the *Tarkhan* burst six feet above the deck, sending a shower of lethal fragments to shatter the quarter-boat and the davits from which it was suspended and tear splinters from the deck planking. Kirkoff came abruptly to a standstill, his bearded face stiffening in dismay.

"My signal lamp is at your disposal, Captain," Phillip called after him.

"You are a madman!" Kirkoff accused. "You have no chance . . . heave-to, in the name of heaven! You . . ." his voice trailed off into a strangled gasp of horror as, clear across the intervening distance, came the reverberating crash of an explosion. It was followed, seconds later, by another and a great tongue of flame soared up the *Tarkhan*'s starboard side, leaping across her upper deck where, Phillip could only suppose, it met some piled ammunition or a reserve of powder which exploded almost simultaneously. He kept his glass trained on the stricken gunboat, the cheers of his own men ringing in his ears.

Thompson had been right, he thought, conscious of more pity than elation as he stared into the clouds of black smoke now rising into the night sky—the Russian ship had run on to both bombs and they had done more damage than he had imagined they were capable of inflicting. They hadn't stopped her, she was still moving at full speed through the water, her paddles churning, but she was ablaze, the wind of her passing fanning the flames which leap-frogged across the dry timber of her planking. There were men fighting the blaze and, as he watched, he saw others run to the rails to fling cases of ammunition overboard . . . she would not fire on him again for some considerable time, he told himself, and shook his head almost angrily to Thompson's shouted request for permission to bring his gun into action.

CHAPTER FIVE

The fort's upper guns belatedly opened fire and, to
Phillip's shocked surprise, pumped two shells into the
now stationary *Tarkhan* before realizing their error and sending a few ragged salvoes of chain and roundshot in the wake
of the fleeing *Constantine.* But they had delayed too long and,
although one or two of their roundshot came unpleasantly
close, she emerged unscathed from the barrage, which ceased
when the range became extreme.

Phillip's tautly stretched nerves relaxed a little, as he
conned her carefully back into the newly-buoyed channel. No
doubt more horsemen would be sent galloping overland to
Ferrikale with warning of her coming, he told himself. The
fort Commander, having recovered from his initial bewilderment, might call up another gunboat to search for the mysterious brig, flying the Imperial Russian ensign, yet behaving as
if she were an enemy but . . . that would take time and time
was on his side now. Within a few hours, this channel would
be swarming with Allied ships; British, French, and Turkish
troops—due to land at Kamiesch at first light—would be marching towards Kertch and Yenikale, and the coastal forts would
be under attack from both land and sea.

He smothered a weary yawn, wishing that he could drop
anchor here to await the coming of the Sea of Azoff flotilla,

instead of running the gauntlet of the Ferrikale batteries a second time. But there were still two of Kirkoff's accursed bombs lying unmarked and unaccounted for—the two that he and Thompson had failed to sight, close to the channel entrance. With the sickening spectacle of the blazing *Tarkhan* fresh in his mind, he knew that he could not leave them where they were if there was even an outside chance of being able to find and destroy them.

It would be an outside chance, he reminded himself. Thompson had said that the evil things were almost invisible in this light and . . . he unrolled the Russian chart, in order to check the position of the last of the red-ink circles and confirm what his memory had told him. The bombs, if they hadn't drifted, lay on the western side of the channel, well within range of the Ferrikale guns . . . perhaps a boat could slip in unnoticed, while the gunners' attention was focused on the *Constantine.* A boat, with muffled oars and a man in the bows, who knew exactly what he was looking for . . . damn it, it was either that or wait for the dawn.

He crossed slowly to the starboard rail, rubbed the sleep from his tired eyes and, taking out his glass, searched the landward side of the channel for any evidence of unusual activity. Seeing nothing, apart from the lights of Ferrikale itself, still some two and a half miles away, he was about to order a reduction in speed when a hail from the masthead stopped him in his tracks.

"Flashing light signal, sir!" the look-out warned. "Fine on the port bow and distant . . . over a mile, I'd say, sir."

"Repeat the signal," Phillip answered. "When you can read it." He bent to pick up the signal lamp and, from the port side of the quarterdeck, Captain Kirkoff watched his approach with narrowed, speculative eyes.

"They are signalling from the Cheska Bank, Captain Hazard," he said. "Do you wish to know for what reason?"

Phillip shrugged. He did not offer the Dollond this time but instead raised it to his own eye. The salt marshes of the Cheska Bank ran from the north-eastern extremity of the Taman Peninsula to form the eastern boundary of the Strait, a curving, flat expanse of land, between two and three miles in width, extending for seven miles southwards from Cape Kamenai. It was on this desolate spit of land that the enemy had recently constructed the three earthwork batteries whose purpose, he was aware, was to guard the deep water channel normally used by their own ships. These batteries—of which the principal, sited opposite the ferry station at Yenikale, was designed to cross fire with the fort—had taken no part in the earlier action and had not opened fire on him when the fort had done so. Mainly for this reason, he had dismissed the possibility of their intervening from his calculations but now . . . he trained his glass on the distant light, automatically counting the flashes. The message was a lengthy one and, although he could not pretend to understand it, either from his own or the masthead look-out's version of the varying flashes of which it was composed, he experienced no surprise when Kirkoff announced, a note of triumph in his gutteral voice, "Warning has been sent to Ferrikale concerning my ship, Captain."

Phillip lowered his glass, shut it with studied deliberation and replaced it in his breast pocket. He said nothing, conscious of so intense a dislike for his prisoner that he could not trust himself to reply to the taunt.

"The gunners have been ordered to sink her!" Kirkoff spat the words at him, shaking off Higgins's restraining hand. "They will do so, unless you hand her over to me, Captain Hazard.

To go on is to cause unnecessary loss of life. You cannot hope to pass Ferrikale."

He was probably right, Phillip thought dully. He ordered the engines to dead slow, aware that he was only playing for time now . . . and that time was on his side no longer. The guns of Ferrikale were waiting for the little *Constantine;* there was nowhere he could hide her, to await the arrival of the Sea of Azoff squadron. If he anchored here, a gunboat would be sent in search of him and the alternative to surrender would be, as Kirkoff had reminded him, unnecessary loss of life. It was possible that he could save his crew—there was the cutter, they might slip by in that, if they crossed the deep water channel and hugged the shadows along the edge of the Cheska Bank. The cutter would make a difficult target for heavy calibre guns and might not be seen at all, although . . . he looked up at the star-bright sky and cursed it silently and with bitterness.

There was a risk, of course, but his men would undoubtedly prefer that to the certainty of capture and . . .

From behind him, Driver asked quietly, "Will I haul down the enemy ens'n, sir, and hoist our own?"

His tone, for all its quietness, was not that of a man contemplating surrender and Phillip's indecision was suddenly at an end. They would finish what they had come to do, he thought, by heaven they would! They would find and destroy those foul bombs and be damned to Kirkoff, who would have the *Tarkhan* on his conscience but no British ship to even the score . . . and then they would take to the cutter, if their luck held. Aware that he was grinning like an idiot, he nodded to Driver. "Yes," he said. "By all means hoist our colours, Bo'sun's Mate. We've worn the enemy's for long enough."

A cheer went up from the men as they watched the Russian flag hauled down and it was redoubled when Driver broke out the White Ensign. Captain Kirkoff listened to them in ludicrous astonishment and then demanded sullenly to be taken below.

"I regret, sir, that I cannot accede to your request," Phillip told him, with icy firmness. "There are still two of those infernal machines of yours in this channel and I intend to get rid of them. You witnessed their effect on one of your own ships and so, alas, did I. They are hideous weapons, sir, against which no ship can defend herself and, if you genuinely wish to avoid unnecessary loss of life, then perhaps you'll assist me to find them."

Kirkoff glared at him in resentful silence for a moment and then, prompted by the boom of a cannon from Ferrikale, he observed almost apologetically, "The bombs which struck the *Tarkhan* had drifted, Captain Hazard—I could not have anticipated that, they were not secured."

"No," Phillip conceded. He turned to watch a hail of shot spatter the water a hundred yards ahead of the *Constantine* and the Russian Captain, following the direction of his gaze, spread his hands in a gesture of resignation.

"Give me the chart," he invited thickly. Unrolling it, he jabbed at the red-inked circles with a blunt forefinger. "The explosive devices you seek are here, where they are marked on my chart and *they* cannot have drifted from their position which, as you can see, lies less than a quarter of a mile from the shore batteries. You cannot destroy them without losing this ship."

"Not even by gunfire, Captain?"

Captain Kirkoff shook his head. He was very pale but he spoke with a calm and logical certainty that, of itself, carried conviction. "These are not floating bombs, they are a different type from the others—larger and more deadly. They are buried in an artificial bank and are detonated by galvanic cells, which can only be set off when a ship's keel strikes them. You cannot reach them with gunfire and you cannot see them." There was another salvo from the fort and Phillip drew in his breath sharply as he assessed the shortening range, but he gave no order to reduce speed and Kirkoff went on, a bitter edge to his voice, "I did not design them, Captain Hazard, and I did not place them in position—that was done by army engineers under cover of darkness and from a boat. But you are right . . . they are hideous weapons. They contain a charge sufficient to blow a ship-of-the-line in half and there are fifty more of them in the arsenal at Yenikale, ready to be placed in the channel."

"Ready?" Phillip echoed, his throat suddenly constricted. Dear God, this was worse than he had imagined—a quarter of that number could destroy Jack Lyons's entire flotilla. "They're not in the channel yet, Captain?" he asked urgently.

Captain Kirkoff shook his head. He launched into technical details and added, "It is a lengthy and dangerous task. Few volunteers could be found to place them in position and our naval Commanders were—and are—opposed to their use. Most of us held that they would constitute a danger to our own ships, even when their positions were marked on our charts, you understand. There is an alternative method of exploding the charges, by means of connecting wires from the forts but . . ." he shrugged. "It was tried and found unreliable, so the combustibles remain in the arsenal."

Could he believe this man, Phillip wondered, a part of his mind shying from the possibility that he could not—dare he believe him? Kirkoff was an enemy; he had behaved as an enemy throughout his captivity on board the *Constantine* but now, for no explicable reason, he appeared to be telling the truth and his own inclination was not to doubt him. Besides, had he not sounded and buoyed the channel up as far as Yenikale and found neither artificial obstructions nor buried explosives, save for the two which were marked on Kirkoff's chart and which, on his own admission, had drifted?

"Sir . . ." it was Driver, his eyes bright with the light of battle. "Permission to open fire on the fort, sir?"

It would be a useless gesture, Phillip knew, remembering the Fleet's abortive attack on the stone-walled defences of Sebastopol Harbour, when great ships-of-the-line, mounting a hundred guns, had been driven out of action, their decks ablaze, their masts and rigging reduced to sprung and tangled wreckage. The small *Constantine,* with her two antiquated guns, could do nothing effective against Ferrikale's casemated cannon, firing from behind the protection of their massive walls. It was doubtful whether, at this range, the brig's guns could even hit—much less damage—the earthwork emplacements close to the shore.

There was one service she *could* perform, though, if Kirkoff had told the truth. He glanced down at the chart, still held in his enemy's outstretched hands, took it from him and straightened slowly, conscious of pain that was not physical as he shook his head to Driver's request.

A roundshot thumped against the hull; a charge of chain clattered through the upper rigging—both were spent and did little damage, but exploding shell fragments splashed like hail into the water ahead and abeam of the labouring brig. They were getting her range now, Phillip thought, his brain ice-cold, as he tried to calculate the odds against the *Constantine* ever reaching the destination he had planned for her. They were fantastically long odds but it would not matter if it were only her empty hulk which survived to drift on to its objective . . . hadn't Kirkoff said that a ship's keel would set off the buried sea-mine? Someone would have to remain at the wheel until the last possible moment, to keep her on course and . . . he swallowed hard, feeling the acid taste of bile rising from his stomach. Driver would have to take command of the cutter . . .

"Jackson," he called. "Tell Mr Curtis to reduce speed to dead slow and then he's to come on deck with his crew, leaving his engines running. Bo'sun's Mate—pipe all hands on deck, if you please, and prepare to abandon ship. Man the cutter and take command of her and I want every man into her, including the prisoner. When you have your full complement aboard, cast off and steer for the Cheska Bank. The *Huntress* should be at the entrance to the Strait to pick you up but, if you need assistance from her, send up a rocket. Put two men— *now*—to bring the cutter alongside and secure her amidships. They'll have to rig hauling tackle and do it fast—understand?"

"Sir?" Taken by surprise at the sheer unexpectedness of these orders, Driver stared at him, jaw dropping, and he snapped impatiently, "Look lively, my lad, for pity's sake! There's no time to be lost. And tell Trevelyan to put a lashing on the wheel before he leaves the deck."

Jackson was already on his way to the engine-room and the boatswain's mate managed a dutiful, "Aye, aye, sir," his expression still bewildered. But he recovered himself and the pipe shrilled, clear and penetrating, above the background thunder of the Russian guns.

"All hands on deck!" he bawled. "Prepare to abandon ship!"

The order was instantly obeyed. The masthead look-out came shinning down from aloft with the speed and skill of long practice and Phillip gave him a quick, "Well done,

Williams," as he thudded on to the deck, to be joined by the two guns' crews and, a few moments later, by Curtis and his sweating, oil-grimed stokers from the engine-room. The hauling tackle was rigged and, with half a dozen willing hands heaving on the lines and Driver and Jackson easing her round, the cutter was secured amidships.

"Abandon ship!" Phillip bade them. "Over the side with you and into the boat. Cast off when you're loaded, Bo'sun's Mate!"

A shell burst on the forecastle, emitting a shower of ominously glowing fragments and Thompson moved instinctively towards his abandoned gun but Phillip called him back.

"Where the devil do you think you're going?"

"Ammunition, sir," the gunner's mate stammered. "I ought to . . ." he gulped. "What about you, sir? You're coming with us, aren't you?"

"I'll join you, if I can," Phillip told him. "But don't delay for me—you'll have a long pull. Carry on, Gunner's Mate . . . and good luck. Get back to the *Huntress* if you have to swim for it!"

"I can't swim, sir," Thompson answered wryly. He hesitated, looked down at the cutter and asked, with a hint of anger, "Why, sir—in God's name, *why?* She's not your ship, you don't have to go down with her. You—"

"Captain Kirkoff will tell you why, lad. Now jump to it, will you, or you'll damned well have to swim."

The boat was loaded, with Kirkoff in the sternsheets looking up at them, an odd expression on his bearded face. Thompson swung himself into the bows and the cutter cast off, to fall slowly astern, a small, dark shape on the moonlit water of the channel, its six pairs of oars moving in rhythmic unison as it headed for the Cheska Bank and, God willing, for safety.

Phillip checked the lashings on the deserted wheel and then went below to the engine-room. Amidst the lamp-lit dimness, deafened by the metallic clank of the engines and the hiss of steam, he could scarcely hear the guns and he smiled grimly to himself as he opened valves and, stripping to his shirtsleeves, shovelled coal inexpertly on to the glowing fires, knocking the furnace doors back into place with his shovel as each was replenished. He had taken a course of instruction on the marine steam engine before being appointed to the *Trojan* and he blessed this fact now, since at least he knew how to make the necessary adjustments to give him the increase in speed he wanted. The pressure gauge rose but the furnaces were voracious and would, he was aware, soon consume the coal he had fed them and the head of steam would start to drop. It could not be helped; he would probably have gained his objective before the engines lost power altogether and speed was essential now, if he were not to offer a sitting target to the fort's gunners.

A thunderous crash from somewhere overhead sent him rushing back on deck, almost losing his footing as the brig shuddered under the impact of the roundshot pounding against her hull. The enemy gunners had got her range now and with a vengeance, he thought numbly, as he stumbled unsteadily across to the wheel, the sweat turning to ice on his weary body and the boom of the guns beating a merciless tattoo inside his head. There was a fire smouldering on the forecastle and a gaping hole in the deck planking, just behind the gun, offered mute evidence that Thompson's spare ammunition must have exploded in the heat from the flames.

During his short absence in the engine-room, chainshot had wrought havoc with the brig's upper rigging and was continuing to do so. As he stared in dismay at the chaotic tangle above him, the foretopmast stays were neatly carried away above the seizing, the mast broke at the cap and, after swaying drunkenly for a moment or two, went toppling over the side, taking futtock shrouds and jib-stay with it.

Phillip freed the wheel of its lashing and, his blistered hands closing about the worn spokes, he brought the ship's head hard round to starboard, to take brief advantage of the shelter afforded by a low, tree-grown promontory jutting out from the shore. She was hulled twice on her exposed port quarter as she answered to her helm but, although she started to take in water, the paddle-wheels were thrusting her on with increased momentum and he took heart from this, the tangible result of his exhausting visit to the engine-room. A number of roundshot passed harmlessly overhead; one buried itself among the trees on the rocky promontory but, when he was compelled to emerge from its shelter, the gunners swiftly found the range again. Twist and turn as he would, they kept their sights fixed on her and, as she began to list and lose speed, Phillip's hopes faded.

He had been mad to imagine that he could bring her through such a cannonade he told himself—as mad as Kirkoff had accused him of being. True, he had had the luck of the devil up till now but now the time of reckoning had come and, if he were to make his own escape, he would have to abandon the *Constantine* . . . run her ashore, so that she did not obstruct the channel, and abandon her. He peered ahead, half blinded by the smoke from the burning forecastle, and a bitter sense of failure stirred in him as he realized that he was within a scant two hundred yards of his objective. The artificial bank ran out from the shore at an angle of 45°, according to Kirkoff's chart . . . he should be able to see it from here.

Leaving the wheel, he crossed the deck at a limping run and dragged himself up into the tattered mainmast shrouds.

Yes, there it was, marked by an irregular line of timber stakes, evidently driven in to hold in place the sunken stones and rubble of which the bank was composed. The stakes could be ship's masts—one of them, at all events, rose high out of the water, casting a long shadow before it and could hardly be anything else, he realized, when he contrived to train his glass on it. So near, so damnably, tantalizingly near and yet the infernal thing might have been two hundred miles away . . . he sucked a painful breath into his lungs, fighting off a spasm of coughing, and staggered, bent almost double, back to the wheel. The *Constantine* barely had steerage way on her now but the current was carrying her down-channel, towards the bank at its edge . . . as well let her drift on to it—if she lasted that long—as run her ashore, he decided.

The spokes of the wheel spun through his hands; he set her head towards the bank and secured the lashing, seized by another spasm of coughing as he did so. Greedy tongues of flame were engulfing the quarterdeck, leaping this way and that as the littered mass of cordage caught alight, like demons in the bowels of hell. Phillip tottered aft, struggling for breath and it was borne on him suddenly that silence had fallen . . . a strange, eerie silence, broken only by the slow, irregular clatter of the brig's failing paddles and the bubbling hiss of steam escaping from her flooded boilers.

The guns were no longer firing . . . he clung, gasping, to the rail, scarcely able to believe the evidence of his own dulled senses. But it was true—no rippling orange flashes pierced the curtain of black powder smoke which hung over the fort, no ragged thunder of cannon fire echoed across the intervening stretch of water to assault his tortured eardrums. The ghastly cannonade had ceased, although he could think of no logical reason why it should have done so, when the *Constantine* had been so clearly at their mercy, awaiting the *coup de grâce,* which a single gun could have delivered.

Unless . . . he stiffened involuntarily, the void that had been his mind starting to function again. The gunners knew the position of the artificial bank and of the charge buried within it—could they have decided to let their hideous sunken weapon do their work for them? It seemed a strange decision, on the face of it, but Kirkoff had said that the sunken explosives were new, the various means by which they were detonated the subject of experiment and even doubt on the part of the Yenikale engineers. Fifty of the things were still stored in the arsenal, waiting to be put into use until a reliable method of detonating them could be found and agreed upon . . . for God's sake, that must be why the guns had ceased fire, there could be no other reason!

They were going to use the *Constantine* to test their infernal device. Battered and blazing, listing heavily, she could be of no value to them if they recaptured her and the gunners had had their target practice with her; now it was the turn of the engineers, some of whom—if he knew anything about them—would probably have ridden flat out from Yenikale in order to demand it.

He retreated before the flames, eyes streaming, hands over his face in an attempt to shield it from the heat. But, in contrast to his sweating body, his brain was suddenly ice-cold and he laughed his relief aloud, as he began to realize the implications underlying the enemy's decision.

Dear heaven, they could not know, could not even suspect that they themselves would be under attack within a few hours! They could have no idea that their test would be made too late or that, however successful it might be, their fifty experimental sea-mines could not now be sunk in time to stop the Allied Azoff squadron steaming up the channel to lay siege to Yenikale.

Evidently they had attached no significance to the buoys he had laid out to mark the channel—either they had not observed them or had supposed them to have been laid by one of their own ships. And, because they had failed to notice the *Constantine,* when she had slipped past the fort on her out-ward journey through the fog, they were now—if he had read the signs aright and interpreted their motives correctly—preparing to let her destroy the last obstacle which remained to block the free passage of the channel. Apart, of course, from their guns, but Jack Lyons would be ready for those . . .

Phillip felt his heart thumping against his ribs. It seemed incredible but it was the only explanation that made any sense to him and he could see no reason to doubt it. In any case, if he was wrong, it made no difference—the result would be the same. Filled with a heady sense of exhilaration, he leaned over the rail, as far out as he could, in an effort to make sure that the brig was still on course. He would have to make his own bid for escape very soon, he knew; the deck was almost unten-able, the heat and smoke overpowering, sapping his strength and robbing him of breath. And he would need his strength, because he looked like having to swim for it—the boats were riddled like collanders, if they weren't smashed to pieces. Even supposing he could lower one, it wouldn't keep him afloat for more than a few minutes, he told himself but, to his own sur-prise, he felt no undue anxiety. His feeling of excitement tran-scended fear and, as he passed a blackened hand over his eyes and glimpsed the raised line of stakes directly ahead, he found himself cheering with a wild abandon for which he would almost certainly have rebuked one of his seamen.

The stakes were very close—thirty or, at most, forty yards from the brig's wallowing bows. She could not miss her objective now, even if her paddle-wheels clanked to a standstill, she must drift on to the submerged bank . . . nothing could stop her. She . . . the cheer died on his parched lips, to be replaced by a prayer, as the maintopmast came crashing down across the deck in front of him, in a welter of torn cordage and splintered wood. The flames licked at it hungrily and then it slid down the canting deck and, still held by stays and shrouds, hung suspended there until—as if in answer to his muttered prayer—the whole mass slipped slowly into the water.

The *Constantine* lost way but, miraculously, regained it and, her paddles still turning, she continued on course, as if, like the fireships of so many earlier naval battles, she knew her destiny and did not shrink from it.

Phillip experienced a pang as he left her, diving cleanly over the stern into the cool, moonlit water, which was balm to his scorched and aching body. Aware that, for his own self-preservation, he ought to put the greatest distance he could between himself and his doomed ship, he swam twenty yards and then, suddenly indifferent to whatever fate might be awaiting him on shore, he trod water, turning to look for her. She was a fearsome sight, from this level, bearing more resemblance to a flaming torch than to a ship but, curiously, her stern was almost untouched and her borrowed ensign flew proudly from its staff, smoke blackened yet lit to an uncanny radiance by the flames that were consuming her.

He resumed his swim, turning his back on her, unable to bring himself to watch her end. It came swiftly, long before he reached the shore, in the boom of a massive explosion, which echoed and re-echoed in his ears and left him in no doubt that the *Constantine* had gained her objective. *A charge sufficient to blow a ship-of-the-line in half,* Kirkoff had said and, fighting against the shock-waves which threatened to swamp him, he did not doubt the Russian Captain's claim as to the force employed. A great spout of water rose into the air, hiding the little brig's death throes behind a curtain of spray, but he knew that there would be nothing left of her and found himself wondering cynically whether the engineers from Yenikale—if they were, in fact, watching it—would be satisfied with the result of their experiment.

A mounted patrol, carrying lighted torches, galloped along the edge of the rocky foreshore as he neared it. They were spread out, evidently searching for him and, as the depth of the water decreased and he was able to stand upright, he could see that some of them had dismounted and were advancing towards him. It was useless to attempt to evade capture—he was too stiff, too exhausted, to go on swimming and to run from them would be to invite them to open fire on him.

As it was, a few musket balls peppered the water about him but he ignored them and when he stumbled on to the rocks, swaying like a drunken man, the firing stopped. Shouts, excited and unintelligible, greeted his appearance but he had no means of knowing if these were addressed to him or were intended to bring more men down from the cliff top. He was partially deafened by the explosion and his eyes, unaccustomed to the semi-darkness of the shadowed beach, seemed unable to focus on distant objects, so he stood where he was and waited, chilled from his immersion in the water and shivering in his thin, damp shirt and dripping trousers. He could dimly recollect having kicked off his boots when he was in the water but could not remember where or when he had removed his jacket. The pistol he had worn, strapped about his wrist, had gone and so had his Dollond but he still had his watch—the elaborately engraved and crested watch that had belonged to Mademoiselle Sophie's father and which she had given him in Odessa. His numb fingers felt for and found it in the pocket of his trousers but, when he opened it, he could not see its face in the darkness. The sky was lightening, though—the moon emerging from behind a cloud.

A voice yelled something in harsh tones which he did not understand but, taking it to be a command from the patrol to advance to meet them, he staggered a few paces up the beach, the watch still in his hand.

The shout was repeated and a horseman—a Cossack from his garb—who had led his horse down the cliff, leapt into the saddle and came charging recklessly over the rocks, his sabre flashing silver in the moonlight as he wrenched it from its scabbard. Phillip had expected no violence and was ill-prepared to ward off his assailant. He attempted to step aside, slipped on the loose shingle, and dropped to his knees. The sabre struck him a glancing blow across the shoulders and was raised again, as the Cossack jerked his small, shaggy horse to a standstill beside him. He lifted both hands to ward off the blade and felt it bite painfully into the muscles of his right forearm. Then a hand came out to wrench the watch from his grasp but he struggled instinctively to retain it and a second rider spurred to the aid of the first, bringing the butt of his pistol savagely down on his unprotected head.

The last sound he heard, before he lapsed into unconsciousness, was the renewed thunder of cannon fire but he could not be sure whether or not he had imagined it.

CHAPTER SIX

A *booted foot* prodded him to wakefulness and Phillip struggled to sit up, flinching from the bar of bright sunlight which filtered through a small window set high in the wall opposite to which he was lying. His whole body ached, his head was throbbing unmercifully, and he could scarcely see. He was as weak as a kitten, he realized disgustedly and, finding the effort to sit up beyond him, he slithered back on to a heap of straw behind him and let his heavy eyelids fall so as to shut out the light.

The foot prodded again with, it seemed, the deliberate intention of causing him pain, and a soldier in a grey uniform thrust a coarse earthenware cup into his right hand. He tried to hold it but his fingers were so stiff that they would not retain their grasp. The cup tilted and the warm, evil smelling liquid it contained spilled over his chest, compelling him to drag himself into a sitting position in order to rid himself of it. The soldier swore at him, deposited a hunk of black bread on the floor at his side and went out, slamming the heavy wooden door of his prison with a force that set every nerve in his head jangling anew. There were guns firing, close at hand—a great many guns, which shook the building with their thunder—and these added to his discomfort.

Phillip eyed the bread distastefully and lay back once

more, to seek refuge from his pain and exhaustion in sleep. The next time he wakened—some hours later, as nearly as he could judge from the position of the sun—he felt stronger and was able to sit up, his back resting against the dank stone wall of his cell. His right arm was swathed in a filthy, blood-soaked bandage, behind which he decided not to look. It was stiff and numb and resisted all his attempts to move it—the Cossack's sabre, he thought, memory returning, must have severed both bone and muscle. If it had, he would lose the arm. His right arm . . . devil take it and the man who had inflicted the wound!

Probing cautiously with his left hand, he discovered a lump the size of a pigeon's egg over his temple, which was painful to the touch and sticky with dried blood. He could have been in a worse state, he told himself philosophically; his Cossack captors could have let him bleed to death, instead of applying a bandage to his arm, or the man who had struck him with the pistol could, as easily, have shot him with it. Evidently they wanted him alive but, recalling Captain Kirkoff's complaints of the treatment meted out to him aboard the *Constantine,* he smiled wryly. Kirkoff had talked of the civilized usages of war and the respect due to his rank but his compatriots, it appeared, cared little for such niceties, when the boot was on the other foot . . .

After a while, finding the silence of his prison unendurable, Phillip managed to crawl over to the window and drag himself up to it, the fingers of his left hand gripping the sill. But he could hear no sounds that had any meaning for him; no gunfire, no voices, no churning paddle-wheels, and he could see nothing. Yet he must be in one of the forts—he could be nowhere else, with walls over ten feet thick and windows like arrowslits . . . and rats, like the pair which were now fighting for the hunk of black bread he had left on the floor.

Yenikale, perhaps? He drew in his breath sharply. Wherever he was, the day was well advanced and the Allied attack—if it had taken place as planned—should, by this time, be under way. Unless there had been another setback such as the one, three weeks ago, when General Canrobert, the French Commander-in-Chief, had ordered the withdrawal of his entire force a few hours before they were due to be landed . . . but surely, surely *that* could not have happened again? It was unthinkable. With fifteen thousand troops, five batteries of artillery, and virtually every ship in the Allied Black Sea Fleets committed to the expedition and lying off Kaffa the previous night, ready to move on to Kamiesch-Bourno for the landings at first light today, Admiral Lyons would have permitted no change of plan. With or without the French, he and Sir George Brown, the military Commander, would have set the troops ashore and Jack Lyons, the Admiral's son, who had been appointed to command the Azoff squadron, would be leading his gunboats and light-draught steam-frigates up the channel to Yenikale. But no cannon were firing . . . for God's sake, what *could* be going on? Kerch was only five miles overland from Yenikale . . . would not the sound of battle have carried, however faintly?

In an agony of uncertainty, Phillip strained his ears but there was nothing. Could he have slept through the battle, he wondered—without his watch, he had no idea for how long he'd lain unconscious in this filthy, rat-infested dungeon. Or— an appalling thought—had the landings been made and repulsed? He tried vainly to drag himself to a level with the sloping window-sill, only to fall back on to the uneven stone floor, gasping with pain, his injured arm crumpled beneath him. Then, as he was making a second attempt to reach the window, a series of dull, booming explosions shattered the silence and he stood, his body pressed against the wall and his heart pounding, endeavouring to count them and identify their source. He heard at least half a dozen before the dreadful throbbing in his head compelled him to draw back, reeling with nausea, the cell walls whirling about him.

It was almost a relief when, about an hour later, two soldiers came into his prison and dragged him roughly to his feet. The orders they shouted at him were unintelligible but a rifle butt, jabbed into the small of his back, made their meaning clear and he staggered out into a dark stone corridor with the men half-driving, half-carrying him between them. Stone steps, which he ascended with difficulty, led to an open courtyard, above one side of which he could see the ramparts of a fort, silhouetted against the setting sun, with heavy iron cannon mounted at each embrasure.

There were artillerymen, in green uniforms, moving about the guns but they were not, as he had expected them to be, working or standing to their guns. They were engaged in spiking them . . . Phillip halted, heedless of the prodding rifle butts, and stared up at them incredulously, as another party descended from the ramparts carrying boxes of ammunition. Then, from somewhere to the rear, beyond his line of vision, he heard a further series of muffled explosions which he identified, after a moment's puzzled thought, as the destruction of other and probably heavier guns by means of blocked charges, set to blow up their barrels.

Dazed though he was, his spirits lifted. If the garrison were putting their guns out of action, it could mean only one thing—the Allied landings had taken place and the attack had been successful. Kertch must have fallen and this fort was about to be evacuated—the Russians were not staying to defend it or to contest the entry of the Azoff squadron into the Strait. He breathed a heartfelt prayer of thankfulness and, buoyed up with new hope, was walking erect and without their aid when his guards opened a door at the head of another flight of stone steps and thrust him into a small room, furnished as an office, which was built into the thickness of the massive wall.

An Officer, in the uniform of a Colonel of artillery, was seated at a desk in the centre of the room, sorting out papers, assisted by two others. He was middle-aged and wore pince-nez and he looked glum and out of temper, his cheeks unshaven and his eyes puffy and bloodshot, as if he had been for a considerable time without sleep. The other two were younger, one a Major in the blue and silver of a Lancer regiment, the other an Engineer Lieutenant, with fair hair and duelling scars, which disfigured his square, Teutonic face.

When Phillip was brought to a halt in front of the desk by his escort, the Colonel glanced up with a flicker of interest in his lacklustre eyes and said, in French, "Ah, this is the man! He appears to be the sole survivor. I can only suppose that he was drunk, since he failed to take to the boat with the rest."

"Or mad," the Lancer Officer suggested with a hint of cynical amusement. "Like those madmen at Balaclava, the English light cavalry, who were annihilated when they charged our guns in the North Valley. We believed them to be drunk but I spoke to some of the men we took prisoner, Colonel, and they swore that not a drop of liquor had passed their lips the whole day! Most of them had not eaten, either, so they must have been mad—there can be no other explanation. I wish, however—and particularly at a time like this—that *I* had a regiment of English madmen under my command. We should not be preparing to retreat if I had!"

"The orders to retreat are not mine, Vladimir Ivanovitch," the Colonel returned sourly. He subjected Phillip to a brief scrutiny, taking in his filthy clothes and unkempt state and snapped an order in his own tongue to one of the escort. The man clicked his heels and left the office. "The unfortunate fellow was roughly handled by the Cossack dogs who took him prisoner," he went on, reverting to French, which he spoke with easy fluency. "And, of course, these cretins of mine have neglected him but"—he shrugged—"I have had other and more pressing matters on my mind."

"Haven't we all!" the man addressed as Vladimir agreed feelingly. He ruffled the pile of papers in front of him and sighed. "Must we really go through all these, Colonel? Surely it would be simpler merely to make a bonfire of the lot?"

"I have my orders." The Colonel's tone was stiff but he thrust two large, unopened bundles across the desk with an impatient hand. "These can be burnt. Attend to them, Walburg."

The Lieutenant said woodenly, "I will read them, if you wish, Colonel."

"There is no need—don't waste time on them. You'll have plenty to do when we receive the order to blow up the magazine."

Phillip maintained a cautious silence, head down and eyes averted. It was evident from the freedom with which they were speaking of confidential matters in front of him, that they believed him to be an ordinary seaman, no more capable than his escort of understanding any language but his own, and he was well content to play the part for which they had cast him. Had they suspected that he was an Officer, he would probably by this time be on his way to Prince Gortchakoft's headquarters at Simpheropol, under heavy guard, but as it was . . . he stared down at his shoeless feet with well simulated indifference as he heard the cavalry Major say, "And what of our mad—or drunken—sailor, Colonel? What do you intend to do with him?"

"Ah, yes—the sailor." The Colonel searched in his pockets. "The watch they found on him puzzled me. It bears the Imperial cypher and the personal arms of the late Grand-Duke Michael who, as you are doubtless aware, died long before this accursed war broke out. I have it somewhere . . . yes, here it is." He produced the watch from his breast pocket and offered it for the cavalryman's inspection. "As you can see, it is a magnificent and extremely valuable timepiece, and I asked myself what an English sailor could be doing with it."

Phillip stiffened involuntarily, feeling a shiver of apprehension course through him but the eyes of all three Officers were on the watch and he breathed again, thankful that he had not betrayed himself.

"I imagine he looted it," the Major said. He smiled, with genuine amusement. "An enterprising fellow, this madman!"

"Quite so," the Colonel agreed dryly. "So I decided to satisfy my curiosity before letting him go. You speak English, Vladimir, do you not?"

"After a fashion, sir, but I've had little practice of late."

The Colonel waved the excuse aside. "Question the man, if you please. Ask him how he acquired the watch and—"

"You surely do not intend to set this man at liberty, Colonel?" the Engineer Lieutenant interrupted, unable to contain his indignation. He was German, from his accent, and there was thinly veiled scorn in his young voice as he added accusingly, "Russian discipline is too lax! In the German Army, looters are shot out of hand. It is the only way to set an example to the others and to make soldiers out of a rabble. This—this enterprising fellow, as Major Stepanoff so humorously calls him—no doubt murdered the Officer from whom he stole that watch. Yet you speak of letting him go unpunished!"

Phillip, endeavouring to follow the conversation without appearing to do so, passed his tongue over his dry lips. His head was throbbing again and it was all he could do to hold himself upright but, to his intense relief, the Russian Colonel exchanged an expressive glance with his compatriot and said curtly, "Attend to your own responsibilities, Lieutenant Walburg, and leave me to mine. As you are aware, I have to evacuate my garrison before nightfall and get them to Arguine before the enemy cut the road. It will be a long march and I have no desire to be burdened by prisoners—least of all wounded prisoners. I am leaving my own sick and wounded behind."

"As you say, Colonel." The fair-haired young German shrugged resignedly. He looked for a moment as if he intended to argue and Phillip waited, stony-faced and silent, having to make a great effort to control the trembling of his limbs.

"In any case," the Colonel went on, with a tight-lipped smile, "I'm sending him to the hospital . . . and the wretched fellow will probably lose his arm. The wound was severe and has been neglected—he'll be of little use to the English Navy when the surgeons have done with him." He held up the watch and nodded impatiently to Major Stepanoff. "Ask him, Vladimir!"

"Sailor," the cavalry Major began hesitantly. "This watch—you see?"

Phillip braced himself. The news concerning his arm was not encouraging but he thrust the thought from him. If the garrison was to be evacuated by nightfall, the surgeons would go with it—certainly they would leave before the arrival of the Allied troops. He nodded and held out his hand for the watch. "If you please, sir," he said, in English. "Give me the watch."

"It is not yours," Major Stepanoff said. "Is it?"

Deciding on a half-truth, Phillip shook his head. "No, sir. It belongs to my Captain—to Commander Hazard, of the Royal Navy. He gave it to me for safe-keeping, sir."

"Safe-keeping?"

"To look after for him, sir."

Major Stepanoff translated for the Colonel's benefit and then asked, "Where did *he* get it? This is a Russian watch, is it not?"

"It was a gift to the Commander, sir, from a Russian Officer—Prince Narishkin. He was killed at Balaclava and the Commander was with him when he died."

"What does he say about Prince Narishkin?" the Colonel asked. He listened thoughtfully to the translation but, before he could express any opinion, a cavalry Officer in a mud-spattered uniform clattered into the room, saluted and proffered the despatch he was carrying. The Colonel read it with furrowed brows, sighed deeply and rose. The room filled, in response to his shout. "We are to leave at once," he announced, as his Officers gathered round him. "Lieutenant Walburg, you will light the fuse to the magazine. And take these with you." He indicated the heap of documents littering the desk. "Dispose of them as best you can . . ." he gave his orders, in a flat, expressionless voice and Phillip, forgotten in the sudden commotion, moved slowly towards the door. He was at the head of the stone steps when Major Stepanoff caught up with him.

"Wait!" he called in English. The guard who had escorted him from his cell was there also, Phillip saw, and he waited, aware that it would be impossible to escape from both of them. The Russian Officer put the watch into his hand. "You are a brave and noble fellow," he said softly. "Whoever you are! I am from Odessa and I have heard of Commander Phillip Hazard of the *Trojan,* so I gladly return his watch to you for safe-keeping. Now . . . this soldier will take you to the hospital. You will be safe there until we have gone and I have given him a note for the surgeon."

He offered his hand and, pocketing the watch, Phillip took it unthinkingly, to see a smile of sudden pleasure light the cavalryman's dark, expressive eyes.

"As I thought—this is not the hand of a common sailor and I suspected when I first set eyes on you that you do not ordinarily walk barefoot. Oh, do not concern yourself, I shall say nothing. Andrei Narishkin was my friend and patron and I held my first commission in the Hussars of Odessa. I wish you Godspeed, Commander Hazard!"

Only when he had gone did Phillip realize that Vladimir Stepanoff had spoken in French and that he had thanked him in the same language. But he was permitted no time for speculation; his escort, anxious to carry out the orders he had been given and join his unit for the evacuation, hurried him down another flight of stone steps and along what seemed an interminable corridor, sparsely lit by rush torches at infrequent intervals. The soldier did not use his rifle butt to enforce his prisoner's compliance; he behaved respectfully and, for most of their journey, offered the support of his arm. When they were in sight of their destination, however, the soldier pointed to it, gave him Stepanoff's note and hurried off, leaving him to his own devices.

For a moment, Phillip was tempted to make his escape into the town but, having little idea of its whereabouts or the situation there, he thought better of it. Without shoes, he could not walk far and his arm was becoming increasingly painful. He looked down at the stained and filthy bandage and sighed.

It would be asking for trouble if he did not, at least, have the dressing changed, and the surgeons would be in as much of a hurry to leave as his escort had been. They would not do more than change the dressing, unless he insisted, and . . . he smiled wryly to himself, as he crossed another courtyard filled with hurrying men. He would ask for no more; if he had to lose the arm, as the Colonel had predicted, he would prefer a British surgeon to take it off for him when he rejoined the Fleet.

The hospital proved to be a cold, cheerless cellar, with little more in the way of furnishing for the wounded than lines of straw palliasses and, scattered here and there, a few wooden tables for the surgeons and orderlies to work from. There was a nauseating stench of mortifying flesh, stale vomit, and excreta rising from the score or so of wounded men who still occupied the ward and he drew back at the entrance, his stomach heaving. Better retain the foul dressing on his arm than submit to being treated here, he thought. This was a place of the dead and the poor devils who were left here were being left to die . . .

He was limping slowly away when a grey-haired man, with a neatly trimmed beard and wearing a smock over his uniform, emerged from a small room opening off the corridor and called out to him by name, in tones of startled recognition.

Phillip turned, equally startled. Both face and voice were familiar, although he could not, at first, recall the man's name or remember where they had encountered each other before. Yet evidently they had—the newcomer had addressed him correctly by rank and name, and he was a surgeon, judging by the bloodstained smock and the case of instruments he was carrying.

"Sir," he began uncertainly, "surely you are . . ." still the name would not come but now he remembered the circumstances of their last meeting, more than six months ago, when he had been a prisoner-of-war in Odessa. After he and poor young O'Hara had been dragged, half-frozen, from the icy sea, this man had marvelled at their powers of survival . . . and he had lent them his own set of chessmen, to while away the long hours of their captivity. "You are Dr Bozenko!" he exclaimed.

The surgeon bowed. "And you, it would appear, are once again in need of my services, Commander Hazard," he said, in his precise and careful French.

"I regret to say I am, Doctor. But—"

"You are only just in time—I was preparing to leave. Well, come in and let me see what I can do for you." Dr Bozenko motioned to the room behind him, in which a stove glowed redly, emitting a pleasant warmth. He smiled faintly. "Should one enquire what you are doing here? This time, presumably, you are not a prisoner, since you have come here without an escort . . . but once again from the sea, I observe. Do you lead an advance party of the British force from whom we are about to retreat?"

Evading the question, Phillip gave him the note.

"Ah, this is from Major Stepanoff," he said, the smile widening. "He asks that you be given what medical treatment is necessary and then instructs me to leave you here . . . so I will do as I am bidden and ask no questions. Sit down, Monsieur Hazard, if you please, and permit me to examine your wound."

The surgeon cut away the soiled bandages and thrust them hastily into the stove. An orderly, in response to his shouted instructions, brought in fresh linen and a steaming bowl of water and, with much tongue-clicking, he cleansed and made a careful examination of the wound, wrinkling his nostrils delicately as he inhaled the odour of putrefaction which was starting to emanate from it. Phillip caught a whiff of this too and had again to fight down the waves of nausea which threatened to overwhelm him. It was the same ghastly stench that had hung over the ward and he knew, only too well, what it portended . . .

"Flex your fingers, if you please," the doctor requested. "So . . . do you feel, when I touch the palm of the hand? Now the wrist . . . ah, there is sensation there, not much, but still a little. Now try to close your hand." Phillip tried, the perspiration breaking out with the intensity of his efforts, but the hand would not close. He looked up to meet the surgeon's pitying gaze.

"It is my right hand, Doctor," he said wretchedly.

"Even so, Monsieur Hazard," the doctor began, "You . . ." a tremendous explosion drowned whatever he had been about to say. The whole building shook and Phillip was toppled from his chair, as windows shattered and a shower of tinkling glass covered the floor beside him. Bozenko assisted him to his feet. "That was the magazine," he stated breathlessly. "Excuse me for one moment—I must see to the men next door."

He was gone, and the orderly with him, for almost twenty minutes and as he waited, Phillip came very near to despair. He had seen men lose limbs in battlefield casualty stations and in the tossing cockpit of a ship but familiarity with the ghastly mutilations which had, of necessity, to be performed had not lessened the horror of it, so far as he was concerned. And this was his right arm . . . he shivered, looking down at the wound with sick disgust.

"Monsieur Hazard!" The dapper little doctor returned, agitated and apologetic, his face and hands begrimed, his grey hair dishevelled and plastered with dirt. "I have orders to leave immediately, so I must ask your forgiveness for having to desert you. I will dress this arm but it should come off, you understand—it *must* come off. Your people will be here tomorrow—Kertch has fallen to them and already there are English and French ships in the Strait." He took a bottle of colourless liquid from his case, lifted Phillip's limp arm and with a murmured, "This will pain you but it may help to ward off the infection," poured its contents over and into the wound.

Phillip had to bite back the anguished cry which rose involuntarily to his lips and Dr Bozenko, with quick sympathy, placed the bottle in his left hand and invited him to drink what was left. The raw spirit burned his throat but it had the desired effect and the pain had eased a good deal by the time a fresh dressing had been deftly secured about his arm.

"I regret that I can do no more for you," the doctor told him, with genuine distress. "Remain here, in this room, and get what sleep you can. There are shoes and some clothing in the closet—help yourself to anything you need. And the samovar is full." His orderly appeared in the doorway, calling out something Phillip did not understand but glancing round, he saw that there were three or four women with him, shadowy figures in the dim light dressed in dark robes, with shawls about their heads. Dr Bozenko gestured to them. "These women have offered to stay and care for the wounded until your troops and medical staff arrive. They are Jews and Armenians and they speak no English but they are good women, who have served us well, and they will do what they can, for you and the others. Although, God knows, there is little enough they *can* do for the others." He closed his instrument case, gave it to the orderly and stripped off his smock.

Phillip started to thank him but was cut short. "Take this, Monsieur Hazard." To his astonishment, he saw that the doctor was pulling a pistol from the tail-coat pocket of his uniform. It was a large, unhandy weapon and he shook his head. "No, Doctor," he objected. "I shan't need it, I—"

The pistol was placed on his knee. "You may, Monsieur Hazard, if the accursed Turks get here first. I would beg you, if you can, to protect these good and innocent women from them—even if you are unable to protect my wounded men in there. I ask you this, as one Christian to another."

He was gone before Phillip could bid him farewell, the orderly clumping after him, glum faced and stoical.

A little later two of the women came in, long dresses rustling as they walked, and shyly offered him food, which he fell upon ravenously and washed down with tea from the doctor's samovar. He felt better when he had eaten and, impelled by his conscience, managed to don a pair of boots, which he found in the closet and stumble unaided to the main ward. He felt curiously light-headed and his legs barely had the strength to hold him up but he contrived somehow to drag himself the length of the ward, no longer nauseated by its stench and conscious only of the need to satisfy himself that the occupants of the ward were being well cared for by the silent, dark-robed women.

Evidently guessing his intention, they did not attempt to stop him, content to follow his unsteady progress with their eyes and only when his strength gave out did one of them, a grey-haired Jewess with a gentle smile, come to his assistance and, an arm about his waist, lead him back to the doctor's room. They had made up a bed for him by the stove, he saw and, unable to argue with his smiling nurse, he let her help him to it, pull off his borrowed boots and cover him with a blanket.

Silence fell over the deserted fort, broken only by the

far-off crackle of musketry and an occasional moan from one of the Russian wounded. Phillip dropped at last into the exhausted sleep, from which he wakened, hours later, feeling as if his whole body—with the exception of his wounded arm—were on fire. The arm, by contrast, seemed to be ice-cold and try as he would, he could not lift it. He stirred restlessly and cool, soft hands moved soothingly about his burning face, while others gently restrained his threshing limbs and someone, he had no idea who, held a cup of water to his parched and straining lips, murmuring words of reassurance in a language he did not understand.

After a while, lulled by the voice, he slept again.

CHAPTER SEVEN

Two *Turco-Tunisian* regiments were the first to reach Yenikale, which they entered—firing indiscriminately at anyone they met—at a little before noon on 25th May. They were not officially the advance guard of the successful Allied invasion force, which left Kertch two hours after them but, with the connivance of their Commander, Faruk Bey, they had slipped out under cover of darkness to make a rapid march along the coast road, killing and burning as they went.

Phillip's first reaction to their arrival was one of shocked disbelief, for it was heralded by the smoke rising from burning buildings and the terrified screams of their inhabitants, as they sought vainly for escape. Listening eagerly for the pipes and drums of the Highland Brigade, he was bewildered by the sounds he heard and unable to account for the presence of a mob of vengeful Turks, who appeared to be running wild without any semblance of discipline, slaughtering all who stood in their way.

It was only afterwards that he learnt, from an Officer of the 93rd, the events which had led to their presence. The town of Kertch, Captain Campbell told him—occupied without opposition the previous day—had been sacked and brutally plundered by the five thousand strong Turkish contingent, which had been among the first to be landed. Appeals to their

Commander-in-Chief, Reschid Pasha, to restrain his troops, had been met with the extraordinary assertion that this could not be done and that, in any case, it was contrary to Turkish military policy to deny the spoils of victory to the victorious.

When some French Colonial regiments had followed their example and a few rapacious seamen from the British troop transports had also—albeit belatedly—come ashore to seize their share of the looted wine and provision stores, the situation had threatened to get out of hand. With part of the town already in flames, the British military Commander, General Sir George Brown, clamped down firmly on the rioters, sending in the well-disciplined Highland Brigade to restore order, protect the townsfolk, and assist them to fight the fires. This done, he issued instructions that any member of the Allied force, if caught looting or maltreating the inhabitants, was to be arrested, whatever his nationality, and flogged without the formality of a trial.

The order—reminiscent of the great Duke of Wellington, under whom Sir George had served in the Peninsular War—was carried out with French support and strict impartiality but, inevitably, most of those arrested were Turks and feeling began to run high among the Sultan's Officers.

With a score of his men under arrest and awaiting humiliating punishment at the hands of infidels—who clearly did not know how to make war or understand that plunder was often the only pay a Turkish soldier received—Faruk Bey had started on his self-imposed mission in a spirit of bitter resentment against his British allies. Now, having left a ghastly trail of destruction in their wake, his men were beyond his power to control. They had raped, tortured, robbed and murdered, burnt crops and set peaceful dwelling places alight, and they were laden with plunder of every description.

It had not been part of the Bey's plan to enter the Russian

stronghold of Yenikale; he had no means of knowing whether or not the fort was still defended and he would gladly have called a halt, had he been in a position to do so, but his soldiers had tasted blood and were deaf to the promptings of caution. They charged in, without skirmishers or reconnaissance, ignoring the shouted commands of the more responsible of their Officers and, meeting no resistance, went on a rampage in the town. There Faruk Bey lost most of them but, aware that the main body of the Allied land forces could not now be far behind and anxious to salvage what he could of his reputation, he gathered a handful of them and advanced boldly on the deserted fort.

Warned of their approach by the fusillade of shots which preceded it, Phillip made what preparations he could to receive them. His first responsibility was to the women and, with no illusions as to the fate which would be in store for them if the Turks suspected their presence, he herded them all into the small room in which he had spent the night and warned them, by signs, to bar the door. They behaved with a courageous dignity that won his admiration; if they were afraid, they did not show it and were reluctant to abandon the men in the ward until he held up the pistol Dr Bozenko had left with him and indicated that he would use it to defend their charges.

He could find no spare ammunition and wondered wryly for how long he would be able to defend even himself with so inadequate a weapon, if the Turks were really determined on slaughter. Not for the first time, he regretted the loss of his uniform jacket, which might have lent him sufficient authority to order them to seek their victims elsewhere and, conscious that he cut a singularly unimpressive figure in his stained blue trousers and filthy shirt, he positioned himself at the entrance to the ward.

He felt considerably better after his night's sleep and,

although his right arm was ominously numb and the throbbing in his head continued unabated, he was able to stand without experiencing attacks of vertigo and to walk without too much difficulty.

The Turks were quite a long time finding him and he was starting to hope that they would fail to penetrate the labyrinth of corridors and cellars which constituted the lower regions of the fort, when he heard voices and the scrape of booted feet on the steps leading down from the rear courtyard. Like jackals in search of carrion, he thought disgustedly, they had tracked down the hospital with its dead and dying Russians and their excited shouts suggested that they were aware that their hunt was at an end.

Drawing himself up to his full height, Phillip waited, the pistol held, out of sight, in his left hand. The voices came nearer—there were between twenty and thirty of them, as far as he could make out, bunched at the end of the corridor. He called out to them in English and in his best quarterdeck manner to halt and the leaders did so, only to be thrust forward by those behind them, who either had not heard or chose to ignore the order. He repeated it, in the nearest he could get to a stentorian bellow and this time they did stop, eyeing him uncertainly from a distance of fifteen yards.

"There's nothing for you here, soldiers," he told them, still in English. "Return to your duties."

A tall, dark complexioned Officer, holding a drawn sword, marched up to him arrogantly. "Who are you, to give orders to my soldiers?" he demanded in passable French.

Relieved that at least he would be able to make himself understood, Phillip returned crisply, "I am Commander Hazard of Her Britannic Majesty's ship *Huntress,* sir. And you?"

"I am Faruk Bey of the Army of His Magnificence the Sultan of Turkey," the tall Officer supplied sullenly. He scowled, his eyes bright with suspicion as he took in Phillip's torn clothing, the bandage on his arm, and his unshaven cheeks. "You are not in uniform," he observed. "What are you doing here?"

"I am—that is to say, I was—a prisoner-of-war until the Russians evacuated the fort yesterday evening."

"The Russians fled yesterday?" The Officer sounded surprised. Despite his claim to be Turkish, he was of Arab ancestry, Phillip decided, and so were most, if not all, the men with him. His heart sank. The Turco-Tunisian mercenaries were among the most cowardly and the worst disciplined in the whole of the Turkish Army . . . he remembered their behaviour at Balaclava. Entrusted with the defence of the redoubts covering the vital Woronzoff Road, they had fled without firing a shot, abandoning their guns to the enemy. Worse still, as they ran screaming towards the harbour, they had attempted to loot the camp of the 93rd as they passed through it . . . and these men, judging by the bloodstained state of their garments and the sacks they carried, had been engaged in looting on their way here. Looting and killing . . . he said sternly, "Perhaps Your Excellency would be good enough to withdraw your men. There is nothing of value for them to steal here."

"Nothing?" Faruk Bey was not placated by Phillip's courteous use of his title. He advanced to within a foot or two of the ward entrance, attempting to peer into the dark interior. "No Russians? The swine cannot all have fled! Let me pass, Commander Hazard—if that is indeed who you are, which I take leave to doubt. Your ship, the *Huntress,* was amongst those which covered our landing. I fancy you are a deserter, whom the Russians did not choose to take with them. You have no uniform. The boots you are wearing are Russian."

Phillip ignored the accusation. "The men in there are dead or dying," he stated with dangerous calm.

"They are Russian curs! Death is what they deserve—let us at them!"

"They are dying of disease, as well as from wounds. I do not advise you to enter for your own sake, Faruk Bey. In any case, they have nothing worth plundering. I request you to withdraw." Phillip did not raise his voice but his quiet air of authority was not lost on the Tunisian.

Faruk hesitated. "You, too, are wounded," he suggested unpleasantly, flicking at the bandage with the point of his scimitar. He continued to hold his ground, encouraged by murmurs of approval from the men grouped about him, some of whom had evidently followed their conversation—or enough of it to realize that the hospital was not deserted. "And you are alone! One man, against many . . . stand aside, Englishman!"

Like a wolf pack scenting blood, there was a concerted howl from the Tunisians and one or two started to edge cautiously forward.

"I am also armed," Phillip countered coldly. "And I shall shoot the first man who attempts to pass me." He displayed the pistol and had the satisfaction of glimpsing sudden fear in the dark eyes, as those who had pressed forward thought better of it and hurriedly stepped back. They might have gone then—they were undecided, Phillip sensed—but, at that most inopportune of moments, he heard a soft rustling sound behind him and turning, saw to his dismay that the grey-haired Jewish woman with the gentle smile was coming to range herself beside him.

Somehow, when he had urged the others to take refuge in the doctor's room, this woman must have eluded him, he thought bitterly, wishing her in perdition rather than where she was, although his heart applauded her selfless courage. The Tunisians stared at her open mouthed, momentarily taken

aback by her sudden appearance and he bundled her uncere-
moniously behind him.

"For God's sake!" he whispered in English. "Hide yourself!
Back to the ward!" She understood the urgency in his voice, if
not the words, and attempted to obey him but it was too late.

"So you have women here—women, as well as pigs of
Russians!" Faruk Bey snarled at him.

His men took up the cry. Like the wolf pack to which, a
few moments before, he had compared them, they came surg-
ing towards him with the Bey at their head, flanked by two of
his Officers with drawn swords, and Phillip was compelled to
retreat into the ward to avoid being knocked over. From somewhere in the distance he heard the faint skirl of Highland
pipes and the tramp of marching feet but they, too, his mind
registered despairingly, were too late . . . the hospital would
be a shambles if he waited until the British advance guard
arrived.

Several muskets exploded in the confined space of the corridor outside and one ball struck the vaulted ceiling high above
his head but there were too many men milling about there to
permit of accurate shooting and he paid the would-be marksmen no heed. He kept his pistol levelled at Faruk Bey's close-
cropped head, holding it steadily just beyond the reach of his
henchmen's swords and said uncompromisingly, "I shall not
hesitate to use this, if you compel me to, sir."

"Against an ally, Commander? And in defence of those
who are our mutual enemies?"

"In defence of wounded and helpless enemies. It is not a
British custom to slaughter wounded after a battle, or to make
war on women." Phillip controlled his rising temper but the
strain was becoming well-nigh unendurable and he could feel
the sweat pouring off him, as the foul stench of the ward once

again threatened to choke him. One of the wounded Russians, evidently aware of the danger he was in, made an abortive attempt to get to his feet and Faruk shouted something to the Officer beside him, who turned with a grin to obey him. The curved scimitar he carried was razor-sharp and it descended with the force of a guillotine on the back of the wounded man's neck. The Russian dropped with a strangled cry, his head not quite severed from his falling body and as his assailant prepared to complete his grisly task, Phillip took careful aim and fired from a range of six feet. The ball took the Tunisian squarely in the chest and he collapsed in a crumpled heap beside his victim.

"You have killed him!" Faruk Bey exclaimed, backing away. He was visibly shaken and Phillip, the empty pistol smoking in his hand, seized upon his momentary advantage to drive the whole mob of them, step by step, back towards the door of the ward. For how long he could have held them he was never to know; just as he was beginning to doubt his ability to do so, the corridor was filled with scarlet uniforms, and a party of Marines, with bayonets fixed, drove a purposeful way through their shrinking ranks. Sick with relief, he let the pistol fall, the roof of the cellar whirling about his head in crazy circles as he stumbled to meet his deliverers. From what seemed a long way away he heard a voice, which he dimly recognized as that of Faruk Bey, screaming in execrable English to the Marines to arrest him.

"He is a pig of a Russian spy, claiming that he is an English Officer! Do your duty—arrest him—he has in cold blood killed one of my men!"

Before he could say a word in his own defence, a rifle butt struck him on the side of the head and he slipped, almost gratefully, into oblivion . . .

*   *   *

"Phillip . . . Phillip, old man, can you hear me?" Phillip stirred weakly. He recognized the voice but it was too much of an effort, just then, to acknowledge it. "Phillip, I shall have to go very soon. We're entering the Sea of Azoff, with my father's flag about to be hoisted aboard the *Miranda,* but I want to speak to you before I leave. You—"

"Hold on, sir," a second voice requested. "The poor chap's pretty far gone." Someone lifted him, a hand supporting his shoulders and a cup was held to his lips. He sipped gratefully and felt the strong spirit course through his weary body, giving it new life. Brandy, he thought, brandy . . . and opened his eyes, to see Jack Lyons bending anxiously over him.

"That's better," Lyons approved. "How are you feeling, Phillip?" He gestured to the man who was with him. "Give him some more of that brandy, Doctor. It seems to be helping . . . and my God, he's earned it, if anyone has!"

Assisted by the *Miranda*'s surgeon, Phillip sat up. His head swam for a moment or two and then his vision cleared a little. He was in the room in which he had spent the night, he realized—Dr Bozenko's room—but now it was cold, because the stove had gone out. "What about the women, Jack?" he asked thickly, scarcely recognizing his own voice. "The ones who were here? I locked them in because they—"

"You need not explain why you locked them up, my dear Phillip," Captain Lyons put in grimly. "That mob of Turkish and Arab cut-throats would have given them short shrift if you hadn't. I've seen some evidence of what they did in the town before we got here. Don't worry about your Good Samaritans— not a hair of their heads was harmed, and I've just sent them back to their homes under guard."

"How long have you been here?" Phillip asked.

"A few hours. I anchored within sight of the fort—and out of range of the batteries—last night. We didn't realize the enemy had evacuated the place . . . I wish to heaven we had! There was a tremendous explosion when they blew up the magazine, of course, but I expected them to leave troops here, to defend the fort, so we waited until daylight to make sure. Sir George Brown was held up at Kertch and my orders were to wait until his troops were on the way . . ." Lyons supplied a few details and added, smiling, "But now, as perhaps you didn't hear me trying to tell you earlier—the Sea of Azoff squadron is about to gain its objective."

"I heard," Phillip admitted. "And the Admiral is going in with you?"

"Yes, he is—and Admiral Bruat too, with Sedaiges. They'll both rejoin their own flagships tomorrow, I think, and leave us to carry out our orders." There was a note of deep satisfaction in Jack Lyons's pleasant voice. "They've both waited long enough—and worked hard enough—for this moment, haven't they? And it *will* shorten the war, Phillip, I'm convinced of that. Sebastopol will fall, once the supply routes from the Sea of Azoff are cut . . . the only pity is that we could not embark on this expedition three weeks ago. However"—he laid an affectionate hand on Phillip's shoulder—"I must not keep the Admirals waiting, but I wanted a word with you, my dear fellow, before I left. I wanted to thank you, of course, for the splendid job you made of buoying the channel for us, and for clearing it of those infernal machines the enemy had waiting for our ships. If you—"

"Jack . . ." memory returned and Phillip interrupted apologetically, "Forgive me but my men, my prize-crew from the *Constantine* . . . did they get back all right?"

"Yes, indeed—the *Huntress* and the *Snake* picked them up, just north of the Yujnaia Spit. They'd had a long pull but there were no casualties, apart from those you incurred earlier, when you took the brig. And your poor little mid, of course."

O'Hara, Phillip thought, feeling a knife twist in his heart. "You heard what happened?" he asked painfully.

"Your brother made a full report." Jack Lyons rose. "I'm sorry, Phillip, I shall have to leave you. I—er . . ." he avoided Phillip's eye. "The *Huntress* is with my squadron, under your brother's command, and—"

Sensing from his manner that all was not well, Phillip asked, his throat tight, "Am I not to rejoin her, Jack? Is that what you are trying to tell me?"

Jack Lyons inclined his head regretfully. "Yes," he admitted, "I'm extremely sorry to say it is—you're being sent to Therapia, Phillip. Partly on medical grounds"—he exchanged a glance with the surgeon, who nodded his confirmation—"that arm of yours isn't in too healthy a state, I'm afraid. But the surgeon thinks there may be a chance of saving it, with proper care, which you'll get, of course, at the naval hospital at Therapia."

"I see." Well, he could accept that, Phillip thought—indeed, he had half-expected it, and anything was better than losing the arm but . . . he looked up into the face of his boyhood friend and said flatly, "There's another reason, is there not?"

Jack Lyons smiled. "Yes, there is . . . but don't worry about it, for heaven's sake. I'm sure it will blow over, if you stay out of circulation for a few weeks, Phillip. A complaint has been made against you, through official channels, by the Commander of the brig you captured." Phillip drew in his breath sharply. Kirkoff, of course—Kirkoff had lodged the complaint, as he had threatened he would—oh, damn Kirkoff to hell! "I see you know from whom it has come," Jack observed. Again he laid a friendly, comforting hand on Phillip's shoulder. "The fellow's temper, understandably in the circumstances, is a trifle frayed but he'll probably forget the whole thing, given time—or early exchange and repatriation, which I shall suggest to my father as a possible solution." He sighed, his smile fading. "The unspeakable Faruk Bey is, alas, less likely to forget, I'm afraid—he, too, has lodged a complaint against you and—"

"Faruk Bey! Oh, for God's sake, Jack! You said yourself that he was no better than a cut-throat and—"

"And I shall go on saying that, my dear Phillip," Lyons asserted. "His accusations cannot possibly be substantiated, they are wildly improbable. Unhappily, however, he did not make them to me or I'd have told him, in no uncertain terms, what he could do with them! The man you shot was his brother—or so he claims—and he ran, yelling blue murder, to General D'Autemarre. The French are, at the moment, rather sore because of the behaviour of their Colonial troops in Kertch and, almost certainly for this reason, the General has passed on Faruk's complaint—also officially—to my father."

"Then"—Phillip could hardly believe his ears—"there may have to be an inquiry?"

"It's possible," Jack Lyons admitted. "And I thought I should warn you. But don't worry about it—the result will be a foregone conclusion and I'll back you to the hilt. I also intend to recommend you for a decoration. That's to say if—" there was a knock on the door and he broke off as a midshipman came, cap in hand, to deliver a message from the Admiral. "My summons, Phillip," he said, unable to keep the excitement from his voice. "I'll have to leave you now. But good luck, my dear chap, and God go with you."

"And with you!" Phillip called after him. His brief anger died and, when Surgeon Corbett called a stretcher party in and took his leave, he decided to follow Jack Lyons's advice and refrain from worrying about the possible result of the complaints which had been made against him. There was little to be gained by brooding over them and, in any case, his arm was of more immediate concern to him than a court of inquiry into his conduct, which might be held sometime in the future.

The 36-hour passage to Therapia in a crowded transport proved something of an ordeal. He ran a high temperature and suffered considerable pain, for which the over-worked medical staff could do little, apart from suggesting immediate amputation. Phillip rejected this with an obstinacy that aroused their resentment and he was heartily glad when, at the end of a nightmare voyage, he was transferred to the Palace Hospital and, 24 hours later, from there to the comparative comfort and spaciousness of the hospital ship *Bombay*.

Good food, excellent nursing, and skilful medical care wrought, between them, a steady improvement in his health although, once again, he had to use all the powers of persuasion he possessed in order to escape the drastic cure the surgeons repeatedly urged upon him.

"Delay may cost you your life, Commander Hazard," he was warned, when the arm refused to heal and his temperature soared to dangerous heights, but he had recovered the use of his hand and fingers and, when feeling slowly and agonizingly began to return to the arm itself, the surgeons admitted that his gamble had been justified.

Mortality from post-amputation shock and infection was high, even in the wards of the well-staffed *Bombay*, and higher still in the hospital on shore, and Phillip's gradual recovery was hailed as something of a miracle when, a fortnight after his arrival, he was finally pronounced out of danger.

The chaplain, the Rev. Mackenzie, who had prayed daily at his bedside, exchanged his prayer book for the newspapers and, in response to his eager request, read aloud the reports which told of Jack Lyons's successful operations in the Sea of Azoff. And these had been brilliantly successful, Phillip learnt with delight. In the first four days, the squadron had seized nearly two hundred fifty ships carrying provisions for the enemy forces in the Crimea; Arabat had been shelled, its magazines blown up; and stores of corn and flour at Berdiansk and Genitchi—amounting to nearly four months' rations for one hundred thousand men—set on fire.

Vast stocks of coal, found abandoned at Kertch, were being put to good use by the British and French fleets; over a hundred guns had been captured; six war steamers had been sunk or scuttled by their own crews. Boat parties from the *Miranda, Swallow,* and *Wrangler* had blown up a further seventy transport and cargo vessels at their moorings, despite the threatening presence of a force of close on a thousand Cossacks.

By 2nd June, Captain Moore, cruising in the *Highflyer,* reported that the enemy were preparing to evacuate Anapa and Soujak—their last remaining strongholds on the coast of Circassia—which were reputed to be garrisoned by upwards of seven thousand troops. By the 5th, they had gone, leaving the two forts in the jubiliant hands of Serfir Pasha and his guerrillas, to whom Rear-Admiral Houston Stewart paid a visit a week later, in his flagship *Hannibal.*

The Admiral's wife was staying at Therapia, as a guest of the Ambassador, Lord Stratford de Redcliffe, and it was from her that Phillip obtained this last item of news. Mrs Houston Stewart had become a regular visitor to the naval hospital and she took to reading him extracts from her husband's letters, for which reason Phillip welcomed her visits with increasing eagerness. His eagerness was soon succeeded by impatience to return to the scene of action but, despite his pleas to be allowed to rejoin his ship, the doctors would not hear of it. Day followed empty day and he lay fuming in enforced idleness, forbidden to leave his bed, his only distraction the news his visitors brought him which, by its very nature, added to his restlessness.

A letter from Graham gave a graphic account of the operations against Taganrog, Marioupol, and Geisk, in which his own *Huntress* had taken an active part. The squadron, skilfully commanded by Jack Lyons—having shelled military targets in all three towns—had again sent boat parties ashore and, in the face of determined opposition by a force of some thirty-five hundred cavalry and infantry, had succeeded in destroying guns, munitions and more vast stores of grain intended for the Crimea.

"*It was pretty hot while it lasted,*" his brother wrote. "*But we are now in complete control of the Azoff Sea, from Arabat to the Gulf of Taganrog, and the Don River barges come to an abrupt halt at the river mouth. Not bad for a campaign of barely three weeks' duration, is it?*

"*I hear a strong rumour that both Admirals intend to return to Sebastopol very soon and that Jack Lyons—who has covered himself with glory—will return with them, which suggests that great things may be brewing there very shortly. Sir George Brown is also to return to the siege on 15th, leaving only five hundred British troops to 'stiffen' the Turkish garrison at Yenikale and the French, too, are said to be leaving only a token force.*

"*Our orders are to remain here, to continue operations on a somewhat reduced scale, under the command of Sherard Osborn. If I were you, I would endeavour—as Jack Lyons is doing—to rejoin the Admiral's flag, because that is where the action is going to be. There's talk of another naval attack on the harbour defences and a big land-based assault on Sebastopol itself. Here it is virtually over, I fear, although it's possible that I am mistaken . . . but I am not, I assure you, offering you this advice solely because I shall be reluctant to hand back your command to you. Every member of your ship's company will be eager to welcome you back . . ."*

The letter ended with many anxious enquiries as to his health, which added considerably to Phillip's frustration, and there was a postscript, which he had to read twice before he really took it in. *"Do not be surprised,"* Graham warned, *"if you receive a visit from Miss Moray. I heard from her recently, to inform me that she had returned to Constantinople as chaperone to the two daughters of a Mrs Mark Pendleton and, needless to say, I replied at once, telling her of your circumstances and whereabouts, so I feel sure she will get in touch with you, before long."*

Catriona Moray, Phillip thought, pleased . . . indeed, it would be good to see Catriona again. He left word with the kindly Mrs Mackenzie that, should Miss Moray enquire for him, he was anxious to see her and, on the first day that he was allowed to dress and sit up in a chair, Catriona presented herself. To his chagrin, she was not alone; she brought her charges with her—two pretty but excessively pert young girls of sixteen and seventeen—and they set themselves coquettishly to the task of entertaining the invalid, so that he was able to exchange only a few words with her in private, and even these were mainly concerned with his brother Graham and Catriona's correspondence with him.

She promised, however, to repeat her visit as soon as this could be arranged with her employers. The Pendletons were, it seemed, a wealthy family. They had travelled to Constantinople by chartered steamship, with a number of friends, and

Mr Mark Pendleton had now hired a yacht, with a Turkish crew, in which he proposed to sail to Balaclava in order to tour the battlefields of the Crimea and visit various high-ranking friends and relatives in the British Expeditionary Force. Phillip was faintly shocked by the idea that wealthly non-combatants should consider such a tour desirable and Catriona, reading his thoughts, explained wryly, "It is the latest fashion—the modish thing to do these days. The newspapers often publish advertisements for steamer trips to the theatre of war."

"But that was not why *you* returned, was it?"

She shook her head, flushing under his critical scrutiny. "No, it wasn't. I had . . . other reasons, I—well, there's no time to go into them now. We've stayed long enough and tired you, I'm afraid. I will try to come again, if you would like me to and—"

"You know I should be delighted to see you." Phillip accepted her extended hand regretfully. She had changed, he thought, changed almost out of recognition, and he found it difficult to reconcile his memory of her, toiling beside the other Highland women among the Balaclava wounded, with the young lady of fashion whose small, gloved hand he was now holding in his own. Yet her smile was the same; her low, charming voice, with its faint suggestion of a lilt, had not altered . . . it was only her outward appearance, with its revelation of a beauty he had not realized that she possessed, which—strangely—had created the illusion of change. This and, perhaps, the brash manners of her two young charges. "Please come again," he begged. "But alone, if that is possible. I should so much like to talk to you, Catriona."

"I *will* try," Catriona answered. "But we may be leaving here within the next day or two. I . . . I will let you know." She withdrew her hand, as if suddenly shy of him and, calling

to her companions, took her leave with a finality that he found
at once puzzling and—in view of their previous relationship—
a trifle hurtful.

Next day a brief note was delivered, to tell him that the
Pendletons were sailing for Balaclava earlier than she had
anticipated and apologizing for her inability to pay him a second visit. Phillip was disappointed and still more puzzled when
an enquiry as to the whereabouts of the yacht revealed that
it was still lying in the Golden Horn, awaiting the completion
of its crew.

That evening, however, all thought of Catriona was driven
from his mind by the unexpected appearance of the *Miranda.*
The frigate dropped anchor and a boat put off with unusual
haste, carrying a wounded Officer, with the surgeon, Dr
Corbett, in attendance. Phillip guessed, long before the sick
man was carried on board the hospital ship, who it was—the
surgeon's anxiety, the grief of the men who bore the stretcher,
told him that it was their Commander and that he was gravely
wounded.

Surgeon Corbett, recognizing him, sought him out after
the patient had been settled in one of the after cabins. "It was
such a small wound, Commander Hazard," he said bleakly.
"Not as severe as yours—and he need not have incurred it!"

"What happened, Doctor?" Phillip asked, sick with pity.

Corbett sighed. "Oh, there's to be a new land-based assault
on Sebastopol and an attempt, agreed to by Lord Raglan and
General Pélissier, to take the Malakoff and the Redan. A diver-
sionary attack by the Fleet was asked for and nine of our
frigates, including the *Miranda,* and supported by rocket
boats from the flagship, launched an experimental night
attack on the seaward defences. On the 16th, that was. Lord
Clarence Paget set out marks, as a guide for our gunners, and

he commanded the operation, which was highly successful. Quite a lot of damage was done—mostly by the rockets—and we sustained no casualties, so it was decided to repeat the attack the following night. The *Miranda* should not have been in the attacking squadron at all—they were queueing up for the privilege. But you know our Commander."

Phillip echoed his sigh. "Yes, I know him."

"The enemy were waiting for us," the surgeon told him grimly. "They ranged some of their big guns on our marks and we ran into a terrible barrage. The *Sidon* was in trouble—she lost fifteen, killed and wounded—and we went to her assistance. Captain Lyons was struck by a shell fragment, as he was directing our fire. His left leg was lacerated but he made light of it, tied a tourniquet round it himself and did not send for me to attend him until the squadron returned to the anchorage. By that time, the harm was done. I wanted to amputate but, like you, he wouldn't hear of it. 'Do you think I'm going to go around on a peg leg for the rest of my days, Doctor?' he said. 'Pensioned out of the Service at thirty-five? Life wouldn't be worth living—I'd rather take a chance and try to save my leg, if I can.' "

"Can you not save him?" Phillip managed. "Surely something can be done?"

The doctor shook his head, near to tears. "I'd give my own right arm if it would do any good but I'm very much afraid it's too late, Commander Hazard." He spread his hands in a despairing gesture. "It was really too late when I suggested taking the leg off—that was why I did not insist. He'd had the tourniquet on too long, you see, and the flesh had started to mortify. He said it was just a scratch and that he forgot about it! But I brought him here in the hope that the surgeons may be able to do for him what they've done for you. They're examining him now but I . . . I could not stay whilst they did so. I know what their verdict will be, Hazard. It will take a miracle to save him."

The miracle that had been vouchsafed to him, Phillip thought—surely, oh surely God, in His infinite mercy, would not deny that same miracle to Jack Lyons? Jack, with his splendid prospects, his outstanding courage and upright character, who was beloved by every Officer and seaman who had ever served with him . . . and who was the pride of his father's heart. He asked huskily, having to make an effort to hide his emotion, "Does the Admiral know, Doctor?"

The doctor bowed his head, "I tried to prepare him but I don't think he believed me, I don't think he could bear to. They're very close, you know. The Admiral thinks the world of his son. 'He's done well, hasn't he, Corbett?' he kept saying to me. 'He's proved himself in the Azoff operations and he'll go to the top, as I always knew he would . . . right to the top, in the best Nelson tradition.' And now this! It'll break his father's heart, Hazard, as it's breaking mine . . . and it was such a small wound. If only he had called me sooner!"

Phillip took his arm. There were no words of comfort he could offer and his own grief matched his companion's as, in numb silence, they paced the *Bombay*'s shadowed deck and watched the sun sink below the horizon in a blaze of glory. At last an orderly came to summon the doctor to a conference with his colleagues and he said, in a low voice, "This is it, then . . . God help him! Go to him, will you Hazard? He was asking for you as soon as we brought him on board. There's something troubling him on your account—something he says he failed to do for you. I should be grateful if you could set his mind at rest."

"Of course," Phillip promised. "I'll do anything in my power, Doctor." He laid a hand on the doctor's bowed shoulder. "And we shall all be praying for a miracle."

Jack Lyons received him with cheerful affection. His face had a grey, pinched look but he waved aside the suggestion that he was in pain. "Good Lord, I can't feel a thing! I've slept the clock round since it happened—that's proof enough, is it not? And the sight of you is a tonic, Phillip my dear chap— you're a whole man, with all your limbs, but the sawbones would have had that arm of yours off in a trice, if you'd let them. How are you? You're looking better than when I last saw you, anyway, although you've lost the devil of a lot of weight."

"I'm all but recovered, Jack. The staff here are truly wonderful. They'll do for you what they've done for me and—"

"No." The interruption was quiet but Phillip stiffened in dismay as he heard it. "No," Jack repeated. "I fear they cannot, Phillip. It's too late for me . . . and through my own stupid fault, not Corbett's. Poor devil, he's done everything humanly possible and he's perjured himself a dozen times, in his well meaning efforts to hide the truth from me. No, for pity's sake"—as Phillip tried to protest—"don't *you* start lying to me as well. We've been friends too long for that. Shipmates, too, Phillip . . . remember those good old *Pilot* days, when you were newly-promoted Lieutenant and I was in all the glory of my first command?"

"Yes, I remember. They were damned good days. I shan't forget them, as long as I live. I . . ." Phillip broke off, realizing what he had said but Jack smiled at him mockingly.

"And nor shall I, my dear chap. I wish this didn't have to be . . . I don't want to end my life now, Phillip, with everything I've ever wanted, everything I've worked for within my reach. But if it is God's will, who am I to question it?" He spoke without bitterness and Phillip's heart went out to him in helpless pity. "I'm worried about my father, though—he'll take it hard, I fear. See him for me, if you can, would you please, when it's . . . when it's over. Tell him he must carry on, it would be a national loss if he did not, if he let what's happened to me bring about his premature retirement. And tell him"—Jack's smile lost its mockery—"tell him there never was a son who was fonder or prouder of his father than I've been, all my life. He always modelled himself on Nelson, you know, even as a young man, and he has the Nelson touch. *I* think so, anyway. Indeed, I may speak out now and confess that I believe my father to be our greatest Admiral, and a man fitted for the times we're living in. Tell him that, will you, Phillip my friend?"

"I'll tell him," Phillip promised. He could feel his control slipping but somehow he managed to steady his voice.

"Thanks," Jack acknowledged. "There's one other thing, which I must get off my conscience. I've let you down, Phillip. I never intended to but I have and—"

"You've never let me down. You—"

"I'm afraid I have. You're in trouble, old man, and you shouldn't have been, if I'd been able to keep my promise to back you to the hilt. But we've been pretty busy in the Sea of Azoff—you'll have heard, no doubt, what's been going on there—so I put off writing a full report on your particular operations. I thought I had plenty of time and—"

"Forget it, Jack, please!" Phillip besought him. "It doesn't in the least matter, I assure you. It—"

"Oh, but it does matter, old son, and I shall write that report if it's the last thing I . . . oh, damn it, I intend to see it's written. You'll need it, Phillip, because you'll be facing a

Court Martial when you—" Dr Gorbett put his head round the door of the cabin.

"Excuse me, sir," he began. "But they want to transfer you to the Palace Hospital and . . ." his carefully assumed smile faded when he glimpsed his patient's flushed face. "I beg you not to overtax your strength, Captain Lyons. You should rest for a while now. I'm sure that Commander Hazard won't mind. He can visit you again later, when you're—"

Jack waved him to silence. "I've not quite done, Doctor," he said. "And this is something I *must* get off my conscience. Give me five minutes, will you please? And tell them I don't want to be moved—I'm very comfortable here."

When the doctor had rather unwillingly departed, he turned to Phillip again, his expression troubled. "Your Court Martial will be a pure formality, my dear fellow. The decision to prefer charges against you was not made by my father willingly, as I feel sure you'll realize. He was compelled to yield to pressure from high places. That great bear of a Russian Captain you took prisoner, allied to—what's his name, the Arab? Faruk, isn't it? Yes, Faruk Bey, who has pulled every string he could lay his filthy hands on . . . *they* are responsible, I'm afraid. Most of the pressure has come from our Ambassador, Lord Stratford de Redcliffe, between ourselves. He fears that good relations with the Porte might be damaged by a refusal to enquire into Faruk Bey's complaints and Their Lordships appear to have taken his word for it. The Secretary has advised my father privately that it's considered best to afford you the opportunity to refute the charges, once and for all, rather than attempt to hush the matter up . . . with which view I trust you will agree?"

Shocked by this news, Phillip was at pains to hide his dismay. He managed a smile, as forced as Dr Corbett's had been, and said guardedly, "Naturally I shall do as Their Lordships see fit to command, Jack. I—do you know what the charges will be?"

"Not precisely, no. Faruk wants to charge you with murder, which is, of course, quite absurd. Captain Kirkoff seems to have dug up all kinds of obscure clauses in the Articles of War—ours and the Russian equivalent—in an effort to prove that you violated his rights as a prisoner-of-war . . . whatever those may be. I confess I'm not clear—are you?"

"No, I'm not. But you—"

"My report will settle the matter," Jack said with certainty. "So you've nothing to worry about. As I told you, the trial is a pure formality." He lay back, suddenly exhausted, and held out his hand. "I'm ready for old Corbett's ministrations now, if you'd tell him. Good-bye, Phillip my dear fellow. You'll remember the message for my father, won't you? God bless you and the best of luck!"

Phillip grasped the proffered hand in both his own, blinded by grief and unable to say a word, a deep and abiding sense of loss tearing the last remnants of his control to shreds.

Jack Lyons died 24 hours later, on 23rd June, conscious almost until the end, resigned and uncomplaining, and courageous beyond belief. Phillip shared the vigil at his bedside and, with some of his *Miranda* Officers, helped him to make his will and, at his dictation, took down a letter to his father and messages for his family and close friends. He started to dictate the report he had promised to one of the Lieutenants from the *Miranda,* Cecil Buckley, but it had progressed no further than the first paragraph when strength and memory failed and it had to be abandoned.

"I hadn't the heart to urge him to continue, sir," Buckley apologized. "He said he'd given you his word that he would write it, but I knew you'd understand. Yesterday was his birthday, you know. He told me how fortunate he had been to live for thirty-six years, and then he said, 'This is the way the Captain of a man o' war should die, Cecil, if it is not granted to him to die instantly on the deck of his ship and in the heat of action.' And then his mind wandered a bit and he was back aboard the *Miranda*. 'Steady as you go, Quartermaster,' he shouted. And then to the First Lieutenant, 'Ease her, Mr Mackenzie. Stop engines.' Those were his last words, sir." Lieutenant Buckley unashamedly wiped the tears from his eyes, handed Phillip the few lines he had written, and added, with conscious bitterness, "He's to have a grand funeral, sir. Lord Stratford and his suite are to attend, with the French Ambassador and dignitaries representing the Porte, I believe. But we're to be permitted to supply a bearer party and a guard of honour, so we'll see him to his rest, as he'd have wanted us to. And the First Lieutenant and I have chosen the spot, with the Chaplain's aid, in the garden of the Palace Hospital. He'll be near the sea there, sir. I think he'd like that, don't you?"

Phillip nodded. "Yes," he agreed. "I think he would, Mr Buckley."

The funeral, held on the 25th, was as grand as young Buckley had predicted, but it was also deeply moving, for when the time came for his Mirandas to take final leave of their Commander, even the battle-hardened seamen drawn up at the grave-side were weeping.

Phillip returned to the hospital to find an Officer from the *Hannibal* waiting for him. "I have orders to place you under arrest, Commander Hazard," he said formally. "And to escort you aboard the *Hannibal* to face a general Court Martial, on charges of which you will be informed in due course. May I ask you for your sword, if you please?"

Phillip said wryly, "I don't possess a sword, I'm afraid, Commander, but doubtless I shall be able to borrow one, if my own does not reach me in time. Come to that, I haven't a uniform."

"No full dress uniform, do you mean, Commander?"

"No uniform of any kind, I regret to say. My ship is with the Azoff squadron."

"Arrangements will be made for your kit to be collected," the Officer volunteered. Abandoning formality, he smiled. "My name's Macdonald, John Macdonald. I—er—forgive my curiosity but what the devil's been happening to you, Hazard? No sword, no uniform, and you look as if you've scarcely recovered from a severe wound. In fact, you—"

"You'll hear my story in court," Phillip assured him. "Although"—he became aware, suddenly, of a haunting fear—"it occurs to me to wonder whether the story you'll hear will bear any relation to the truth. Now I come to think of it, I rather fear it may not, because the evidence I'd intended to call in my defence has just been interred in the hospital garden, together with the body of one of the finest men I ever knew."

Commander Macdonald stared at him in astonishment. "I understand," he said sympathetically, "that you've just come from laying poor Jack Lyons to rest."

"Yes," Phillip confirmed. He expelled his breath in a long-drawn sigh. "Permit me to take my leave of the staff, if you please, and then I shall be ready to accompany you."

CHAPTER EIGHT

An *indefinable air* of gloom and disillusionment was the first thing Phillip noticed on his return to Sebastopol. Morale had been high, prior to the departure of the Kertch expedition but it was at rock-bottom now, even in the Fleet. Among the Army Officers he met, this was even more apparent; few spoke of victory any more and most seemed to have abandoned all hope of seeing a successful end to the siege.

The French attack on the Malakoff—launched prematurely by General Pélissier without the usual French practice of a heavy preliminary bombardment—had failed and, despite the desperate heroism of the attackers, they had been driven back with appalling losses. In a vain attempt to save his allies from further slaughter, Lord Raglan had ordered two British columns to attack the Redan at dawn but they, too, had been repulsed in some of the heaviest fighting of the war, fifteen hundred of them falling beneath a ghastly hail of cannon and musket fire. The Naval Brigade, which had taken part in this attack, had also suffered heavy casualties which had included the gallant Captain Peel, who was severely wounded in the right arm.

Listening to different accounts of the battle, Phillip was horrified, as much by the thinly veiled hints of confusion and mismanagement, as by the sickening details of the inferno of shot and shell in which so many brave men had gone to their deaths. Under open arrest, the date of his Court Martial not yet announced, he went ashore, accompanied by John Macdonald, to visit friends in both naval and military camps and it was on one such visit that he heard the tragic news that Lord Raglan himself was dying.

"He looked quite done up when he returned to his head-quarters, after the battle on the 18th," a Coldstream Guards Major told him. "Pélissier bungled the whole affair; it was not Lord Raglan's fault—the French went in against his advice and hours earlier than had been agreed between them. But His Lordship took it to heart . . . the defeat, the loss of so many Officers and men, with nothing to show for their sacrifice. Oh, he was at pains to appear cheerful and confident at dinner that night—he was pleasant and kind, as he always is. But afterwards, I heard him telling Colonel Steele that it had been a catastrophe, and Burghersh said he spent half the night in prayer. Then, on Sunday, he visited the hospitals, and called to see General Estcourt, who died next day of cholera."

"You mean that he—that Lord Raglan has *cholera?*" Phillip asked, shocked.

His informant shrugged despondently. "Dr Prendergast, who is attending him, says not. He is exhausted, weak from an attack of dysentery and . . . heartbroken. It's rumoured that he is sinking fast. The Chaplain is with him. Poor, gallant old gentleman—his will be an irreparable loss, to the Army and to the nation. It may even cost us this ill-omened war!"

And it would deal a grievous blow to Admiral Lyons, Phillip thought, recalling the brief interview he had had, when he had requested permission to deliver Jack's last message to him. The Admiral, normally the most courteous and kindly of men, had stared through him as if unable to recognize him and had dismissed him with a wave of the hand, without saying a word.

First his son and now, it seemed, Lord Raglan who was, perhaps, his closest friend outside his own naval circle . . .

Lord Raglan died that evening and the news, unexpected and sudden to the ordinary soldiers and seamen, cast an even deeper gloom over camp and ship alike. General Pélissier, already nicknamed *"l'homme brutal"* by his own troops, was reported to have stood for upwards of an hour beside the simple iron camp-bed on which the body of his English colleague lay, weeping like a child. Everywhere, men spoke in hushed voices, expressing regret. "It's as if," one young soldier said sadly, "we had all of us lost a near relative. It won't be the same, now he's gone from us. We didn't see much of him, except when we were under fire—he was always there then, in the thick of it, too. And he came to the hospital, to give us a word of cheer when we'd been wounded. He never failed us, not when it really mattered."

The funeral took place on 3rd July and it left a confused impression on Phillip's mind. Looking back afterwards, he remembered that the sun was shining and that—strangely—both the Allied guns and those defending Sebastopol were silent, as the cortège left Lord Raglan's farmhouse headquarters at a little after four in the afternoon. The coffin, borne on a nine-pounder gun carriage, was draped with a Union Jack, on which lay the sword and plumed hat of the late Commander-in-Chief. To the roll of drums and the solemn music of the Dead March, the gun carriage—with General Simpson, the new British Commander-in-Chief, General Pélissier, Omar Pasha, and General della Marmora riding on either side of it and the other Allied Commanders following behind—passed between double ranks of British and French infantry, to wend its slow way down to the landing stage at Kazatch.

There a launch was waiting, to take the coffin out to the *Caradoc*—the little despatch steamer, in which Lord Raglan had made his first reconnaissance of the Crimean coast. She steamed out of the bay, to begin the long journey back to England, with guns booming in salute and a signal-hoist at her masthead, which Phillip read, with a lump in his throat, as the single word *"Farewell."*

The troops marched off, to return to their duties in the camps and trenches on the Upland; a groom led off Lord Raglan's riderless charger; General Pélissier climbed into his carriage, which bore him swiftly away; and Omar Pasha and della Marmora rode back to the farmhouse with Lord Raglan's successor.

Admiral Lyons, on medical advice, did not attend the funeral but Phillip heard later that, on his instructions, the *Caradoc* brought-to under the stern of his flagship to enable him to make his personal farewell, standing in salute on the *Royal Albert*'s lofty poop-deck, where he remained, his head bowed in sorrow, until the *Caradoc* was out of sight.

A week afterwards, on 10th July, Phillip's Court Martial was convened on board the *Hannibal*.

The atmosphere, when he presented himself before his judges, was formal but far from hostile. Most of the members of the Court were known to him by name and repute, if not by sight, but he was a trifle disconcerted to learn that Captain Crawford—now in command of the *Trojan*—was acting as President.

Normally, naval Courts Martial were conducted without spectators being present, although, in fact, all such Courts were legally open to members of the public, few ever took advantage of their right to attend. Today, however, there were six chairs placed to the left of his own and he saw, with some surprise, that these were occupied by two French Officers, both from Colonial regiments; three Turkish Officers, and a British civilian, whom he recognized as a member of Lord Stratford de Redcliffe's diplomatic staff.

"Interested parties, one can only suppose," John Macdonald whispered, when Phillip uneasily drew his attention to them. "I shouldn't let them worry you." But he frowned, clearly puzzled, as the prosecuting Officer accepted a small package of papers from the well-dressed young diplomat before taking his own seat.

"*Politically* interested parties in search of a scapegoat, Hazard," his defending Officer qualified, laying a consoling hand on Phillip's knee. "But they are here as observers only— they cannot influence the Court." He smiled, without amusement. "I shall make mincemeat of them if they try, never fear!"

Commander James Fraser was a cousin of the *Trojan's* surgeon and Phillip had received his offer to act in his defence with gratitude and relief, when old Angus Fraser had sought him out to pass on the offer. The Commander was an astute, grey-haired Scot, with outspoken views and a strong radical bias, who had retired on half-pay many years before and had been a writer to the *Signet* in Edinburgh until the outbreak of war had brought him back to the Royal Navy. In their preliminary conferences, Fraser had expressed a heartening and almost aggressive belief in his ability to refute the charges, which he described indignantly as venomous and beneath contempt, but Phillip found it increasingly difficult to share his confidence. He felt ill and depressed, unable to shake off the conviction that he was, indeed, being made a scapegoat in an affair which had been deliberately exaggerated out of all proportion to its importance. The Admiral's silence—although not difficult to account for—added a great deal to his depression and, at one stage, he had wanted to plead guilty in order to have done with the whole unhappy affair.

"You'll be broken, if you do," James Fraser had warned him. "You'll need to fight, man, or see your career in ruins. These are malicious charges, brought by men with ulterior motives, who are out to smash you so that they may save themselves. And those who are backing them have each an axe to grind, too! All you'll have to do is to stand up there and tell the truth . . . leave the rest to me. I'll get you off, I give you my word, just so long as you don't leave me to fight alone."

He had given in, in the end, of course, but he cherished only faint hopes and even Fraser's confidence had been a trifle shaken when he had been informed officially, just before the Court opened, that the witnesses from the crew of the *Huntress* had, for some inexplicable reason, failed to arrive. His ship was still with the Azoff squadron, Phillip knew, but he found it hard to believe that the two men he had chosen— Thompson and Higgins—would, on their own account, have let him down. Or that his brother Graham would have done so, if he had received Fraser's request in time. Indeed, he . . .

Commander Fraser nudged him and he rose to his feet. The charges, their venom hidden beneath the legal phraseology in which they were couched, sounded unsensational as they were read out to him but, when he entered a formal plea of Not Guilty, he knew that it was going to be difficult, if not impossible, to prove his innocence with neither witnesses nor the report from Jack Lyons, which might have enabled him to justify his actions.

He resumed his seat and the prosecuting Officer, a Commander named Danvers, after a brief opening address, called Captain Kirkoff as his first witness. His examination, to Phillip's surprise, was conducted through an interpreter, and it occupied most of the morning. As he listened to question and answer, laboriously translated, his surprise turned to stunned dismay. There was a basis of truth in every assertion his one-time prisoner made but each incident, small enough in itself, had been twisted, added to and even misinterpreted, so that a damning picture was built up of himself and the men he had commanded. He was shown as a ruthless glory-hunter, out to distinguish himself no matter what the cost, whilst at the same time imposing a minimum of discipline upon his crew.

The fight which, heaven knew, the Russian had brought upon himself, became—as Kirkoff now described it—a brutal and quite unjustified attack on his person, aimed at compelling him to betray his country by revealing the secrets of a new weapon which, rather than besmirch his honour, he had tried to destroy. Even poor young O'Hara's death was misrepresented as yet another example of lack of discipline, and the responsibility for it laid, fairly and squarely, at the door of the man who, as Commander, should have prevented it. Phillip had to exercise iron self-control to prevent himself voicing a bitter denial when Kirkoff, dark eyes bright with malice, referred to "the gallant young Officer, hardly more than a boy," whose life had been needlessly thrown away.

Predictably, he glossed over the *Tarkhan's* unhappy fate, laying emphasis instead on the fact that he had been compelled to remain on deck whilst the brig *Constantine* was under fire, under the added threat of a rifle held to his head, in an attempt to force him to disclose the Russian recognition signals.

When the Court was adjourned, at mid-day, his evidence had just concluded and Phillip, sick at heart and unable to eat, paced the cabin in which he was confined, living for the moment when James Fraser would be given the opportunity, in cross-examination, to make the bearded Russian retract some, at least, of the lies he had told. His blood was up, he was seething with anger, as ready to fight now as, before, he had been apathetic and resigned but all the fight went out of him when the Court resumed and he had to listen, in impotent silence, to the failure of all Fraser's efforts to shake the Russian Captain's testimony.

Kirkoff was unshakable; he retracted not one word. His gaze fixed unflinchingly on the President, he insisted that the account he had given was true in every particular. When Fraser pressed him, he took shrewd refuge behind the not very competent interpreter, delaying his replies until the defending Officer, losing patience, brusquely repeated the questions he had asked and received a reprimand from the President for his pains.

Finally, in a well-simulated show of indignation, the Russian complained that his honour was being impugned and the Court adjourned with his cross-examination still unconcluded and the President's sympathies clearly directed towards him.

Phillip spent a sleepless and miserable night. His worst fears had been realized and he now regretted having taken Fraser's advice and agreed to defend himself against the charges. Had he pleaded guilty, he would not have had to endure the calumny which had been heaped upon his head, he told himself wretchedly—he would have been broken, probably, but that, at least, would have been the end of it . . . and he looked like being broken in any case.

When Fraser joined him early next morning, he was in the depths of despair.

"For heaven's sake!" he exclaimed bitterly. "Kirkoff complained that *his* honour was impugned, after lying himself hoarse . . . but what has he left me of mine?"

"We're not beaten yet, Hazard, we're not by any means

beaten," the Scotsman assured him. "I've spent most of the night going through his testimony and I've found three or four instances when he contradicted himself. Once just here, do you see?" He indicated the notes he had been working on. "When he stated that those bombs of his were defused and harmless. And then, a few minutes later, he said just as positively that they were not."

"I fear that won't help," Phillip objected. "It's a very minor detail, after all."

"Ah, but if I can catch him out and make him admit one inaccuracy, I'll have him on another. Don't lose heart, my friend. He's a tough nut to crack, I grant you, because he has no compunction whatsoever about lying to his enemies, but he'll go too far and when he does, I'll make him eat his words."

He fulfilled his promise, within a few minutes of resuming his cross-examination and for the first time since he had faced them, Phillip sensed that the members of the Court had begun, at last, to doubt Kirkoff's veracity. His flagging hopes revived a little and they remained high when the Russian was permitted to stand down, on the plea—made through the interpreter—that he felt unwell and could not continue.

"We shall recall Captain Kirkoff later on, if we deem it necessary," the President announced. "In the meantime let us hear evidence relating to the second charge, if you please, Commander Danvers." He consulted his papers, eyeing Phillip thoughtfully before adding, "That is to say the charges brought by Faruk Bey."

Faruk gave his evidence truculently, as if expecting his claims to be challenged. They were extravagant claims and they had neither the ring of truth nor the authority which— at any rate until his final cross-examination—had characterized Kirkoff's. It was obvious, even to Phillip, that the members of the Court Martial were inclined to doubt his statement that his precipitate march to Yenikale had been undertaken for any of the reasons he gave. Captain Crawford and at least one of the junior Captains had been with the expedition to Kertch; they had, presumably, witnessed the looting which had taken place there and knew who had been responsible for it, and they were probably aware that a Turkish force had laid waste a number of villages on the coast road, between Kertch and Yenikale.

When it came to his account of his arrival at the underground hospital, however, Faruk's description was accurate enough.

"There were Russians in this cellar," the interpreter translated. "Soldiers of the garrison, who were in hiding in what appeared to be a fortified place and who, for all the Bey knew, were armed and prepared to resist capture. In his zeal, he was about to take them prisoner but a man, without uniform, in his shirtsleeves and armed with a pistol, positioned himself at the entrance and threatened to shoot the Bey, if he permitted his soldiers to enter. The man was unknown to him. He might have been a Russian or a European mercenary, in the employ of the Tsar's forces—he had no identification and he made no attempt to prove who he was. He—"

"Ask the Bey, if you please, whether he is now able to identify the man he has described," the President requested.

There was a brief consultation between Faruk and his interpreter and the Tunisian inclined his head sullenly.

"He is the Officer on trial, your honour," the interpreter said carefully. "Commander Hazard. But he was not in uniform at the Yenikale Fort, he had not shaved and he was wearing boots of Russian manufacture."

"Did he claim to *be* Commander Hazard?" the President persisted. "Did he tell the Bey that he was a British Naval Officer?"

After a slight hesitation, Faruk nodded again.

"His excellency the Bey wishes me to tell your honour that at this time Commander Hazard bore no resemblance to a British Officer."

"That is understood. Ask the Bey to continue."

Faruk continued his evidence and Phillip was forced to concede that, if still delivered in a truculent tone, it was accurate enough, although no mention was made of the sudden appearance of the Jewish woman, which had so inflamed his men. Describing the shooting of his brother, however, Faruk's omissions became more blatant and, encouraged by the fact that neither Captain Crawford nor Commander Danvers interrupted him, his version was a travesty of the truth.

"I did not shoot the fellow in cold blood," Phillip whispered to Fraser. "He'd decapitated an unfortunate Russian, who had attempted to drag himself to his feet, long before I fired at him."

Fraser made a note and smiled. "This one is a poor liar," he answered. "He'll be easy to break down."

His cross-examination was brief but telling. Taxed with his omissions, Faruk simply but unconvincingly denied them, losing his temper in the process.

"Ask the Bey, if you please," Fraser pursued relentlessly. "To describe Commander Hazard's manner."

"His manner, sir?"

"Yes—how did he appear? Was he angry, excited, threatening, or did he seem calm when he denied the Bey's entry to the hospital?"

"He was excited and angry," Faruk answered eagerly. "I believed him to be mad . . . a mad Russian mercenary, not a British Officer!"

"How many soldiers had accompanied you to the cellar? Twenty, thirty perhaps?"

"About twenty-five or thirty."

"Thirty armed soldiers," Fraser said gravely. "And one man, whom you believe to be an enemy—one man, with a severely wounded arm and a pistol as his only weapon—barred your way to the cellar! Why did you not shoot *him?* Why did you not order your soldiers to shoot him down?"

"Because he held a pistol to my head," Faruk admitted furiously. "He held it a few centimetres from my head."

"In his left hand," Fraser observed. Again addressing the interpreter, he went on, "Did Commander Hazard not tell the Bey that the hospital contained only dead and dying Russian soldiers? Did he not warn him that his men would find no plunder there?"

"The Bey says he did not," the interpreter answered, looking down at his feet.

"Dr Corbett will confirm that this was the case, sir," Fraser told the President. He asked a few more mildly phrased questions and then, as Faruk was becoming more self-assured, taxed him concerning his brother's attack on the wounded Russian.

"The Russian was endeavouring to escape. He ran at my brother," the Bey said.

"And your brother moved to prevent his escape?"

"Naturally he did. The Russian swine could not be permitted to escape."

"Was it *natural* for your brother to strike the man's head from his body? That was what he did, was it not, with his scimitar?" Fraser paused. "And *then* Commander Hazard fired at him, as he had repeatedly warned you that he would?"

Faruk shrugged and remained silent.

"Dr Corbett of the *Miranda,* whom I intend to call as a witness, will tell the Court that he saw the decapitated body of a Russian soldier in the hospital, sir," James Fraser stated

quietly. "I shall also call Sergeant Playforth, of the Royal
Marines, to offer confirmation, not only of this but of the fact
that Faruk Bey informed him that Commander Hazard was a
Russian spy, masquerading as a British Officer, and ordered
the sergeant to arrest him."

"Commander, I doubt whether that evidence will be necessary," Captain Crawford told him. He glanced enquiringly at
the other members of the Court, and on receiving their nods
of agreement, consulted his watch and announced an adjournment.

Despite his observation, however, the hearing continued,
with several of Faruk's Officers being called to support their
Commander but they made a poor impression and, at the end
of the day, James Fraser was jubilant. "I shall call you to speak
in your own defence tomorrow morning, Hazard my friend,"
he said. "And that, I am sure, will be the end of this strange
and unhappy affair. You'll be cleared of all charges."

Phillip hoped fervently that he was right but he experienced some uneasiness when he saw the young diplomat but-
tonhole Captain Crawford and another member of the Court
and proceed to detain them, talking volubly, whilst the others
filed out. Significantly, the French and Turkish Officers, with
whom he had been sitting, also remained behind but, when
he pointed this out to Fraser, his defending Officer assured
him that there was no reason for anxiety.

"They cannot dictate to the Court, Hazard. They are here
as observers only and have no legal right even to discuss the
Court's proceedings whilst your case is still *sub judice.*"

Nevertheless, when the hearing was resumed the following morning, Commander Danver's request to recall Captain
Kirkoff was granted. His re-examination was mainly concerned
with the death of Midshipman O'Hara and, although the

Russian had little new evidence to add, he contrived to make several damaging references to the poor state of discipline of the prize-crew, to which—by implication—he suggested that the boy's death was due. James Fraser's efforts to shake him had almost no effect and Phillip was in an anxious and unhappy frame of mind when the Court adjourned for luncheon. He was a trifle cheered by a note he found waiting for him from Captain Keppel, of the *St Jean d'Acre,* under whose command he had served as a midshipman in the frigate *Maeander.*

"My dear Phillip," the note read. *"As you may—or may not— be aware, I have recently assumed command of the Naval Brigade, vice Commodore Lushington, who is going home. The brave William Peel, who was wounded on the 18th, is also leaving us and our losses, during the ill-fated attack on the Redan were, alas, heavy.*

"I am therefore anxious to obtain the services of some more good young Officers—especially of your calibre—so, if you should have any thought of applying to join my new command, be assured that I should welcome you warmly."

Phillip frowned, as he folded the note and placed it in his pocket-book. He had always had a great admiration for the fiery, courageous Henry Keppel and was grateful for the kindness which had prompted his one-time Captain to write to him in these terms but . . . *why* had he done so? What could have prompted the kindness, unless . . . he felt a sudden, nagging fear that would not be assuaged.

There must be rumours that his trial was going badly for him, he thought, otherwise why should Keppel have had the note delivered to him here, on board the *Hannibal,* before the Court's findings were known? And why should he have suggested an application for appointment to the Naval Brigade to a young Officer, who had only recently been given his first sea command, unless he knew or had a shrewd suspicion that he was about to be deprived of his command? There was never any shortage of volunteers for the Naval Brigade—Captain Keppel had no need to seek them out, just as he had never had to seek good seamen to man any ship he put into commission. His reputation was enough and yet . . . Phillip was conscious of a bitter taste in his mouth and the elation he had felt on first receiving the note swiftly faded.

When the Court resumed, James Fraser opened the case for the defence. His opening address was a model of its kind, pithy, factual, and admirably clear, but it soon became evident that he was not going to be permitted to develop his arguments. His witnesses were heard and dismissed with extraordinary haste, Commander Danvers cutting short their examination with a smooth, "I concede the facts you are seeking to establish, sir. Further questions are unnecessary, since the Court accepts them also."

Fraser said apologetically, when Dr Corbett had been allowed to do no more than testify as to the nature and severity of Phillip's wounds, "Your two seamen from the *Huntress* still haven't made their appearance, Hazard, so I've no choice but to put you on the witness stand now. I've made enquiries for the men and they'll be brought here the instant they report but"—he spread his hands helplessly—"we'll need to do the best we can without them, I'm afraid. Keep cool, try not to lose your temper and allow me to lead you as much as I can." Phillip nodded, tight-lipped, and his defending Officer laid a hand on his arm. "The pattern is starting to emerge, I think. They will try to have you on two counts—responsibility for the loss of your midshipman, and exceeding your authority in your treatment of Captain Kirkoff and Faruk."

This forecast proved an accurate one. Phillip was tense and apprehensive as he took the oath and began to tell his

story but James Fraser questioned him so skilfully that gradually the tension drained out of him and he found himself able
to give his account of what had happened as easily and naturally as if he were making a report to an ordinary gathering
of senior Officers. He felt that he had made a reasonably good
impression until, reaching the point in his narrative which
covered O'Hara's unexpected attempt to tow away the bomb,
the President intervened.

"I wish to be quite clear on this matter, Commander
Hazard," he said. "You had not ordered Midshipman O'Hara to
tow the Russian infernal device away from your paddle-
wheels?"

"No, sir," Phillip answered, careful to speak without heat.
"I had ordered him to lower the gig and to stand by at the mid-
ship chains. I intended to deal with the infernal device—that
is, the floating bomb, sir—myself. My gunner's mate had prepared a charge, with which to—"

Captain Crawford cut him short. "Your intentions have no
bearing on what happened. In fact, Mr O'Hara was acting without orders when he made his attempt to remove the bomb?"

"Yes, sir, he was. But he was a very keen and very courageous young Officer. He acted on impulse, with the intention
of sparing me by taking my place and—"

Again Captain Crawford interrupted. "We are not concerned with intentions, Commander Hazard, only with facts.
Midshipman O'Hara is not here to testify as to his intentions,
is he? The unfortunate boy is dead."

Phillip felt the blood drain from his cheeks. Suddenly he
was back on the *Constantine*'s paddle-box, peering down at
O'Hara, seeing his face, hearing his voice, strained and fear-
ful. *"Sir . . . the bomb's yawing an awful lot. I don't think I can
hold it . . . I'll have to fend it off. My—my hands are slipping, sir."*

"In our pursuit of facts"—Crawford's voice broke into his thoughts, sounding cold, even hostile—"what steps did you take to save this inexperienced midshipman of yours from the consequences of his unauthorized action?"

Phillip told him conscious, as he did so, of how inadequate his efforts sounded. James Fraser made an attempt to intervene but the President waved him to silence.

"Continue, Commander Hazard, if you please. Since your rescue operation apparently took so long, why did you not simply order Midshipman O'Hara to leave the bomb where it was and row himself to safety in the gig?"

"I feared that if I ordered him to release the bomb, sir, it would strike against my paddle-wheels and explode. If it had, he would not have reached safety. He—"

"In the event, he did not—he was blown up when the bomb did explode, was he not? At least you might have given the boy a chance of escape. Were you, perhaps, afraid that he would *not* obey you, if you ordered him to release his hold on the bomb?"

Phillip shook his head. "No, sir," he answered bitterly. "I was not afraid of that." There was a murmur from the assembled Officers and Crawford went on relentlessly, "You had the advantage of having secured a set of Russian plans, diagrams of these infernal machines, which clearly showed their construction and the means by which they were detonated, on your own admission. Did you at any time show these diagrams to Midshipman O'Hara?"

"No, sir."

"Why not? He was acting as your second-in-command surely? He was the only Officer in your prize-crew."

"I showed them to my gunner's mate, sir. I considered him to be—"

"Ah, your gunner's mate—Thompson, is his name, I believe. Well, he's not here to support your testimony, is he?"

"He has been sent for, sir," James Fraser put in. "But as I explained to the Court, neither he nor the other witness from the *Huntress* has yet reached this anchorage and—"

"The Court is aware of the absence of these two witnesses," Crawford said brusquely. "And has ruled on it. Pray continue, Commander Hazard."

The questions came, coldly voiced, accusing, unanswerable and Phillip could only reply in stiff, monosyllabic denials which, even to his own ears, sounded unconvincing.

"Search your conscience, Commander Hazard," Captain Crawford finally invited. "And tell me frankly—do you or do you not consider yourself to blame for the death of this gallant and promising young Officer?"

Phillip faced him, a sick feeling in the pit of his stomach but it was O'Hara's voice he heard, shrill and eager, calling up to him a second or two before the bomb had burst. *'I've got the hang of it, sir . . . it's coming quite easily. All you have to do is hold it steady . . .'* Oh, for God's sake, of course he had been to blame! There was no need to search his conscience, no point in trying to hide the truth.

"I hold myself solely to blame, sir," he said firmly, ignoring Fraser's warning headshake.

Satisfied, the President leaned back in his chair. After a pregnant silence, he motioned James Fraser to continue but the harm was done and Phillip knew, from the expression of dismay on his defending Officer's craggy face, that he had condemned himself. And yet, he thought, with numb resignation, he had told the simple truth—O'Hara's death would be on his conscience to the end of his days.

He gave the rest of his evidence with a harsh brevity which, he could see, distressed the man who was trying, with all the skill at his command, to defend him but Fraser was fighting a lost cause now and they both knew it. His carefully planned effort to enlarge on the heroism of Phillip's single-handed dash down channel in the stricken *Constantine* would have done credit to any of a dozen of the most eminent Queen's Counsel on the London circuit, but it was defeated as much by Phillip's own lack of response as by Commander Danvers's assurance that the facts were not in dispute.

Captain Crawford did not intervene again until Phillip was giving an account of his clash with Faruk Bey but, once again, by means of a few accusing questions, the President forced the admission from him that he had acted entirely on his own initiative.

"You had received no orders to prevent Allied troops from taking prisoner any of the Yenikale garrison remaining in the fort?"

"No, sir."

"You had, in fact, no communication with any senior Officer from the time you went aboard the brig *Constantine* until the late Captain Lyons came ashore from the *Miranda* and found you being held by a party of Royal Marines, under Sergeant Playforth?"

"No, sir, none at all," Phillip was compelled to admit.

"And you made no attempt to identify yourself as an Officer in the Royal Navy to Sergeant Playforth?"

"I was unable to do so, sir. I was unconscious. One of Sergeant Playforth's party struck me on the head with his mus-ket butt and—"

"We have heard the sergeant's evidence to that effect, Commander Hazard. If *he* found it hard to recognize you for what you are, how much harder must it have been for Faruk Bey, who is an Officer in the Turkish Service?"

"Nevertheless, Commander Hazard," James Fraser put in

quickly. "You did inform the Bey of your identity, did you not?"

"Yes," Phillip confirmed wearily. "I did. In French, which is a language he appeared to speak and understand, until he was called upon to give evidence to this Court."

"The members of this Court are not all as fluent as you claim to be," Crawford returned. He shook his head firmly to Fraser's request for an adjournment. "I hardly think it will be necessary, Commander Fraser. The cross-examination will not take long, I am confident, and it seems to me that it is not beyond the bounds of possibility that we may be able to conclude this trial today, if you have no more evidence to offer. It has already occupied the valuable time of a number of Officers whose presence is urgently required for the prosecution of the war. I myself have orders to proceed to Kinburn as soon as I am free of my duties here." He glanced enquiringly round the table. "In fact, gentlemen, with your agreement, I propose that we sit late, if necessary, in order to avoid our having to give another day to it."

There were murmurs of assent. "But, sir," James Fraser began indignantly. "Surely you cannot—"

Captain Crawford silenced him with an imperiously raised hand. "I am fully aware, Commander, that this may preclude you from calling witnesses to testify to the accused Officer's previous good conduct and character. But the Court is more than willing to concede that Commander Hazard bears an exemplary character and that he has a distinguished record in the Service. Furthermore, it has before it a written statement from the Commander-in-Chief to the effect that, at the request of his son, the late Captain Edmund Lyons, he has drawn the attention of Their Lordships of the Board of Admiralty to Commander Hazard's gallantry, in the affair of which we have heard this afternoon. This will be taken into account by the

Court, you may be sure, when it arrives at its findings . . ." he talked on but Phillip scarcely heard him.

The Admiral had not abandoned him, he thought thankfully. Even in his grief, he had remembered and taken effective action, and this despite the fact that Jack had been unable to write the full report he had intended to submit . . . meeting Fraser's mutely questioning gaze, he nodded, and the defending Officer bowed and resumed his seat.

Commander Danvers rose to take his place, with the announcement that he had only three questions to ask. All three concerned the treatment meted out to Captain Kirkoff, all three contained the subtle suggestion that Phillip had acted without orders and without regard for Kirkoff's rank and status as a prisoner-of-war, and he replied to all three with crisp and confident rejections.

"I am ready to admit, sir," he said, addressing Captain Crawford, "that, had I been in Captain Kirkoff's situation, I should have refused—as he did—to co-operate with an enemy. On the other hand, I do not, in all honesty, believe that I should have offered the provocation this Officer saw fit to offer to seamen, of inferior rank, who were restrained by their respect for naval discipline from retaliating. None of my men retaliated, sir, I give you my word. They only laid hands on Captain Kirkoff on my instructions, in order to prevent him from damaging the *Constantine*—and thus placing our mission in jeopardy."

"The Court will accept your assurance," Captain Crawford answered. "It is with your own actions that we are concerned."

"Yes, sir, I appreciate that," Phillip said quietly. "My actions are for you to judge, so I will offer no excuses. I also accept full responsibility for the death of Midshipman O'Hara, which I regret with all my heart."

"Very well, Commander Hazard. Have you anything else to say on your own behalf?"

Phillip shook his head. What else, he wondered wearily, was there to say? He was about to return to his seat when Commander Danvers asked sharply, "One last question, Commander Hazard. Were you ordered to capture the Russian brig *Constantine* for the specific purpose of sounding and buoying the Yenikale channel or were your orders to do so in your own ship, the *Huntress?*"

"I . . ." unprepared for this question, Phillip caught his breath. "My orders were to sound and buoy the channel," he answered, after a brief hesitation. "If possible without making the enemy aware of my presence or my purpose and without taking unnecessary risks to my ship and her crew. I took—that is to say, I came upon the *Constantine* unexpectedly, in the fog, and decided that I could best carry out my orders by putting a prize-crew aboard her and using her instead of my own ship."

"Then from the outset," Danvers suggested unpleasantly, "you were acting according to your own interpretation of your orders, even contrary to them?"

Phillip inclined his head in wordless assent and, walking stiffly, went back to his seat. He listened to but did not consciously hear Danvers's closing address and took in little more of James Fraser's. Then, escorted by John Macdonald, he rose, bowed to the Court and left its members to their deliberations, returning to the cabin which had been placed at his disposal to await the verdict.

"I've lost, haven't I?" he said, when Fraser joined him there about twenty minutes later. "And it's entirely my own fault— you did everything you could."

James Fraser clapped a consoling hand on his shoulder.

"Aye, you've lost," he agreed. "But you've no reason to be ashamed of the manner in which you lost, Hazard. Like many a good man before you, you've been condemned for showing initiative and for refusing to make excuses for what you did. In other circumstances—and if it hadn't been for that scoundrel of a Turk—they would be pinning a medal on your chest, instead of giving you a reprimand."

Phillip sighed. "Do you honestly think that's all they'll give me—a reprimand?" he asked, afraid to believe it.

"Before heaven, they can hardly give you more!" Fraser asserted with conviction. "And they would not have been able to give you that if those two seamen of yours had got here in time. I hear there's been a severe storm in the Sea of Azoff, by the way . . . that may have delayed them." He smiled. "You did damned well, my young friend! I'd sooner lose in your company than win in that of a fellow like Kirkoff, believe me. Well, I've one or two matters I must attend to, so I'll see you in Court. They'll not be very long in making up their minds, if Captain Crawford has anything to do with it."

Phillip thanked him and settled down to wait. An odd calm possessed him. He was no longer anxious or strung up; the worst was over, he told himself, the ordeal he had been dreading was at an end and, if James Fraser was right, he would not lose the *Huntress.* That had been his greatest fear—he could live down a reprimand but the loss of his command was quite another matter.

There was a tap on the cabin bulkhead and John Macdonald, returning the salute of the Marine sentry posted at the door, came in, smiling.

"This is it, Phillip old man," he said cheerfully. "If you're ready. They haven't wasted much time, have they?"

"No," Phillip said. He hadn't expected them to but he

wondered, as he led the way back to the *Hannibal*'s spacious stern cabin, whether they had all agreed on the verdict. He saw his sword which, throughout the trial, had lain across the table in front of the President, and the last faint hope to which he had clung was dashed when he realized that its point was now facing towards him. So they had found him guilty but not, surely not on *all* the charges . . . instinctively he glanced over to where the six observers were sitting. They kept their faces studiously averted, not even looking round as he went to his own seat and it was not until he drew level with them that he saw, to his dismay, that the young man from the Ambassador's staff was smiling. Dear heaven, that augered ill for him, it was . . .

"Steady, Phillip," John Macdonald whispered, a hand on his arm. "They can't hang you, you know."

That was true, Phillip reflected wryly. He drew himself to attention and waited, outwardly calm and controlled but inwardly sick with apprehension, his heart thudding against his ribs as he tried vainly to concentrate on what was being said to him.

The first two charges brought by Kirkoff were dismissed; the third upheld—well, he had brought that on himself when he had accepted responsibility for O'Hara's death, he knew, and given the chance again, he would still have accepted it. But . . . he listened incredulously. Two out of three of Faruk's charges were held to be proven . . . it wasn't possible, it couldn't be happening. Faruk was a cowardly murderer, a rogue who had lied quite blatantly about the reason for his presence in Yenikale and yet a board of British Naval Captains had taken *his* word, accepted *his* evidence . . . Phillip gasped, feeling as if he were living a nightmare, cold sweat prickling out on his body.

His judges, their faces grim and unsmiling, avoided his gaze; he listened to the sentence, the blood pounding in his ears, and was hard put to it to maintain his rigid, disciplined pose and the pretence of calm which went with it. The sentence of the Court was that he was to be severely reprimanded and dismissed his ship—Captain Crawford's clear, cold voice seemed to echo from end to end of the shadowed cabin, sounding the death knell of all the hopes he had cherished, all the dreams, all the ambitions. He had lost the *Huntress* . . . and, he thought dully, she probably would not even be given to Graham, which might have been some slight consolation. He hadn't enough seniority—they would appoint another Commander and . . .

" . . . this Court wishes it to be placed on record," the President was saying, "that, whilst the accused Officer has been found guilty of exceeding his authority and acting in accordance with his own interpretation of the instructions he was given, these findings in no way detract from his personal gallantry, which was of an exceptionally high order . . . and will, it is hoped, in due course merit suitable reward."

The members of the Court Martial filed out; the observers went off with Commander Danvers and two clerks busied themselves collecting papers before they, too, hurried out of the cabin. John Macdonald, his cheeks suffused with angry colour, took Phillip's sword from the baize-covered table and assisted him to buckle it on.

"I don't know what to say," he began awkwardly. "Except that it was a parody of justice . . . and I hope the blasted Turks choke on their pound of flesh! I wouldn't in the least mind shooting Faruk myself, Phillip. For God's sake, I—"

"They didn't hang me," Phillip pointed out. He offered his hand. "I'll take my leave of you, John. My truly grateful thanks for all you have done—you were the best and most considerate of escorts. And you—"

"Devil take it!" Macdonald exploded. "Don't thank me,

Phillip, I did nothing. Come and have a drink with me, won't you? My cabin's at your disposal."

"Thank you . . . but no. It's kind of you but I have business ashore. If you'd procure me a boat, I'll be on my way."

"Yes, of course. I . . . I really am most damnably sorry about all this. I—"

"Forget it, please," Phillip begged. They walked over to where James Fraser was standing by himself, staring out of the stern windows. He turned at their approach and said gruffly, "The sentence has yet to be promulgated. I shall appeal to the Admiral and—"

"No," Phillip bade him, his tone one that precluded argument. "I want no appeal. Let it stand."

"The papers will go to him in any case, Hazard. As Commander-in-Chief, he has the right to decide whether or not to confirm the sentence, so—"

"I want no appeal, Fraser. But I thank you sincerely."

They faced each other for a moment and then the one-time lawyer bowed his greying head. "As you wish, then. But my cousin Angus won't forgive me as easily as you have, I'm afraid." He shook Phillip's extended hand, avoiding his gaze. "Where are you going?"

"Ashore—to procure my next appointment." Phillip forced a smile. "I'm happy to say that I've already been offered one by my old Commander, Captain Henry Keppel. He has just assumed command of the Naval Brigade and he suggested— before the Court's findings were known—that I should volunteer to serve under him again. I intend to do so at once."

"Then God go with you," James Fraser answered and turned away to hide the pity in his eyes.

CHAPTER NINE

Life in the Naval Brigade had a strange, unrealistic quality to which—to his own surprise—Phillip quickly and even gladly adjusted himself. There was plenty of action; the guns fired night and day for long periods at a time, casualties were high, and the risk of death never far away.

Captain the Hon. Henry Keppel, renowned for his cool courage and love of action, was in his element, inspiring the Officers and men under his command by his own example, always ready to share any dangers they faced and swift to praise and appreciate the daring of others. He was under five foot in height, with red hair and a charm none could resist and, within a few days of assuming command of the Naval Brigade, he had won the respect and affection of every member of the Brigade. The men cheered him whenever he appeared and would have followed him anywhere. A new spirit of optimism and aggression had been born with his coming and the talk was now of victory, not defeat.

The Naval Brigade Camp was situated at the head of a ravine between the French camps and British Army Headquarters at Khutor Karagatch. It had its own field hospital, a supply of fresh well-water, and—a blessing to men returning cold and soaked to the skin after a night of rain in the batteries—a drying-room for clothing. The sanitary arrangements were a legacy from the previous Commander, Captain Lushington, and were so well organized that the general health of the men was excellent, the proportion of deaths from disease much lower than in the Army camps, where less attention was paid to hygiene. Each morning, the seamen were paraded to drink hot cocoa or coffee under the supervision of their Officers and, in addition to regular issues of lime juice and quinine, a ration of hot soup, prepared by the cooks, was served to every man when he came off duty.

As a result, morale was high and the men did their work with a will. They served their guns uncomplainingly—from the thirty-two-pounders, which normally formed the main armament of a man o' war, to the giant Lancasters, whose range was thirty-six hundred yards—repaired damaged emplacements and carried up shot and shell, often under fire, with the greatest nonchalance. They were a splendid body of men and Phillip, who had at first tended to shy away from the company of his fellows, soon found himself taking both pride and pleasure in their company. He worked as hard as they did, frequently for longer at a time, and gradually the sense of loss he had felt, after being removed from his own command, became less acute.

To his surprise, his brother Graham was left in acting command of the *Huntress* and he was gratified to learn that, in a spirited action with several other ships of the Azoff squadron at Genitchi, Graham had held off an attack on a shore party and received immediate promotion. As an acting Commander, he might have been superceded at any time but now, with a step in rank, his position was secure and Phillip could not find it in his heart to begrudge his elder brother's good fortune.

By the end of August, he had himself become wholly

involved in the day-to-day activities of the Naval Brigade, thinking and caring for little else. News of the arrival off Balaclava
of the Pendletons' yacht *Fedora,* a few weeks before, had left
him unmoved. He had made no effort to seek out Catriona
and even when the hospitable Captain Keppel had given a dinner party at the camp, to which her employers had been
invited, he had chosen to stay on duty in the battery in pref-
erence to attending. Keppel, who dined fairly frequently on
board ships of the Fleet commanded by his friends, had now—
to Phillip's secret relief—given up asking him to accompany
his party. With the understanding kindness that made him one
of the most popular Commanders afloat, Harry Keppel left
him to work out his own salvation at the guns.

"You feel bitter now, Phillip," he said. "And I fancy you
have good reason to—they made a scapegoat of you and gave
you less than justice. But if there's a lesson to be learnt from
your experience, it is that throughout life there's precious little justice. Few men get the rewards they deserve and not all
that many are punished as they ought to be. You have to take
the rough with the smooth, my dear boy. Keep faith with your
Maker and 'to thine own self be true,' as the Great Bard so
aptly put it . . . you can't do more than that. In any event, it's
an ill wind that blows nobody any good—*I'm* glad to have you.
And you'll have no regrets when Sebastopol falls to our final
assault, because you'll be in the thick of it, as a fighting man
should be, and you'll know that you've played your part in
bringing this war to an end."

The final assault was now the main topic of conversation,
in mess tent and battery; everyone believed that it would come
soon and that, this time, it would not fail. The French had
pushed their saps up to the *abattis* round the great Malakoff
Tower, until they were a scant thirty paces from the ditch

which surrounded it and there were over two hundred British guns—fifty of these manned by men of the Naval Brigade— ranged on the enemy defences. The Russians were reported to be constructing a floating bridge, from the south side of the harbour and opinion was divided as to their reason for doing so. Some Allied Officers believed that it was for the purpose of bringing in more troops and munitions, in case of assault, but others—who included Admiral Lyons—held that the enemy were contemplating retreat from the city.

Phillip was uncertain, finding it hard to believe that, after their epic resistance, the Russians would abandon Sebastopol, but he joined in the general acclamation when Captain Keppel assembled his Officers to announce that a bombardment had been ordered, to commence on 5th September, and continue for the next two days.

"If we can make sufficient impression on the defences, the assault will take place, gentlemen," he told them, blue eyes gleaming. "A Council of War was held yesterday and, I'm told, a definite decision will be made on the 7th. I can only hope that it will be an affirmative decision because this may well be our last chance of taking Sebastopol before winter is upon us. The plan is for the French to attack the Malakoff Tower at about 11:30 in the morning and our signal to attack the Redan will be when the French hoist the Tricolour from the top of the tower. As before, we shall supply ladder parties to go in with the first wave of assault troops, but our main task will be to bring down the defences of the Redan and I am confident that we shall succeed in doing so. Failure will mean a second winter on these bleak Heights, so I do not contemplate failure."

A cheer went up and everyone was smiling when Keppel dismissed them.

The cannonade opened next morning, supported by fire

from rocket and mortar-vessels in Streletska Bay, which was directed against the Quarantine Battery and the enemy ships-of-the-line at anchor in the harbour. The bombardment was continued for two more days with telling effect—several enemy ships were hit and burnt to the waterline, and both the Malakoff and the Redan suffered so tremendous a pounding that, for the first time in almost a year, the return of fire from both slackened noticeably. On 7th September, as Captain Keppel had predicted, the men of the Naval Brigade learnt that the attack was to be launched, as planned, the following morning.

"The French will attack with four divisions, under General Bosquet," Keppel told his Officers. "MacMahon's division, with the Zouaves, will lead the assault on the Malakoff, and two others will be sent simultaneously against the Little Redan and, assisted by a Sardinian brigade, they will attempt to capture the Central Bastion and then wheel right, to take the Flagstaff Bastion in the rear. The fourth division will advance against the Curtain." He indicated the various points of attack on his map. "They have learnt their lesson from the last costly failure, when over-crowding in the forward parallels permitted the assault troops only to advance in twos and threes and support was late in reaching them. They have built a road, fifty yards in width, cutting straight through the parallels and, at present, hidden from the enemy by gabions, which are merely laid in position and can easily be removed when the attack is due to begin."

"How about our attack, sir?" Captain Moorsom, his second-in-command asked, a faint edge to his voice. "Have *we* learnt our lesson?"

Henry Keppel sighed. "I am not sure," he admitted. "It is not for me to criticize military decisions made by the High

Command. But we are sending in two divisions only—General Codrington's Light Division, which is bled white and the Second, both of which, as you know, failed and suffered heavy losses in the last attack on the Redan on the eighteenth of June. These two have been given 'the honour of the assault,' as the Commander-in-Chief calls it, in consequence of their having defended the batteries and the approaches to the Redan for so many months. Their losses have been made up by large intakes of raw boys, who have never seen action and cannot be expected to fight like the gallant veterans of the Alma and Inkerman, whom they have replaced." The little Captain repeated his sigh. "If the choice had been left to me, gentlemen, I confess that I would have entrusted this crucial attack to Sir Colin Campbell and his Highland Brigade, which still contains a high proportion of splendid veterans, and to the Third Division, which is also unimpaired by recent losses. As it is, both these will act only as the second line of reserves."

There were murmurs of agreement with this view, in which Phillip joined with some feeling. He had been at the Battle of Balaclava as naval liaison Officer to Sir Colin Campbell and had the greatest admiration and respect for the Highlanders and their tough, experienced Commander. And it was, he knew, a maxim of war that troops which had suffered a severe defeat should go to reserve for a considerable period and not be used again in an identical operation. He leaned forward to study the map which Henry Keppel had spread out for this purpose. The Redan, which had been the main target for the Naval Brigade's guns for so long, was a familiar sight to him but now he was seeing it with new eyes and from a different angle, as a fortress to be taken by assault—and by soldiers on foot, who would charge with the bayonet.

It was built on a vineyard some three hundred feet above

sea level and it had two faces, each seventy yards long, which met at an angle of 65°. Its base was a fortified line of earthworks, in front of which lay a ditch, twenty feet in width and fourteen in depth. Above this, the Redan rose to a height of fifteen feet, forming an escarpment nearly thirty feet from top to bottom, which could only be surmounted with the aid of scaling ladders. It was defended by over fifty guns, Phillip was aware, some of them in two tiers, sited behind well constructed embrasures, with traverses to the rear. To reach it, the assault troops would have to cross two hundred yards of uphill ground, exposed to the fire of batteries to right and left, as well as those of their objective, and they would have to negotiate an *abattis* of felled trees and intertwining branches, fifty yards in front of the ditch. It would be a daunting prospect for seasoned troops, he thought, and for half-trained replacements, who had never been in action . . . he found himself echoing Keppel's sigh.

"Now as to the plan of attack, gentlemen," the Naval Brigade Commander went on. "As I told you a few days ago, the signal for our attack will be the hoisting of the French Tricolour on the Malakoff. There will be a covering party of two hundred, a ladder party of three hundred and twenty, a storming party of a thousand, and fifteen hundred support troops. These—"

"Are we to supply ladder parties, sir?" a youthful Lieutenant asked eagerly.

"These will be supplied in equal numbers by the Light and Second Divisions," Captain Keppel said, as if there had been no interruption. Turning to the boy who had asked the question, he added with a wry smile, "Like Sir Colin Campbell's Highlanders, we shall be in reserve. That is to say, we shall have a reserve party of fifty volunteers, standing by—the rest of the Naval Brigade will stand to their guns. It is no exaggeration to say, gentlemen, that your shooting tomorrow, if it is accurate and rapid, may make a material contribution to the success of the assault. Whilst we cannot hope to silence fifty enemy guns, we shall do all in our power to put out of action as many of those guns as shot and shell can reach." He issued precise orders as to the supply and allocation of ammunition and then turned to Phillip, lowering his voice, "Have I read your thoughts aright, my dear boy . . . would you welcome the opportunity to rid yourself of the scapegoat stigma you have borne so patiently?"

"Indeed I would, sir," Phillip assured him, his throat suddenly so tight that he had difficulty in getting the words out. "I'd give anything in the world for such an opportunity, sir."

"It may cost you your life," his Commander warned.

"I wouldn't consider the price too high, sir."

Keppel eyed him thoughtfully from his diminutive height and nodded. "No, I don't believe you would! Very well—you shall have the task every Officer in this Brigade would like me to give him. Take charge of the ladder party, Phillip. Volunteer fifty reliable men but remember—yours is a reserve party. You will only go in if the others fail to reach their objective."

Phillip gave him a grateful, "Aye, aye, sir," and went to choose his men.

The assault troops paraded at nightfall and were in position long before dawn. Unlike the French, the British had not built a concealed road or even an adequate *banquette* to enable an extended line of attackers to make their advance on a wide front. The men had to move forward from parallel to parallel through zig-zag communication trenches, in some confusion in the darkness and often slowed to a snail's pace. When they reached the fifth and final parallel, they found themselves halted since the forward saps, which could accommodate only twenty files at a time, were already occupied by the covering and ladder parties, whom they had been instructed to follow.

A long wait ensued, which sorely tried the courage and patience of even the most seasoned campaigners and reduced many of the inexperienced youngsters to shivering panic. The day dawned at last and a strong northerly wind, which had risen during the night, drove clouds of stinging dust into the faces of the tensely waiting troops and added considerably to their discomfort. But the British batteries were keeping up a vigorous and accurate fire, to which the enemy gunners, in both the Malakoff and the Redan, made only desultory reply and spirits started to rise, although an Officer of the 88th, who had survived the first attack in June, confided grimly to Phillip, "They've not been put out of action. They know we're about to attack and they're conserving their ammunition until we do."

At 11:30 a bugle-call from the French lines heralded the opening of the attack and General MacMahon's Zouaves charged across the intervening 25 yards in fine fashion and were into the Malakoff with scarcely a shot fired. With the rest of the division, followed by artillery, advancing to their support along the specially constructed roadway, the Russians were taken by surprise and their resistance lasted for only a short time. As they were driven back, the French Tricolour could be seen floating from the ramparts, and the order was given to the waiting British troops to advance on the Redan.

They did so, in some disorder, due to the narrowness of the saps and trenches from which they had to climb, and the hitherto silent guns of the Redan met them with a withering fire of grape and roundshot and cannister, which drowned the cheers they had given so eagerly as they started across the two-hundred-yard expanse of open ground which separated them from their objective. The ranks of the covering and ladder parties were thinned long before the Rifle Brigade skirmishers reached the *abattis;* those who managed to get past it came under musket as well as cannon fire, from guns mounted *en barbette* at the top of the escarpment. A number of green-uniformed Riflemen reached the ditch but got no further, flinging themselves into it or into such cover as they could find in shell-holes or behind rocks, where they lay, seemingly paralyzed by the terrible hail of shot and shell raining down on them, unable to go on. A few blazed away uselessly at the towering fortifications with their new Lee Enfields but most lay motionless, pinned down by the barrage.

Only about six of the Light Division's twenty scaling ladders were carried as far as the ditch; the rest were scattered amongst the rough, tussocky grass which covered the approach to it, the bodies of the men who had borne them piled about them or crushed beneath their rungs. As the first wave of the storming party prepared to leave the trench, Phillip turned to his waiting seamen.

"Come on, my boys!" he bade them. "It's our turn now. Follow me—but don't bunch close together and keep your heads down!"

They could scarcely hear him for the roar of the guns but they understood his gestures and raised sword and obeyed without hesitation. With eight men to each of the 24-foot ladders they ran, bent double and in silence, not wasting their breath in an attempt to cheer or urge each other on, for they had seen what had happened to those who had gone before them. The smoke and dust afforded them some cover but the Russian guns were laid accurately on the open ground which they must cross and the gunners needed neither sight nor sound of their target—they had only to fire and keep on firing.

Phillip stumbled through the inferno like a sleep-walker, now tripping over a dead or wounded soldier lying in his path, now reeling from the blast of an exploding shell. Before he had covered twenty yards, he had to take the end of a ladder from whence the bearers had vanished somewhere in the smoke, one with his head blown from his body. He was choked and half-blinded, convinced that each breath he drew into his tortured lungs would be his last. Only instinct and an obstinate determination to see his ladder in position drove him on, for this was worse, infinitely worse, than anything he had ever experienced before. The enemy fire never slackened, men were falling like ninepins all about him and he knew that it would be a miracle if one of his ladders reached the escarpment.

Hearing a scream of agony behind him, he turned to see that another of his party had fallen, a big gunner's mate, who had reminded him of Thompson and who now lay on the rocky, dust-covered ground clutching a shattered leg. There were now only four of them staggering drunkenly under the weight of the ladder, where before there had been twice that number, but he glimpsed two of his other parties—incredibly with their numbers intact—to his left and he pressed on into the smoke, with no idea of how far they had come or how much further they had still to go. Then he saw the ditch directly ahead of him, with a party of engineers working like beavers, under the direction of an Officer, to construct a ramp across it. The Officer grinned at him, his teeth gleaming white in his powder-blackened face, and raised a hand in welcome.

"The Royal Navy, God bless 'em!" he yelled. "Be the first to take advantage of our bridge, Commander!"

Phillip found himself grinning back, as he waved his two parties to go ahead of him. "I'm a bit short of hands," he said breathlessly. "If you could lend me a couple to get our ladder across, I'd be grateful."

"I'll lend you a hand myself," the young Lieutenant offered. "My job here is finished, thank God." He gripped the end rung of the ladder with a hand that was raw and bleeding and said grimly, his mouth close to Phillip's ear, "These aren't properly organized stormers, for heaven's sake! They are coming up in driblets, by ones and twos, stunned and paralyzed. They've none of the dash and *élan* one expects from British soldiers in an assault. Look at them! They're just clinging to the foot of the escarpment, where they are out of the line of fire, and letting their Officers go in through the embrasures alone."

He was right, Phillip saw, looking up. As he watched a youthful ensign, in the uniform of the 90th Foot, who had clawed his way up the crumbling slope on hands and knees, hurled himself over the top of the parapet with sword held high and a cheer on his lips, but not a single one of the soldiers with him followed his example. They stayed where they were, crouched under the over-hanging gabions of the gun embrasures, and did not stir.

"They're young soldiers," he defended. "Most of them have only been out here a few weeks and the poor little devils have spent all their time in the trenches, I understand, learning to keep their heads down and little else."

"Then why pick them for this vital assault?" the Engineer Lieutenant demanded unanswerably. "God forgive whoever made *that* decision!" He sighed, as Phillip and his party placed their ladders in position. "Well done—you've added fifty percent to the number we had here. Perhaps it'll encourage some of the poor little trench warriors to mount 'em. Er—my name is Ranken, by the way—George Ranken."

"And mine is Hazard. Are more ladders wanted, do you think?"

"The ones we have are not being used," Lieutenant Ranken pointed out. "But here come some of the 88th—perhaps, after all, Commander, we have not laboured in vain."

The 88th was an Irish regiment which, Phillip knew, had distinguished itself in the earlier battles at the Alma and Inkerman and he waited expectantly as a party of about sixty men emerged from the smoke and came pounding across the ramp, led by two young subalterns. Both Officers mounted the nearest ladder without pausing to draw breath but only a dozen men and a grey-haired sergeant, who was bleeding from a wound in the chest, made any attempt to follow them. The rest, as if with one accord, dived for cover at the foot of the slope and when, a moment or so later, the sergeant fell close by them to lie moaning with the pain of a fresh wound, it was Phillip who ran across to drag him to shelter and two of his seamen who volunteered to carry him back in search of medical aid. The men of his regiment did not move.

"You see?" Ranken said bitterly. "And it's not only our men who are behaving like this. The French took the Malakoff in grand style and appear to be holding it, but they have twice been driven back from the Little Redan, I was told. And I saw, with my own eyes, one of their regiments in full flight from the Central Bastion, just before you got here." He gestured wrathfully to the escarpment above their heads and to the red-coated soldiers clinging, face downwards, to its lower slopes. "They would run too, if they didn't feel safer where they are and fear to return through the barrage. In the name of heaven, where are our reinforcements? We shall never take even the salient with those yellow-livered boys!"

"The support troops and reserves have a thousand yards

of zig-zags and parallels to traverse, in single file, before they can advance," Phillip told him, recalling the orders which had been issued a few hours before. "And by this time they'll be hideously congested, I fear, since the wounded are to be evacuated by the same route."

The Engineer Officer groaned. "For which brilliant feat of organization we can thank our General Staff, I suppose! Few of them ever come near the trenches, you know—gilded popinjays that they are. The only one I've ever seen is Henry Clifford, General Codrington's aide, who is a most efficient and gallant Officer. Devil take it, this is the eighteenth of June all over again, except that the butcher's bill is likely to be even higher and—" he broke off to mop his brow as his sergeant, a tanned, imperturbable veteran, came to report the ramp securely in place. "Good!" he approved. "Collect the men, Sergeant, and prepare to withdraw. We'll fall back to the quarries."

Phillip looked at his own battered party, now reduced to fifteen men, armed only with cutlasses, and Lieutenant Ranken, guessing his thoughts, offered the suggestion that they should be sent back with the wounded. "Take them to the quarries. It's closer—they'll only have about fifty yards of open ground to cross. We can do no more here, Hazard. No one can, until the support troops arrive . . . if they ever do. I'm taking my fellows back. They've done all and more than they were ordered to do and they are highly-trained men—there's no sense in getting them killed for nothing. I should suppose the same applies to your men, does it not?"

It did, of course, Phillip thought and, although stretcher bearers were now starting to come up, there were too few of them to deal with all the wounded. His men could make themselves useful and . . .

"Sir—look over there, sir!" One of the seamen, a fair-haired giant named Oxtoby, was pointing excitedly in the direction of the British trenches and Phillip's heart lifted with pride as, through the eddying smoke, he saw a line of red-coated infantrymen advancing with bayonets fixed, in splendid, disciplined deployment.

"The Fusiliers!" Ranken exclaimed. "The 23rd . . . now *that's* the way to come into battle! They make a brave sight, don't they, as steady as if they were on the parade ground."

Their commanding Officer at their head and scorning the sap—which would have brought them out in the driblets Ranken had complained of—the 23rd were coming from the main forward trench as a whole regiment. As they crossed the open ground, they had to run the same terrible gauntlet of fire as their predecessors but they did not falter. Inevitably they suffered casualties but they closed ranks and retained their formation until they were right up to the ditch. Reaching it and cheered on by their Officers, they crossed and made for the scaling ladders, ascending to the parapet and, still as a cohesive whole, jumped on to it and over, into the interior of the Redan. A few of the men who had been clinging to the gabions, fired by their example, went after them and Phillip exchanged a swift glance with the Engineer Lieutenant.

"Let's try and rally some support for them, shall we?" he suggested and Ranken nodded, the light of battle in his eyes. "They deserve no less," he agreed. "But I shall still send my men to the quarries. They're not infantrymen."

He rapped an order to his sergeant but, before Phillip could do the same, Oxtoby drew his cutlass.

"We're with you, sir," he stated firmly. "All of us—we didn't carry them bleeding ladders all this way for nothing, sir."

With his fifteen seamen at his back, Phillip climbed up to

the parapet, yelling at the top of his voice to the scattered infantrymen to join them. One or two did so but the majority appeared too shocked even to hear him, until a bare-headed young bugler of the 55th scrambled past him and with complete disregard for his own safety, stood on the broken sandbags at the summit of the escarpment and sounded the advance.

"Good man!" Ranken shouted hoarsely. "Oh, good man!"

Inside the Redan was a shambles and Phillip recoiled in horror at what he saw. Bodies lay scattered everywhere he looked and the men of the gallant 23rd had been brought to a halt at last under a terrible cross-fire from an enemy they could not see. The Russians were sheltered behind strong defences and they were well supplied with ammunition. Musket balls, shells hurled by hand, their fuses lit, and grape from guns which had been turned inward rained down on the scarlet-uniformed attackers, until the salient was strewn with their dead. Here and there, small pockets of men were engaged in desperate, hand-to-hand struggles with Russian infantrymen brought in as reinforcements but, hack and thrust though they might, they were being steadily, mercilessly driven back.

There were plenty of weapons lying about and, directing his party to arm themselves with muskets, Phillip was able to pour in a telling volley which put out of action the crew of a brass cannon, which had been spraying grape with devastating effect on a knot of men of different regiments, who had formed themselves into a defensive square. But there was no spare ammunition and the infantrymen, when they had emptied their pouches, could only resort to the bayonets and panic spread swiftly, when more and more enemy reserves came pouring from concealment to meet them. Finding themselves outnumbered, the young soldiers broke and fled back from whence they had come, flinging themselves over the parapet in blind terror. Russian marksmen, firing down from the safety of their embrasures, picked off those who managed to gain a foothold on the crumbling slope, and the Officers, endeavouring to cover their men's precipitate retreat, died where they stood in twos and threes or small, heroic groups, refusing to surrender.

"This is hopeless, Commander Hazard," Ranken gasped, seizing Phillip by the shoulder as they were pushed back towards the apex of the salient. "For God's sake, the enemy are bringing up fresh reserves and we have none!" He pointed with a broken, bloodied sword at an advancing column of tightly-packed Russian infantrymen which, as he spoke, fanned out to fire an echoing volley into the remnants of a company of Fusiliers and then knelt to reload. "We'd better try to make an orderly withdrawal, if even that is possible."

Phillip, having no breath to speak, nodded his assent. He contrived to keep what was left of his party together and they retreated to the parapet, fighting off Russian bayonets for as long as they could with any weapons that came to hand. The giant Oxtoby was a tower of strength. He laid about him valiantly, first with the butt of a newly-issued Rifle Brigade Lee Enfield, then with his cutlass and finally with his bare fists, a grin of pure pleasure lighting his round, moon face, which only faded when a fragment from a bursting shell took him in the chest.

"I'm finished, sir," he whispered, when Phillip dropped to his knees beside him. "But it was worth it! I . . . I had me . . . bleedin' money's worth. Before heaven . . . I did."

He died seconds later, the grin miraculously returning to his blackened, blood-flecked lips as his great body slumped to the ground.

It seemed half a lifetime afterwards that Phillip found himself, with Ranken and four of his seamen, slithering down into the ditch at the foot of the escarpment. The ramp had gone and the ditch was filled with a mass of bodies, some living but most of them dead. Somehow, still keeping together, they managed to struggle free and drag themselves out on the far side, just as a landslide of earth, smashed gabions, and broken ladders came hurtling down from the slope behind, to fill the ditch with choking clouds of dust and a fresh cascade of bodies.

The cannon fire from the Redan had slackened but the open ground was still under musket fire from the enemy reserves and a battery to the left—the one the French had been driven out of, Phillip remembered dimly—continued to vomit a deadly hail of roundshot and grape as, with a hundred or so others, he set out to cross it once more. There was a deadweight on his back and he was only able to stumble a yard or two at a time, pause for breath and then stumble on in the same direction as all the others, which he could only hope was that in which safety lay.

He lost sight of Ranken and, at times, seemed to be almost alone, until another wave of running men caught up with and passed him but he made no attempt to increase his pace. Musket balls passed overhead like swarms of angry bees and occasionally a shell burst and the ground about him was pockmarked in half a hundred places, but he felt curiously unmoved and quite unafraid and scarcely troubled to step aside to avoid the holes which appeared like magic in his path. It was as if all that he had seen and endured during the attack on the Redan had rendered him immune to such normal human emotions as fear or hatred or pity and even the instinct for self-preservation seemed largely to have deserted him.

He passed wounded men, who cried out feebly for help or water, or a bullet to put an end to their pain, and was deaf to their entreaties, but to a young ensign with a shattered leg, who was limping along supported by a rifle, he gave his arm and, before they gained the British forward trench, the contents of his water-bottle. It was only when the boy sobbed his thanks that he became fully aware of his presence and he did not realize, until someone relieved him of his burden at the trench parapet, that the dead-weight on his back was one of his own seamen, for he had no recollection of having picked the man up.

"He's dead, I'm afraid, sir." The soldier who had come to meet him spoke sadly and Phillip stared at him in hollow-eyed bewilderment, unable to understand either his words or the pity in his eyes.

"Who's dead?" he asked hoarsely, choking on dust.

For answer, the soldier gestured to the limp body at his feet. "Your bluejacket, sir, the one you brought in. Shot through the head, poor sod, clean as a whistle. And I think you've been hit in the head too—better let me take you along to the dressing station, sir. It's not far and they've shifted most of the wounded to the rear now, so you won't have to wait too long."

Hours later, the wound in his head dressed and conscious of no pain, Phillip set off through the darkness to walk back to the Naval Brigade Camp. He was still in a shocked state and wearier and more despondent than he had ever felt in his life. As he plodded slowly along the well-worn track, he was startled to hear the sound of a massive explosion coming from the south side of the harbour. It was followed by another and suddenly the night sky was illuminated by a succession of vivid flashes. Tongues of flame were rising from the beleaguered city and, his weariness forgotten, he ran on and upwards until he could look down on it and was able to see that the whole of the suburb of Karabelnaya was ablaze.

Explosions were coming from the anchored ships now and he watched in stunned amazement as, one after another, the powerful first and second rates—once the pride of the Russian Black Sea Fleet—started to burn. He saw the *Twelve Apostles* catch alight, then the 84-gun *Sviatolaf* and the splendid *Grand Duke Constantine* of 120, and finally the gallant little *Vladimir* steamer, which had fought many actions against British frigates during the siege. Their magazines blew up; shattered masts and spars flew into the air to vanish in the dense black pall of smoke which was beginning slowly to cover the stricken town, as the fires grew in strength and reached out to consume everything which lay in their path. Houses, the dockyard buildings, domed churches, the great bastions and forts which had resisted a year's bombardment—all were going, in a terrible holocaust of destruction created by those who had so stubbornly defended them.

Phillip drew in his breath sharply, scarcely able to believe his ears when he heard an explosion from the Redan itself. Was he dreaming, he wondered dazedly, could this be part of his earlier nightmare? The assault on the Redan—which had cost so many lives and which he had judged an ignominious failure—must, after all, have succeeded . . . surely that wasn't possible? He *must* be dreaming—had he not been among those who had fled from the carnage of its interior, driven back in defeat by the seemingly endless columns of grey-uniformed Russian reserves? Why, in the name of heaven, were the victors abandoning the scene of their victory?

Still uncertain whether he was awake or living a nightmare, he returned to the track. Dawn was breaking when he reached the Naval Brigade Camp and the sound of cheering, coming from the mess tent, sent him towards it at a run, his heart suddenly quickening its beat.

Captain Keppel was there, surrounded by most of his Officers, some of them wearing uniform greatcoats over their night-clothes and obviously just roused from sleep. Their faces held relief and incredulity and a strange sort of wonder as if, like himself, Phillip thought, they could not quite believe what they had seen and heard.

"Sir Colin Campbell has sent an Officer, gentlemen," the Naval Brigade Commander was saying, "to tell me that his men are in Sebastopol and that they met with no resistance. The enemy have abandoned the city and are in full retreat to the north. They crossed by the bridge of boats, after destroying their magazines and setting fire to the principal buildings, and the ships in harbour have all been burnt or scuttled. Sebastopol—or what is left of it—is ours."

"And the Redan, sir?" Captain Moorsom enquired. "I heard a rumour that the enemy have abandoned that also."

"It's more than a rumour, sir," one of the others put in eagerly. "A patrol of the Rifle Brigade entered the Redan an hour ago, and it was deserted, save for our dead."

Henry Keppel saw Phillip and, as another cheer greeted the announcement that the Redan had been abandoned, he strode over with hand extended. "Well done, my dear boy!" he exclaimed. "I've heard glowing accounts of how well you and your ladder party acquitted yourselves . . . but with such losses that I am thankful to see you alive." His smile was warm as he wrung Phillip's hand. "Let me be the first to congratulate you!"

"Congratulate me, sir?" Phillip echoed, seeing Oxtoby's dead face, still wearing its defiant grin. "On being alive, do you mean, sir? Because I . . ." he choked and could not go on.

"That, too, of course. But not only that." Keppel's smile widened. "The Admiral has asked me to tell you that you will probably receive one of the new awards for valour, recently instituted by Her Majesty—the Victoria Cross, it's to be called. The recommendation made by his son Jack, which Sir Edmund passed on to Their Lordships, has been approved. In view of which the sentence passed on you at your Court Martial has been reconsidered and commuted to a simple reprimand, so you will return to the command of your ship. Needless to say, I am delighted for you, my dear boy."

Phillip could not speak. Indeed, he could hardly take in what had been said to him, save for the one thing he had wanted, above all else, to hear—he was to return to his command, to the *Huntress.*

"I . . ." he found his voice at last. "Thank you, sir. Thank you very much indeed."

"Nothing to thank *me* for, dear boy," his Commander assured him. "If poor Jack Lyons hadn't put you up for that award, I should have done so, after today's affair—but you got it without any help from me. They'll give your brother a new command, I imagine, so there's nothing to stand in your way now, is there? You'll soon live down the reprimand." He took his watch from his pocket and then glanced round the tent. "I shall be going on a tour of inspection of Sebastopol in two hours' time, with Sir Colin. Get yourself a shave and something to eat and join me, eh? And after that, you can go back to your *Huntress.* We'll all be going back to our ships in a few days, I understand, and I can't say I'll be sorry." His blue, seaman's eyes looked into Phillip's and he added softly, "Thank God this war is all but over!"

"Amen to that, sir," Phillip said, meaning it with all his heart. "Amen to that!"

His brain was slowly losing its numbness. He would call on Catriona, he thought, if her employers' yacht was still at Balaclava and apologize for his churlish discourtesy. And then he would go back to his *Huntress* to prepare for the long voyage home . . .

BOOKS CONSULTED
ON THE CRIMEAN WAR

GENERAL

History of the War Against Russia, E. H. Nolan (2 vols., 1857)

History of the War With Russia, H. Tyrell (3 vols., 1857)

The Campaign in the Crimea, G. Brackenbury, illustrated
W. Simpson (1856)

The War in the Crimea, General Sir Edward Hamley (1891)

Letters from India and the Crimea, Surgeon-General
J. A. Bostock (1896)

Letters from Headquarters, by a Staff Officer (1856)

The Crimea in 1854 and 1894, Field-Marshal Sir Evelyn Wood
(1895)

The Destruction of Lord Raglan, Christopher Hibbert (1961)

Battles of the Crimean War, W. Baring Pemberton (1962)

The Reason Why, Cecil Woodham Smith (1953)

Crimean Blunder, Peter Gibbs (1960)

The Campaign in the Crimea, 1854–6: Despatches and Papers,
compiled and arranged by Captain Sayer (1857)

Letters from Camp During the Siege of Sebastopol, Lt.-Colonel
C. G. Campbell (1894)

The Invasion of the Crimea, A. W. Kingslake (1863)

With the Guards We Shall Go, Mabel, Countess of Airlie (1933)

Britain's Roll of Glory, D. H. Parry (1895)

Henry Clifford, V.C., General Sir Bernard Paget (1956)

BIOGRAPHIES

The Life of Colin Campbell, Lord Clyde, Lt.-General
L. Shadwell, C.B. (2 vols., 1881)

A Life of Vice-Admiral Lord Lyons, Captain S. Eardley-Wilmot,
R.N. (1898)

NAVAL

The Russian War, 1854 (Baltic and Black Sea), D. Bonner-
Smith and Captain A. C. Dewar, R.N. (1944)

Letters from the Black Sea, Admiral Sir Leopold Heath (1897)

A Sailor's Life Under Four Sovereigns, Admiral of the Fleet the
Hon. Sir Henry Keppel, G.C.B., O.M. (3 vols., 1899)

From Midshipman to Field-Marshal, Sir Evelyn Wood, V.C.
(2 vols., 1906)

Letters from the Fleet in the Fifties, Mrs Tom Kelly (1902)

The British Fleet in the Black Sea, Maj.-General W. Brereton
(1856)

Reminiscences of a Naval Officer, Sir G. Gifford (1892)

The Navy as I Have Known It, Vice-Admiral W. Freemantle
(1899)

A Middy's Recollections, The Hon. Victor Montagu (1898)

Medicine and the Navy, Lloyd and Coulter (vol. IV, 1963)

The Price of Admiralty, Stanley Barret, Hale (1968)

The Wooden Fighting Ship, E. H. H. Archibald, Blandford (1968)

Seamanship Manual, Captain Sir George S. Naes, K.C.B.,
R.N., Griffin (1886)

The Navy of Britain, England's Sea Officers, and *A Social
History of the Navy,* Michael Lewis, Allen & Unwin
(1939–60)
The Navy in Transition, Michael Lewis, Hodder & Stoughton
(1965)
Files of *The Illustrated London News* and *Mariner's Mirror*
Unpublished Letters and Diaries

*The author acknowledges, with gratitude, the assistance
given by the Staff of the York City Library in obtaining books,
also that given by the Royal United Service Institution and
Francis Edwards Ltd.*

More Action, More Adventure, More Angst . . .

This is no time to stand down! McBooks Press, the leader in nautical fiction, invites you to embark on more sea adventures and take part in gripping naval action with Douglas Reeman, Dudley Pope, and a host of other nautical writers. Sail to Trafalgar, Grenada, Copenhagen—to famous battles and unknown skirmishes alike.

All the titles below are available at bookstores. For a free catalog, or to order direct, call toll-free 1-888-BOOKS-11 (1-888-266-5711). Or visit the McBooks website, www.mcbooks.com, for special offers and to read excerpts from McBooks titles.

ALEXANDER KENT
The Bolitho Novels

___ 1 Midshipman Bolitho
0-935526-41-2 • 240 pp., $13.95

___ 2 Stand Into Danger
0-935526-42-0 • 288 pp., $13.95

___ 3 In Gallant Company
0-935526-43-9 • 320 pp., $14.95

___ 4 Sloop of War
0-935526-48-X • 352 pp., $14.95

___ 5 To Glory We Steer
0-935526-49-8 • 352 pp., $14.95

___ 6 Command a King's Ship
0-935526-50-1 • 352 pp., $14.95

___ 7 Passage to Mutiny
0-935526-58-7 • 352 pp., $15.95

___ 8 With All Despatch
0-935526-61-7 • 320 pp., $14.95

___ 9 Form Line of Battle!
0-935526-59-5 • 352 pp., $14.95

___ 10 Enemy in Sight!
0-935526-60-9 • 368 pp., $14.95

___ 11 The Flag Captain
0-935526-66-8 • 384 pp., $15.95

___ 12 Signal – Close Action!
0-935526-67-6 • 368 pp., $15.95

___ 13 The Inshore Squadron
0-935526-68-4 • 288 pp., $13.95

___ 14 A Tradition of Victory
0-935526-70-6 • 304 pp., $14.95

___ 15 Success to the Brave
0-935526-71-4 • 288 pp., $13.95

___ 16 Colours Aloft!
0-935526-72-2 • 304 pp., $14.95

___ 17 Honour This Day
0-935526-73-0 • 320 pp., $15.95

___ 18 The Only Victor
0-935526-74-9 • 384 pp., $15.95

___ 19 Beyond the Reef
0-935526-82-X • 352 pp., $14.95

___ 20 The Darkening Sea
0-935526-83-8 • 352 pp., $15.95

___ 21 For My Country's Freedom
0-935526-84-6 • 304 pp., $15.95

___ 22 Cross of St George
0-935526-92-7 • 320 pp., $16.95

___ 23 Sword of Honour
0-935526-93-5 • 320 pp., $15.95

___ 24 Second to None
0-935526-94-3 • 352 pp., $16.95

___ 25 Relentless Pursuit
1-59013-026-X • 368 pp., $16.95

___ 26 Man of War
1-59013-091-X • 320 pp., $16.95

___ 26 Man of War
1-59013-066-9 • 320 pp., $24.95 HC

DOUGLAS REEMAN
Modern Naval Fiction Library

___ Twelve Seconds to Live
1-59013-044-8 • 368 pp., $15.95

___ Battlecruiser
1-59013-043-X • 320 pp., $15.95

___ The White Guns
1-59013-083-9 • 368 pp., $15.95

Royal Marines Saga

___ 1 Badge of Glory
1-59013-013-8 • 384 pp., $16.95

___ 2 The First to Land
   1-59013-014-6 • 304 pp., $15.95
___ 3 The Horizon
   1-59013-027-8 • 368 pp., $15.95
___ 4 Dust on the Sea
   1-59013-028-6 • 384 pp., $15.95

DUDLEY POPE
The Lord Ramage Novels

___ 1 Ramage
   0-935526-76-5 • 320 pp., $14.95
___ 2 Ramage & the Drumbeat
   0-935526-77-3 • 288 pp., $14.95
___ 3 Ramage & the Freebooters
   0-935526-78-1 • 384 pp., $15.95
___ 4 Governor Ramage R. N.
   0-935526-79-X • 384 pp., $15.95
___ 5 Ramage's Prize
   0-935526-80-3 • 320 pp., $15.95
___ 6 Ramage & the Guillotine
   0-935526-81-1• 320 pp., $14.95
___ 7 Ramage's Diamond
   0-935526-89-7 • 336 pp., $15.95
___ 8 Ramage's Mutiny
   0-935526-90-0 • 280 pp., $14.95
___ 9 Ramage & the Rebels
   0-935526-91-9 • 320 pp., $15.95
___ 10 The Ramage Touch
   1-59013-007-3 • 272 pp., $15.95
___ 11 Ramage's Signal
   1-59013-008-1 • 288 pp., $15.95
___ 12 Ramage & the Renegades
   1-59013-009-X • 320 pp., $15.95
___ 13 Ramage's Devil
   1-59013-010-3 • 320 pp., $15.95
___ 14 Ramage's Trial
   1-59013-011-1 • 320 pp., $15.95
___ 15 Ramage's Challenge
   1-59013-012-X • 352 pp., $15.95
___ 16 Ramage at Trafalgar
   1-59013-022-7 • 256 pp., $14.95
___ 17 Ramage & the Saracens
   1-59013-023-5 • 304 pp., $15.95
___ 18 Ramage & the Dido
   1-59013-024-3 • 272 pp., $15.95

JAMES L. NELSON
___The Only Life That Mattered
   1-59013-060-X • 416 pp., $16.95

DEWEY LAMBDIN
Alan Lewie Naval Adventures

___ 2 The French Admiral
   1-59013-021-9 • 448 pp., $17.95
___ 8 Jester's Fortune
   1-59013-034-0 • 432 pp., $17.95

ALEXANDER FULLERTON
The Nicholas Everard WWII Saga

___ 1 Storm Force to Narvik
   1-59013-092-8 • 256 pp., $13.95

PHILIP McCUTCHAN
The Halfhyde Adventures

___1 Halfhyde at the Bight of Benin
   1-59013-078-2 • 224 pp., $13.95
___2 Halfhyde's Island
   1-59013-079-0 • 224 pp., $13.95
___3 Halfhyde and the
   Guns of Arrest
   1-59013-067-7 • 256 pp., $13.95
___4 Halfhyde to the Narrows
   1-59013-068-5 • 240 pp., $13.95

V.A. STUART
Alexander Sheridan Adventures

___ 1 Victors and Lords
   0-935526-98-6 • 272 pp., $13.95
___ 2 The Sepoy Mutiny
   0-935526-99-4 • 240 pp., $13.95
___ 3 Massacre at Cawnpore
   1-59013-019-7 • 240 pp., $13.95
___ 4 The Cannons of Lucknow
   1-59013-029-4 • 272 pp., $14.95
___ 5 The Heroic Garrison
   1-59013-030-8 • 256 pp., $13.95

The Phillip Hazard Novels

___ 1 The Valiant Sailors
   1-59013-039-1 • 272 pp., $14.95
___ 2 The Brave Captains
   1-59013-040-5 • 272 pp., $14.95
___ 3 Hazard's Command
   1-59013-081-2 • 256 pp., $13.95
___ 4 Hazard of Huntress
   1-59013-082-0 • 256 pp., $13.95
___ 5 Hazard in Circassia
   1-59013-062-6 • 256 pp., $13.95
___ 6 Victory at Sebastopol
   1-59013-061-8 • 224 pp., $13.95

DAVID DONACHIE
The Privateersman Mysteries

___ 1 The Devil's Own Luck
1-59013-004-9 • 302 pp., $15.95
1-59013-003-0 • 320 pp., $23.95 HC

___ 2 The Dying Trade
1-59013-006-5 • 384 pp., $16.95
1-59013-005-7 • 400 pp., $24.95 HC

___ 3 A Hanging Matter
1-59013-016-2 • 416 pp., $16.95

___ 4 An Element of Chance
1-59013-017-0 • 448 pp., $17.95

___ 5 The Scent of Betrayal
1-59013-031-6 • 448 pp., $17.95

___ 6 A Game of Bones
1-59013-032-4 • 352 pp., $15.95

The Nelson & Emma Trilogy

___ 1 On a Making Tide
1-59013-041-3 • 416 pp., $17.95

___ 2 Tested by Fate
1-59013-042-1 • 416 pp., $17.95

___ 3 Breaking the Line
1-59013-090-1 • 368 pp., $16.95

JAN NEEDLE
Sea Officer William Bentley Novels

___ 1 A Fine Boy for Killing
0-935526-86-2 • 320 pp., $15.95

___ 2 The Wicked Trade
0-935526-95-1 • 384 pp., $16.95

___ 3 The Spithead Nymph
1-59013-077-4 • 288 pp., $14.95

C. NORTHCOTE PARKINSON
The Richard Delancey Novels

___ 1 The Guernseyman
1-59013-001-4 • 208 pp., $13.95

___ 2 Devil to Pay
1-59013-002-2 • 288 pp., $14.95

___ 3 The Fireship
1-59013-015-4 • 208 pp., $13.95

___ 4 Touch and Go
1-59013-025-1 • 224 pp., $13.95

___ 5 So Near So Far
1-59013-037-5 • 224 pp., $13.95

___ 6 Dead Reckoning
1-59013-038-3 • 224 pp., $15.95

Military Fiction Classics

R.F. DELDERFIELD
___ Seven Men of Gascony
0-935526-97-8 • 368 pp., $16.95

___ Too Few for Drums
0-935526-96-X • 256 pp., $14.95

NICHOLAS NICASTRO
The John Paul Jones Trilogy

___ 1 The Eighteenth Captain
0-935526-54-4 • 312 pp., $16.95

___ 2 Between Two Fires
1-59013-033-2 • 384 pp., $16.95

Classics of Nautical Fiction

CAPTAIN FREDERICK MARRYAT
___ Frank Mildmay OR
The Naval Officer
0-935526-39-0 • 352 pp., $14.95

___ The King's Own
0-935526-56-0 • 384 pp., $15.95

___ Mr Midshipman Easy
0-935526-40-4 • 352 pp., $14.95

___ Newton Forster OR
The Merchant Service
0-935526-44-7 • 352 pp., $13.95

___ Snarleyyow OR The Dog Fiend
0-935526-64-1 • 384 pp., $16.95

___ The Phantom Ship
0-935526-85-4 • 320 pp., $14.95

___ The Privateersman
0-935526-69-2 • 288 pp., $15.95

RAFAEL SABATINI
___ Captain Blood
0-935526-45-5 • 288 pp., $15.95

WILLIAM CLARK RUSSELL
___ The Yarn of Old Harbour Town
0-935526-65-X • 256 pp., $14.95

___ The Wreck of the Grosvenor
0-935526-52-8 • 320 pp., $13.95

A.D. HOWDEN SMITH
___ Porto Bello Gold
0-935526-57-9 • 288 pp., $13.95

MICHAEL SCOTT
___ Tom Cringle's Log
0-935526-51-X • 512 pp., $14.95

The Alexander Sheridan Adventures

BY V. A. STUART

FROM THE Crimean War to the Sepoy Mutiny, the Alexander Sheridan Adventures deftly combine history and supposition in tales of scarlet soldiering that cunningly interweave fact and fiction.

Alexander Sheridan, unjustly forced out of the army, leaves Britain and his former life behind and joins the East India Company, still in pursuit of those ideals of honor and heroism that buoyed the British Empire for three hundred years. Murder, war, and carnage await him. But with British stoicism and an unshakable iron will, he will stand tall against the atrocities of war, judging all by their merit rather than by the color of their skin or the details of their religion.

"Stuart's saga of Captain Sheridan during the Mutiny stands in the shadow of no previous work of fiction, and for historical accuracy, writing verve and skill, and pace of narrative, stands alone."

—*El Paso Times*

V. A. STUART wrote several series of military fiction and numerous other novels under various pseudonyms. Her settings span history and the globe. Born in 1914, she was in Burma with the British Fourteenth Army in WW II, became a lieutenant, and was decorated with the Burma Star and the Pacific Star.

The Nelson and Emma Trilogy
by David Donachie

PART ONE
On a Making Tide

Young Nelson and Emma begin to make their ways in the world with corresponding recklessness and precocious ambition: Nelson enters the Royal Navy at the age of twelve and quickly develops a reputation as a daring yet benevolent leader. At the same time, teenage Emma rises quickly up the ranks from bawdy house prostitute to noblemen's courtesan to celebrated artist's model.

ISBN 1-59013-041-3
416 pages, maps • $17.95

PART TWO
Tested by Fate

In a string of spectacular naval battles—Cape St Vincent, Tenerife, the Nile—the ravages of war take their physical toll on Nelson, even as he gains the fame and honour he desperately craves.

Emma, now Lady Hamilton, meets the mercurial Nelson in Naples, and she is inexplicably drawn to the brash sea captain. All the doors of Europe are open to her—but how can she forget Nelson when he has not forgotten her?

ISBN 1-59013-042-1
416 pages, maps • $17.95

PART THREE
Breaking the Line

To a nation consumed by war, Admiral Horatio Nelson is a hero. Nelson's lover, the disreputable Lady Emma Hamilton, is another matter. Yet the two are inseparable, and defy friends and enemies alike to stay together. Fate has other plans, however, as Nelson moves inexorably toward the stunning conclusion of his career.

ISBN 1-59013-090-1
368 pages, maps • $16.95

The 3-part biographical novel that chronicles the rise of Horatio Nelson, Britain's greatest naval hero, and his legendary mistress, Lady Emma Hamilton.

"**The strength of Donachie's writing lies in his convincing dialogue that brilliantly conveys the personalities of Nelson and Hamilton.** The author certainly has done his homework . . . historical facts are very cleverly intertwined into the story."
—*Bookpleasures.com*

Available at your favorite bookstore, or call toll-free:
1-888-BOOKS-11 (1-888-266-5711).

To order on the web visit **www.mcbooks.com** *and read an excerpt.*